Cassidy Lane

Cassidy Lane

Maria Murnane

LAKE UNION
PUBLISHING

Text copyright © 2014 Maria Murnane

Published by Lake Union Publishing, Seattle

www.apub.com

Amazon, the Amazon logo, and Lake Union Publishing are trademarks of Amazon.com, Inc., or its affiliates.

Cover photo by Blend Images/Jon Feingersh
Cover design by Debbie Berne

ISBN-13: 9781477849941
ISBN-10: 1477849947

Library of Congress Control Number: 2013922973

Printed in the United States of America

To Tami and Peggy (aka The Besties),
for always laughing with me
and not at me

Chapter One

"**WHERE ARE YOU?** I'm dying here."

Cassidy sat down on the bed, cell phone pressed to one ear, and pulled her knees up against her chest. "Do I have to go? I'm sort of having second thoughts."

"Stop it. If you don't get down here, and *soon*, I'm going to murder you. I'm talking cold-blooded murder. Probably a stabbing."

Cassidy couldn't help but smile. "Were you this demanding in high school? I don't remember this side of you from when you were attaching shoulder pads to your bra straps. Do you still have those?"

Patti let out a little gasp. "We must never speak of those again, do you hear me? Now stop stalling. You promised I wouldn't have to go to this reunion without you."

"I'm still in my bathrobe."

"So, get dressed."

"My hair's still wet."

"So dry it."

"I have a weird little scrape on my nose."

"So cover it up."

"I don't have anything to wear."

"You're lying. I was with you when you bought your dress at Bloomingdale's a couple of months ago, remember? You were in town for the Fourth of July weekend. We had lunch at Pluto's afterward, and you took approximately nine hours deciding between a grilled chicken sandwich and a salad with grilled chicken. I almost shot you."

Cassidy balled her free hand into a fist. "Damn your encyclopedic memory. How many people are there?"

"There are about fifteen of us so far, plus some slippery guy named Trent who no one remembers. I think he might be in the witness protection program."

"Only fifteen? Why did you get there so early?"

"I didn't get here early. I got here on time."

"I will never understand your obsession with punctuality."

"I will never understand your obsession with marshmallows. Now stop stalling and get down here."

Cassidy sighed, and the truth came out with her breath. "What if everyone is married with kids, Patti? I don't want to be the only single person there."

"Stop it. I bet lots of people from our class are single."

"You're not."

"So? I'm just one person. Besides, anyone can find a husband and pop out a few kids. You've been off writing books, which, believe me, is *way* more exciting than wiping butts. I bet someone here will ask you for an autograph before the night is over."

"Yeah, right."

"Want to bet? Connie Thatcher already asked me if you were coming."

Cassidy winced. "Oh no, not filterless Connie Thatcher."

"Yes, the one and only, and for better or for worse, she hasn't changed a lick. She even has the same unfortunate hairstyle. I'll bet *she'll* ask for your John Hancock."

"She always said the most mortifying things. Remember that time in driver's ed, when she asked me in front of the *entire class* if I could lend her one of the tampons she'd spotted poking out of my backpack?"

"Oh my God, I was so embarrassed for you when she did that."

"You were embarrassed *for* me? Try *being* me in that situation."

"Well, she's here in all her awkward inappropriateness, so be prepared. Jimmy Hanson's here too, although I imagine he goes by *Jim* now that we're pushing forty. Didn't you ask him to a Sadie Hawkins dance and he said no?"

Cassidy leaned her head against the headboard. "You're hardly making a strong case for my attendance tonight. Is anyone there *not* related to one of my humiliating high-school incidents?"

"Get down here and find out for yourself. You flew all the way across the country to come to this, and I'm not letting you bail on me now."

Cassidy ran her fingers through her damp hair and glanced out the bedroom door and down the hall, where she saw the soft glow of the flat-screen TV reflected in the glass French doors leading to the den. "It's sort of fun being at my parents' house. I feel like I'm seventeen again, even though I'm in the guest room now. Maybe I'll just skip the reunion and hang out here with Mom and Dad. All we're missing is my brother and actual videos on MTV, and it would be like the last twenty years never happened."

"Have I been stuttering? Get your butt down here or your life will end tonight."

Cassidy swung her legs onto the hardwood floor. "OK, OK, I'm coming. And for the record, I don't think we would have been friends in high school if you were this mean then."

"I'm not mean, I'm assertive. You're the writer. You really should know your adjectives."

"Believe me, I'm thinking of some adjectives right now. You'd better have a glass of wine waiting for me when I get there."

"You know I will. Unless you want a Bartles and Jaymes wine cooler; Exotic Berry flavor, perhaps? That *was* your signature drink in high school, at least the handful of times I remember you actually drinking back then."

"Only if you have on your signature pair of purple acid-wash GUESS overalls when you hand it to me. See you soon."

Cassidy hung up the phone and stood up, then cinched her robe around her waist and walked into the guest bathroom. She studied her reflection in the mirror as she ran a comb through her hair. Dark and a bit wavy, it never seemed to grow more than an inch or two past her shoulders. She leaned in close to examine her fair skin and gently touched the scrape on her nose with her index finger, then traced the faint lines around the corners of her green eyes. The lines crinkled into tiny ridges when she smiled now, and sometimes even when she didn't.

A rush of insecurity hit her with a force that startled her.

And surprised her.

Do I really have crow's-feet?

Does that mean I'm old?

Do I look old?

Do I look as insecure as I feel?

Why am I so insecure?

Have I done enough with my life?

Will the popular girls still make me feel like they know something I don't?

More importantly, why *do I still care?*

She stared at the mirror for a few moments, then closed her eyes and did her best to push the negative thoughts from her mind. She dried her hair and put on some makeup, then returned to the bedroom and opened the closet. Inside hung the burgundy dress she'd bought to wear tonight. With a fitted waist and cap sleeves, it was simple and classy and grown-up—she'd never been able to stand busy patterns of any kind on her clothes. She put her hands on her hips and tilted her head in thought. Patti had assured her the style and color looked flattering on her five-six frame, but now Cassidy wasn't so sure.

She turned to one side and studied her profile.

Do I look hippy?

Is my belly poofing out?

She'd stayed pretty slender and fit all these years, but even so, this was one of those times she wished she had the superhuman figure of a supermodel.

She faced the mirror straight on and nibbled on her thumbnail.

Is it cute enough?

Does it make me look stiff?

Will anyone care?

Almost without realizing what she was doing, she suddenly held out a hand as if greeting an old classmate, then forced a smile and spoke in a loud voice she barely recognized. "It's great to see you! Can you believe it's been twenty years?"

Cassidy blinked. Where had *that* impromptu rehearsal come from? She had to laugh. She was clearly overthinking this, and she hadn't even left the house yet.

"Angel, are you OK?" A female voice called from the den.

Cassidy hollered back. "I'm fine, Mom. Just talking myself into going to this thing."

"It'll be easier once you have some wine in you. Trust me."

Cassidy chuckled. "Thanks, Mom. You're always a fountain of practical advice."

She gazed back at her reflection. The nervous figure in the mirror looked nothing like the happy, confident, independent woman Cassidy was used to greeting every morning.

She frowned at herself.

Just yesterday you were fine. Yesterday!

Cassidy Lane had five published novels under her belt, one of which had recently become a bestseller. After years of struggle, she finally had a steadily growing fan base that allowed her to write full-time. She lived in Manhattan, traveled—within reason—where and when she felt like it, got paid to basically make up stories, and rarely had to wake up early if she didn't want to. It had been a lot of work to get here, but she was now quietly living a life most people could only dream about.

The woman facing her now, however, still felt like the smart girl no one had asked to the prom.

"Cassidy Lane, how nice to see you! We missed you at the last reunion." A short, plump woman seated at the registration table checked Cassidy's name off the list and held up a crisp white name tag.

Cassidy smiled and pushed a loose strand of hair out of her eyes. "I can't remember where I was for that one, but Patti Bramble told me it was fun."

The woman winked at her. "You were probably off on some book tour."

Cassidy smiled again, this time a bit awkwardly, as she pinned on the name tag and hoped it wasn't too obvious that she had absolutely no idea who this woman was. The registration table was outside the restaurant, and she peeked through the windows to see if she recognized anyone. Thank God Patti was already here.

The woman tapped the shoulder of the man sitting next to her. "Honey, Cassidy's that author I told you about, remember?"

He nodded. "Ah, yes, the famous New York writer. Crystal said you were coming tonight. It's a pleasure to meet you." He held out his hand. "I'm Stanley Bryant."

Crystal! That was her name. Cassidy remembered her now, a cheerleader. She'd been Crystal Hightower back in high school. *Wow, she looks really different.* Cassidy shook Stanley's hand and smiled politely. "It's nice to meet you too. And while I'm flattered by the description, I'm hardly famous. Believe me."

Crystal waved a hand dismissively. "Nonsense, you're famous to *me*. I've read all your novels. I just love a good romance." She turned to Stanley. "Isn't that true, babe? Don't I just love her books?"

He held up his hands. "It's true. She's a big fan. You must be living quite the life out there in the Big Apple."

Cassidy felt her cheeks flush. *If you only knew.* Everyone assumed the life of a published author was all glitz and glamour, especially when they found out she lived in New York City. Maybe other writers lived opulently, but she certainly didn't, and even if that were her style, she would never have been able to afford such a life in Manhattan. The truth was that while she did attend some high-profile events and got dressed up for a photo shoot now and then, those occasions were few and far between. She spent most of her days in her apartment, quietly working alone at her desk, usually dressed in jeans, sometimes even in sweatpants or pajamas.

Actually, who was she kidding? Mostly in sweatpants or pajamas.

Tonight was the most dressed up she'd been in months.

She adjusted the strap of her purse over her shoulder and decided to change the subject back to the reason she was there. "I know everyone must say this, but it's hard to believe it's been twenty years since we graduated. It almost feels like just yesterday, don't you think?" She hoped her mom was right in predicting that conversation with her former classmates would flow more easily once she got some wine in her to soothe her nerves. Otherwise it was clearly going to be a long night.

Crystal's eyes got big. "I know! I was just talking to Stanley about that. Call me biased, but I think we all look exactly the same, just as fabulous as we did in high school."

Cassidy pictured how much thinner Crystal had been back then. A lot thinner. Like fifty pounds thinner. She opted for another change of subject, fearing the look on her face would give away what was really going through her head. "I'm guessing I'm the last one to arrive. Did a lot of people come? Looks pretty crowded." She pointed through the windows.

"Oh yes, it's a full house in there. Go on inside and mingle," Crystal said.

"You two aren't spending the evening out here, are you? It's pretty chilly tonight." One thing that hadn't changed from their high-school days in Northern California was the cool—sometimes downright cold—evenings, even in the height of summer.

"Oh gosh, no. We're just waiting for a couple more stragglers to show up. We'll be closing up shop and joining y'all soon, I'm sure. Go on in and have fun." Crystal shooed her away.

"OK, thanks, Crystal. It was nice meeting you, Stanley." Cassidy hesitated for a moment, then took a step toward the entrance before pausing again.

Don't be so nervous.

It will be fine.

She took a deep breath and pushed open the door. As she walked inside, she immediately felt as if every eye in the room was staring at her, though in reality the place was so loud and packed it was unlikely anyone had even noticed her arrival. She scanned the crowd for Patti and quickly spotted her at a bar to the right. Thank God Patti was tall. Suddenly nervous in the company of so many strangers she used to see every day, Cassidy wanted to break into a trot but refrained. Instead she avoided making eye contact with anyone and walked quickly toward her friend.

She was halfway across the room when a woman to her right backed up unexpectedly. She knocked an elbow into Cassidy's stomach as she did so, spilling some of her drink onto Cassidy's dress.

The woman turned and looked at Cassidy. "Oh, I'm sorry," she said, her words a bit slurred.

Cassidy recognized her as Eliza Wood, one of the most popular girls in school back in the day, if not *the* most popular. Though they'd once had a class together, they had never actually spoken to each other. For four years straight, half the boys in school had chased the beautiful Eliza Wood. With her expensive clothes and perfectly applied makeup, each long eyelash expertly curled, her lustrous auburn locks cascading down her back, and a stream of would-be suitors constantly at her side, she was the epitome of the Popular Girl. Every day she appeared on campus looking as if she'd jumped right out of the pages of *Seventeen* magazine, and Cassidy had quietly envied her from afar, wishing she could be like that, wishing that just one boy would pay attention to her like that . . . just one. Eliza hadn't been much of a student or even particularly nice, but none of the guys seemed to mind. And tonight, her slinky green dress clinging to every curve, a full twenty years later, she looked as stunning as ever, despite clearly being a bit drunk. Or maybe a lot drunk.

Cassidy dug around inside her purse for something to use to blot her dress and found a small pack of tissues. "It's OK, I'm fine." Fortunately, her dress was dark, and the liquid was clear. It could have been much worse.

Eliza pointed at her. "Did we have English together?"

Cassidy nodded, secretly thrilled at the recognition. "Junior year."

Eliza squinted. "You were sort of dorky, right?"

Before Cassidy could respond, Eliza spotted someone else and drifted away with nary a wave, leaving Cassidy standing there alone, holding a wet tissue against her chest. Her cheeks and neck suddenly felt warm. Had anyone heard that? She hoped not. She sighed and, keeping her eyes glued to the floor, made her way across the crowded room toward Patti.

"*Finally*," Patti said as Cassidy approached. "I was about to call the police."

Cassidy nodded. "I know, I'm sorry. I was moving in quicksand getting ready tonight. Fear and inertia teamed up to get the better of me."

Patti picked up a full glass of red wine and handed it to her. "Don't sweat it. Kevin and I have been having fun catching up. Remember Kevin Tyson?" She gave Cassidy a subtle can-you-believe-it look as she gestured toward the tall man standing next to her.

"Yes, of course. How are you, Kevin?" Cassidy tried to mask the shock she felt upon laying eyes on him. Back in the day, Kevin Tyson had been the captain of the Palo Alto High School baseball team, tall and ruggedly good-looking, with an athletic build and a thick head of wavy dark hair, the kind of guy who could probably go camping in the woods for a week and be even more handsome on the way home. Nearly every girl Cassidy knew—including herself and Patti—had secretly been in love with him at one point or another. He still had a nice face, but now he wore glasses and was balding, and he appeared noticeably soft despite his tall frame.

He shrugged. "I'm hanging in. I was just telling Patti about my arthritic knees. Very painful."

"I'm so sorry to hear that." *Arthritis? Already?* Cassidy buried her face in her wineglass and tried not to stare at his bulging midsection. First Crystal, now Kevin? Only five minutes into the reunion and she was already getting a bit depressed. At least Eliza still looked gorgeous, though she was still sort of mean. Why were the bitches always so pretty?

He frowned. "It's not fun. Makes it hard to work in my greenhouse. I was also telling Patti about that."

"Kevin's really into horticulture," Patti said.

"Is that so?" Cassidy tried her best to sound interested but wasn't sure how successful she was. *The guy's not even forty and he's talking about arthritis and gardening?* In a repeat of her encounter with Crystal, she smiled and hoped he couldn't read her mind. She already felt mean enough. This reunion was clearly bringing out not only her insecurities but also her most judgmental side, and she willed both to make a quick retreat.

"Yep," he said with a resigned sigh. "Definitely hard with the arthritis, though."

"I can imagine," Patti said.

"That's too bad." Cassidy glanced at Patti, whose eyes sent an urgent *we've got to escape!*

"It was nice seeing you again, Kevin, but I just spotted Krista Nelson." Patti smiled politely and pointed across the room. "We're going to make our way over there to say hi. Good luck with your knees. And your plants."

Before Kevin could even reply, Patti grabbed Cassidy's arm and pulled her into the crowd. When they were a safe distance away, she spoke under her breath. "Holy sweet mother of Jesus. I like Kevin, I really do, but I was going to light myself on fire if I had to talk to him for one minute longer."

Cassidy stole a peek back at the bar. "What happened to him? I had such a crush on him at Paly. I remember him as being much more fun than that, not to mention way cuter."

"Apparently he grew up and became boring. I know it's mean to say, but I think I almost fell asleep for the last part of that conversation." She tapped the side of her head, pretending to wake herself up.

Cassidy pressed a palm against her forehead. "How did he get so old and depressing? Are we that old and depressing?"

Patti squeezed her arm. "Stop it. We're not old *or* depressing. We are youthful and lively. Or so I choose to believe. My children might tell you otherwise."

As they walked through the crowd, Cassidy scanned the faces around them, a blend of familiar and unfamiliar, together creating a literal memory lane. Some faces looked fresh and vibrant, others faded and weary, and she wondered how much of the difference was due to genetics and how much to life itself.

Marriage.

Kids.

Homeownership.

Divorce.

Arthritic knees.

She hadn't experienced any of those things yet, but she imagined that collectively they could add a lot of city miles to one's appearance. She furrowed her brow in thought. A twentieth high-school reunion? Maybe that could spark an idea for her next book. She was a tad more than halfway through a novel right now, but she'd been dragging her proverbial feet a bit, and her editor was pressuring her to finish it.

They were en route to Krista when Patti whispered under her breath. "Abort! Abort!"

Cassidy turned her head. "What are you talking about?"

"Curses, too late," Patti whispered.

"Hello again," a male voice said.

A tall, skinny man wearing a sport coat and an equally skinny tie approached them. His blond hair was pulled into a ponytail.

Cassidy had no idea who he was.

"Hi again, *Trent*." Patti turned to Cassidy. "Do you remember Cassidy Lane?"

Trent gave Cassidy a quick once-over, then squinted at Patti. "I can't say that I do, but I *would* love some weed. Do you got any?"

Patti held her free palm up. "Sorry, Trent, fresh out."

He looked at Cassidy. "You got any, Cathy?"

"Cassidy," Patti said.

"Yep." He turned and wandered away. "See ya."

"What was *that*?" Cassidy whispered to Patti when he was out of earshot.

"I told you, witness protection," Patti whispered back. "My money's on informant for some huge drug bust."

"Ladies!" Krista suddenly emerged from the crowd and gave them each a hug, standing on her tiptoes to do so. "How are you? You both look amazing! You always did, though. Two of the cutest girls in school."

Patti waved a hand in front of her. "Stop it. We look our age and you damn well know it. You, on the other hand, still don't have a line on your face. What's your secret?"

Krista patted her tiny cheeks. "What can I say? Black don't crack."

Cassidy laughed and glanced around the room. "Did Andre come too?" Krista and Andre had been together since ninth grade and had been voted cutest couple their senior year. They'd gone to different colleges but dated long-distance all four years and married shortly after graduation. Now they had three adorable daughters, all spitting images of their mother. If Krista weren't so darned nice, Cassidy would probably be jealous of how her life had worked out. But it was simply impossible not to like her.

Krista pointed toward the far corner of the bar. "He's getting me a drink." She lowered her voice and leaned closer to them. "Did you hear about Eliza Wood?"

Cassidy and Patti both shook their heads.

"Apparently her husband left her . . . for their twenty-five-year-old nanny."

"No!" Patti covered her mouth with her hand.

"Yes," Krista said. "Some young hottie from Sweden. Huge scandal."

"Hotter than Eliza?" Patti raised an eyebrow.

"I think *younger* is the operative word," Krista said.

Cassidy frowned. "I can't believe we're old enough to be having this conversation."

Krista shrugged. "Forty is just around the corner. We might as well face it."

Cassidy tapped her chest. "Eliza ran into me when I first got here, as in *literally* ran into me. She spilled her drink all over my new dress."

Krista lowered her voice. "She's schnockered off her firm little butt and is in oversharing mode. Sounds like it was a pretty messy divorce, although my sources tell me her drinking like a fish had as much to do with the split as the hottie nanny."

"This is truly like being in high school again," Cassidy said. "You still have the best gossip."

Krista snapped her fingers. "It's a gift, what can I say?" She leaned toward them again. "Speaking of gossip, have you seen Kim Harvey yet?"

Cassidy and Patti again shook their heads.

"She looks *a . . . ma . . . zing*. Lost a hundred pounds."

"Wow, that's incredible!" Patti said. "I can't even lose five pounds without them immediately reappearing somewhere else on my body."

Cassidy glanced in the direction of Kevin Tyson and lowered her voice. "I prefer more uplifting reunion stories. Not to sound like a teenager, but finding out that people are getting divorced and going downhill physically is bumming me out."

Krista laughed. "I hate to break it to you, but while not all of us will end up divorced, we're *all* going downhill—sooner or later. That said, if you want to talk about those who have managed to avoid that slope so far, have you seen Brandon Forrester?"

Cassidy shook her head.

"Well, girl, have a good long look when you get a chance. I don't know where he was hiding in high school, but that man is *fine*. Babe with a capital *B*."

Cassidy laughed. "Krista! You're a married woman—to a man in this room, I might add."

"So? No one said I can't look." She touched Patti's arm. "You look, right? I know you do.

Patti nodded. "I promised to be faithful, but I didn't promise to go blind. Roy's on board with that."

Krista looked at Cassidy. "There you go."

Patti scanned the crowd. "I didn't see Brandon come in. Is he here with his wife? I think she and I might have done a tequila shot together at the last reunion. It's all kind of a blur."

Krista put her hands on her waist and slowly shook her head. "*Di . . . vorced.*"

"Was there a nanny involved?" Cassidy asked.

Patti covered her eyes with her free hand. "Please tell me there wasn't. That would make me afraid to hire one, even though I'd love to escape from my kids when they shift into their bratty mode, which is basically all the time these days."

"I don't know the details of what went down, but I don't think it was anything scandalous," Krista said.

Cassidy glanced around the room. "I never really knew Brandon at Paly. Do they have kids?"

Krista nodded. "Twin boys."

Patti took a sip of her drink. "I'm sad to hear that. He was such a nice guy. For some reason we always had math together." She looked at Krista. "He and I and your husband too. What was up with that? We were like the Three Mathketeers."

Cassidy pretended to wince. "Did you learn that joke from your kids?"

Krista gave Cassidy a suggestive smile. "So, my dear . . . Brandon Forrester is divorced *and* looking yummy. I just thought you might find that information interesting."

Cassidy shielded her face with her hand. "Please, don't go there."

Patti pushed her shoulder. "Why not? Weren't you just complaining about being single?"

"I was, but I wasn't looking to find a boyfriend *tonight*. I live in New York, remember? That's a long way from California."

Krista held up a palm. "So? Andre and I live in Seattle, and yet here we are. Have you ever heard of this thing called an airplane?"

Cassidy smirked. "Very funny. But I didn't come here for a round table on the state of my dating life. Can we please talk about something else?"

"Well, hello there, *Brandon*," Patti said over Cassidy's shoulder.

Cassidy felt her face flush and hoped Patti was joking. She slowly turned around and saw Brandon approaching them, followed by Andre.

She hadn't been joking.

And Krista hadn't been exaggerating.

He was gorgeous.

Wow.

He was tall and broad-shouldered, with salt-and-pepper hair and piercing gray eyes. Had he been such an Adonis in high school? She reached into the deepest corners of her memory but came up with nothing. Had they ever had a class together? She didn't think so. From what she could recall, they'd never even met, at least officially. *Funny how high school is like that,* she thought. *Everyone knows who everyone else is, yet so many of us go the entire four years without ever speaking a word to one another.*

"Hi, Krista. Hi, Patti, Cassidy." He made eye contact with each woman as he spoke her name. "It's nice to see you all."

"Hi, Brandon," Cassidy eked out the words, suddenly shy. Out of the corner of her eye, she could see Patti and Krista watching her reaction and trying not to laugh.

Andre handed Krista her drink, then turned to face the others. "Well, if it isn't the one and only Patti Bramble, looking as beautiful as ever," he said to Patti.

Patti did a little curtsy. "It's Patti Baker now, but thank you, my friend."

"And the lovely Cassidy Lane. I'm surprised you made it, what with being a famous author and all."

Cassidy rolled her eyes. "Give me a break, Andre. I bet you couldn't even name one of my books."

"I know they're chick books. Does that count?"

Krista elbowed him. "No."

Brandon cleared his throat. "I'm not technically a chick, but I've read them."

Cassidy looked at him, truly surprised. "You've read my books?"

Patti eyed him with suspicion more than surprise. "You enjoy women's fiction, do you now? Or are you just saying that because Cassidy's rocking that dress?"

"Patti!" Cassidy felt her cheeks flush.

Brandon chuckled. "I guess I do enjoy women's fiction. I'll read anything, though. I've always got a stack of books on my nightstand."

The thought of Brandon Forrester reading *her* novels in *his* bed flustered Cassidy even more, and she quickly buried her face in her wineglass so he wouldn't notice. She glanced at Krista, who winked and gave her a triumphant I-told-you-so look.

"Hey, there's Angela Green," Patti announced. "Let's go say hi." She interlocked her arm with Krista's, then turned to Brandon and Cassidy. "Brandon, it was nice seeing you. Cassidy, we'll catch up with you later." They quickly disappeared into the crowd. Andre wandered off too, leaving Brandon and Cassidy alone.

Cassidy nibbled on her thumbnail and tried to think of something interesting to say to keep him from moving on as well. She cleared her throat. "So, do you still live around here? I'm in New York now."

"Yep, not too far from the house I grew up in, actually. My boys just started kindergarten at Walter Hays this year." He looked around the restaurant. "It's hard to wrap my head around the fact that they go to school there now, especially when I think that I met a lot of the people in this room when *I* was at Walter Hays."

"It's horrifying, isn't it? We're getting so old."

He smiled. "I don't know if I'd go *that* far, but I agree it's been a while since we were kids."

"No really, Brandon, it's *horrifying*. We're closer to fifty than we are to twenty, do you realize that? That means we're closer to wearing dentures than to wearing braces."

"Wow, you're right. Maybe horrifying *is* the appropriate word choice."

"Oh, believe me, it is. I'm quite particular about my adjectives." She sipped her wine.

He laughed. "Were you this funny in high school?"

She shrugged. "Ask the librarian. That's where I spent most of high school."

He gestured to his beer. "Sometimes I wish I'd done more of *that* and less of *this*."

She gestured to her glass. "Sometimes I wish I'd done more of *this* and less of *that*. I probably would have had a lot more fun."

"Life in New York must be fun, especially as a writer. Sounds exciting. How many martinis do you average when you 'do lunch' with your editor?" He made an air quote with his free hand.

She answered with a straight face. "At least three, but never more than four."

He laughed again. "You're quick. I like that. I like that dress too. Patti was right."

The compliment surprised her, and her self-assuredness immediately disappeared. She visualized herself in her New York apartment, alone at her laptop, no makeup on, her hair pulled up into a messy bun, and felt decidedly *un*exciting.

But he didn't have to know that.

She swallowed.

If you only knew what my life was really like.

She decided to change the topic of the conversation, hoping to recapture her wit along the way. "Enough about me. What about you? What did you grow up to be?"

"I'm an attorney. I run a small firm downtown."

"What kind of law?"

"If I told you in detail, you'd fall asleep standing up. But in ten words or less: we specialize in patent disputes for technology companies. I bought the practice from my dad when he retired and moved to Carmel a couple of years ago." He took a sip from his glass, and she found herself wondering what kind of beer he was drinking. Why was she wondering that? Or was it his lips she was interested in?

Mmm.

She blinked and tried to stay focused on the conversation. "Do you like being a lawyer?"

"I do. I guess I enjoy arguing with people."

"I'm terrible at arguing. If they made running from conflict an Olympic sport, I might win the gold." There it was! *Wit, welcome back.*

Brandon chuckled, but before he could say anything, Cassidy felt a tug on her arm.

"Cassidy Lane! How are you?"

She turned and saw Connie Thatcher standing here.

The ever-inappropriate Connie Thatcher.

Oh no.

Cassidy forced a smile. "Hi, Connie." *Please don't embarrass me. Not now. Not in front of Brandon Forrester.*

"Hi, Cassidy! It's great to see you. Are you going to write a book about our reunion? Wouldn't that be fun?"

Cassidy tucked a loose strand of hair behind her ear. "Maybe. I never know where an idea will come from."

Connie poked her shoulder. "I always wonder what parts of your books are from your real life, especially if there's a racy scene." She grinned at Brandon. "Anytime it gets a little hot and heavy, I'm like, *Did Cassidy do this? Go, Cassidy!*" She held up her hand for a high five, clearly proud of her profound insights.

Cassidy winced and lightly tapped Connie's palm to oblige her, then glanced over at Brandon. He had an amused look on his face but let the comment pass. Instead he pointed toward the back of the room.

"I think I'm going to say hi to a couple of guys I used to play tennis with back in the day. I'll let you two catch up. Cassidy, it was really nice chatting with you, and congratulations on the success of your books. Have a safe trip back to New York. Connie, take care."

"It was nice chatting with you too, Brandon." He was really leaving? She wondered if the disappointment she felt was stamped all across her face.

As he blended into the crowd, Connie squeezed Cassidy's arm again. "So tell me, can you totally see the top of my Spanx through my dress?"

"Oh my God, these are even better than I remember them. *De . . . li . . . cious*." Krista spooned out a big lump of chocolate milk shake and downed it. "Want a taste, doll?" She scooped out another spoonful from the silver canister in front of her and held it up to Andre, who sat next to her, across from Cassidy and Patti. The four of them were tucked into a red vinyl booth at the Creamery, a Palo Alto institution.

Patti looked around. "This place has barely changed since high school. Remember how we used to come here after dances?"

Cassidy snapped her neck toward Patti. "Oh my God! Remember when you dressed up like Madonna for every dance sophomore year?"

Patti squeezed her eyes shut. "We must never speak of that again. Do you hear me?"

Cassidy looked at her. "You already said that about the shoulder pads."

Patti shrugged. "I have three children. I'm used to repeating myself."

Andre picked up a curly fry. "I remember your Madonna phase. It was rad."

Cassidy squinted at him. "Did you just say *rad*?"

"I did, man. We *are* at a high-school reunion, after all. And Patti's Madonna phase was most excellent."

Krista scooped another spoonful of milk shake from the canister. "I don't know whether it's this conversation or this restaurant, but I feel like we're in a time warp."

Cassidy nodded. "No kidding. It's like at any moment someone's going to throw on a Walkman and start moonwalking, right here at the Creamery."

Patti closed her eyes and began to sway. "I'm hearing the mixtape in that Walkman right now. It definitely has the Backstreet Boys on it."

"You want some?" Krista held out a spoonful of milk shake to Patti, who shook her head, then slid down the booth a bit and groaned.

"No thanks. After that burger I just inhaled, I think I have an indigestion situation going on here."

Cassidy smiled and lightly patted Patti's stomach. "So, what's the verdict on tonight? What did you all think?"

Krista shrugged. "Overall, I think people looked pretty good."

Cassidy nodded. "I agree. With a few notable exceptions, of course."

"Some of the ladies have let themselves go, that's for sure," Andre said. "Did you see Crystal Hightower? Ouch. Eliza Wood still looked smoking, though."

Cassidy leaned across the booth and poked his shoulder. "Hey now, some of the gentlemen weren't looking so hot either. I'm still trying to erase the image of present-day Kevin Tyson from my brain. Yikes."

Patti sat back up and put her arm around Cassidy. "Brandon Forrester sure looked good."

"Hell *yes*, he did." Krista pointed her spoon at Cassidy. "Girl, you need to get on that."

Cassidy cocked her head to one side. "I need to get *on that*? I can't believe you just said that."

Andre rolled his eyes. "Krista has two drinks and starts talking like Queen Latifah."

"Now Queen Latifah is *rad*," Krista said with a nod.

Cassidy took a sip of her milk shake. "Anyhow, while I agree that Brandon Forrester could probably stop traffic, he is definitely *not* interested in me. He didn't even say good-bye before he left. Plus he has two kids and lives three thousand miles away from me."

Krista shrugged. "He's still a babe."

Just then a dark figure appeared at the end of their booth, and they all looked up.

Trent.

He was holding what appeared to be a joint.

"Any of you know where Eliza Wood went?" he asked with a squint.

Chapter Two

CASSIDY FLEW HOME to New York the next afternoon. It was nearly midnight by the time she opened the door to her modest one-bedroom apartment on the Upper West Side. After wheeling her suitcase across the hardwood floors into the bedroom, she walked back into the living room and plopped down on the couch to go through the stack of mail that had accumulated in her absence. She'd been in California for only a week, but judging by the mound of paper crammed in her mailbox, it looked more like she'd been gone a month.

She flipped through the stack, tossing credit card offers and catalogs into the wicker recycling basket near the couch until she spotted what appeared to be an invitation. She paused, trying to think whether she knew anyone who was getting engaged, but came up empty. She carefully opened the thick cream-colored envelope and smiled at its contents. It was a birth announcement from Sarah, one of her college roommates. Smiling up at Cassidy was baby Sophia Isabel Sanders, delicately swaddled in pink, all six pounds eleven ounces of her.

Cassidy walked into her immaculate kitchen and admired the sparkling linoleum floor, glad she'd scheduled her cleaning lady to come over during her trip. She slid the announcement under a magnet against the refrigerator door, which was already half-covered with photos of her little nieces, Caroline and Courtney. Her brother Tyler lived with his wife Jessica in Saratoga, not far from the childhood home in which their parents still lived, but "just far enough," as he liked to say. Cassidy studied the pictures for a moment, already missing her family a little bit, then poured herself a cold glass of water before climbing into bed.

It was time to switch gears back to her life in New York.

Early one evening the following week, Cassidy laced up her running shoes and set out for a jog through Central Park before it got dark out, which was happening earlier each day, now that September was coming to a close. Many of her friends in New York complained that the Upper West Side was too far uptown, or too sleepy, or too full of baby strollers, but as a lifelong runner, for her its proximity to the park trumped any other consideration. She'd lived there for nine years, and in her current building for three. Though it was hardly the trendy part of Manhattan, she couldn't imagine living anywhere else in New York.

Despite being part of an enormous city, the Upper West Side—in her opinion, at least—had a small-neighborhood vibe that made it feel almost intimate, with enough mom-and-pop shops tucked between the chain stores to rival any midwestern town. It also boasted a respectable number of restaurants and pubs, which made for a robust nightlife—albeit one comprised of a considerably older demographic than in the more "happening" parts of town. One thing Cassidy admired about the Upper West Side was its seamless mix of brownstones and doorman high-rises, an architectural melting pot that reflected the diversity—and beauty—of New York City. She also considered it to be one of the prettiest neighborhoods in all of Manhattan, second only to the West Village. The streets were always clean, the buildings well maintained, the trees abundant and tall. And on clear evenings such as this one, with the sun setting over the Hudson River, she felt lucky to partake in the quintessential New York experience: a run through Central Park.

The Upper West Side would never be the hippest part of Manhattan, but it would always be Cassidy's home away from home.

Plus she'd never considered herself "hip" and wasn't about to start now.

She rode the elevator down to the lobby and waved to the doorman before stepping outside and making her way toward the park. Her building was a high-rise on Seventy-Third Street between Amsterdam and Columbus, just a few steps from the express subway stop, another geographical perk. While part of her missed the charm of the walk-up brownstone she'd lived in before, there was something to be said for a speedy elevator and twenty-four-hour security, not to mention a newer apartment with central air conditioning, a dishwasher, and a washer and dryer right in the unit—no more finding strangers' socks in her laundry! Plus now she had a gym in her building, which gave her no excuse when it was just too hot outside—or too cold—to run. Though she'd never been much of a gym person, the harsh weather of New York often tested her resolve to keep in shape.

But when it really came down to it, the reason she'd moved was to have more space. For several years she'd struggled to pay her bills with a combination of meager book royalties and savings, but she kept writing, and once her novels started selling well enough to generate a steady income, she'd decided to move out of her cramped studio. It was time to start treating herself like a real professional, and that meant having a proper work space. So after years of writing hunched over her laptop on her couch, she'd relocated to a one-bedroom in a building just a few blocks away and set up her "office" in a tidy corner of her living room. The new apartment was hardly opulent, but she had it all to her herself. She thought it funny, if not downright absurd, that for most people in Manhattan, being successful meant being able to afford a decent-sized place without a roommate—no matter what one's age.

As she jogged along her usual five-mile path through the park, she thought about the reunion and the different roads everyone's lives had taken since graduation. By now most of her former high-school classmates probably owned honest-to-God grown-up houses, complete with big backyards, electric grills, and two-car garages. As far as she knew, she was the only one from her class who was living in New York City.

The sun was just beginning to set as she ran, and somewhere along the way the chill of fall had crept into the air. Summer was officially over now, and before she knew it the days of running in shorts and a tank top would be gone as well. Part of her looked forward to the onset of winter, especially that magical first snow-fall, when a soft blanket quietly covered the entire city, everything peaceful and still, the white canvas unblemished, at least for the first few hours, before it all turned to slush and mud. But another part of her knew she'd miss those balmy summer evenings when she could wear a sundress to dinner and never even think about bringing a sweater. She'd never experienced either of those things growing up in Northern California.

Her split affection for the polar extremes of New York weather was similar to the way she felt torn between the two coasts. When she was in New York City, she loved the energy emanating from every corner—the dinners and drinks with friends, the mature social scene in which she never felt old or out of place for being a single woman in her thirties. But every time she went home to see her family in Palo Alto, she couldn't help but imagine herself unpacking her suitcase for good, especially now that Tyler had children and her parents were getting older. After this last trip in particular, she could picture a life of solitary writing on a sun-porch overlooking the rolling hills of Silicon Valley, punctuated by ice cream dates and trips to the park with her nieces. She would rent a small cottage in or around Palo Alto, maybe in Portola Valley or Woodside, and immerse herself in a low-key yet busy life as Auntie Cassie, as Courtney and Caroline called her. Plus Patti was out there, and despite the twenty years since they'd both lived in the same town, Patti was still the only person she could trust to tell her if a pair of jeans made her butt look big.

Opposite coasts, separate lives.

After finishing her loop, she stopped at a bench on Central Park West to stretch for a few minutes before slowly walking back to her building. Would she know when it was time to move back to California? Or would there ever be a concrete signal? She was thirty-eight years old but still didn't have a life plan beyond *finish this novel.*

For now, at least, that was enough.

Back to work.

The next afternoon Cassidy was pondering the latest notes her editor had sent over on her book when the alarm on her phone went off. She picked it up and saw the daily notification for *Respond to reader e-mails.* Was it three o'clock already? She opened a new browser on her laptop and logged into the e-mail account connected to the Contact Cassidy tab of her website. Though she didn't receive a ton of fan mail, she got messages from time to time, and it never ceased to amaze her that readers made the effort to send her a note. Answering fan mail was one of her favorite parts of being an author, if not *the* favorite, because it reminded her that real people were actually out there, enjoying her work and making her feel like she had a calling in life.

Today she had just one message, but it put a smile on her face.

Dear Cassidy,
I love to curl up in bed with a good book and just discovered Gretel Court! *I read it in two days and absolutely adored it!!! I couldn't believe that I found myself nervous for Bonnie when she was tracking down Joe near the end. I was cringing while waiting for his reaction, like they were real people and not just characters. You do such a wonderful job of connecting the reader with the character. I laughed so hard at some parts that I was almost in tears. Thanks for the happy ending too. I'm about to start reading* Montague Terrace *and can't wait to dig in. Keep writing, please!*

She smiled at the e-mail, feeling grateful to Debbie in Chicago for sending it. Maybe she hadn't found the man of her dreams and moved to the suburbs to raise perfect children, but missives like this helped her remember that in the grand scheme of things, she was doing OK.

She replied to the message and had just hit send when a new e-mail appeared in her in-box.

She gasped.

The sender's name was Brandon Forrester.

She opened the e-mail and nibbled on her fingernail as she read.

> *Hi Cassidy, it was nice seeing you at the reunion. I'm not sure if you'll get this or if you're even in town, but I'm going to be in New York next week and thought you might want to grab a drink. Let me know—Brandon*

She stared at the computer screen, her heart suddenly beating a whole lot faster than it had been thirty seconds ago.

No way.

She read the e-mail three more times.

No way.

Had Brandon Forrester just asked her out? Brandon Forrester, the man whose piercing gray eyes and disarming smile had been lingering in the back of her mind since the reunion?

She immediately picked up the phone to call Patti, but it went straight to voice mail. She left a brief message, then hung up the phone and looked at the time. It was 3:28 p.m., lunchtime back in Palo Alto. Patti was a stay-at-home mom, and now that her kids were in elementary school, that meant she spent most weekdays volunteering in one way or another on campus.

She's probably doing yard duty, Cassidy thought. It always made her smile to think of Patti doing yard duty. Patti had told Cassidy she purposefully wore a visor *and* a whistle, just to look intimidating.

She read the e-mail from Brandon again.

Maybe he was just being friendly?

She read it again.

And again.

And again.

What does it mean?

She knew she was putting too much thought into it, knew that he probably didn't know anyone in New York and figured she was better company than the TV in his hotel room. But no matter what his motives, she was going to say yes.

She was *definitely* going to say yes.

She was going to have a drink with Brandon Forrester, and she was already excited about it.

She went on dates now and then, but it had been a while since she'd been invited out by a man with whom she actually wanted to have a drink. Not since Dean.

That realization alone was enough to make her smile.

After dinner that evening, Cassidy's phone rang as she was in the kitchen pouring herself a glass of wine. She was looking forward to curling up on the couch and spending some time with a book other than the one she was writing.

She set down the bottle and checked her caller ID. It was Patti, so she answered right away and skipped the greeting.

"Can you believe it?"

"I'm loving this. Tell me exactly what he wrote. I mean *exactly.*"

Cassidy picked up her glass and walked into the living room. "As in you want me to read you the e-mail?"

"As in I want you to read me the e-mail."

"OK, just a second." She took a seat and set her wineglass on the coffee table, then reached for her laptop and pulled up the message. After she read it to Patti, she leaned back against the couch. "Well? What do you think? Is he interested?"

"Hard to tell."

"I know! I've read it way more times than I should admit."

"Did you respond?"

"Yes." Cassidy recited the message she'd sent, which was brief yet friendly. In an equally brief yet friendly message, Brandon had replied that he'd be in touch when he had his work schedule sorted out.

"You need to look sensational. That means no sweatpants," Patti said.

"Agreed. How do I do that?" Cassidy loved her sweatpants.

"Stop it. You're adorable and you know it. If he's not interested, he's an idiot."

"Thanks, Patti. You always know just what to say to me."

"Just don't forget to show up. Are you going to set an alarm on your phone like you do for everything else in your life?"

Cassidy laughed. "Touché. But I think this is one appointment I'd remember without a reminder."

"Oh Jesus me, Jason's got the remote control in his mouth again. Jason, put that *down*! I'm sorry, Cassidy, but I've gotta run. Keep me posted OK?"

"Will do. Bye."

Cassidy set down the phone, then picked up her glass and twirled the stem between her fingers. She looked around her tidy apartment, which was completely quiet save for the classical music she had playing softly in the background. Her old building had constant street noise, so she treasured the silence here. *Patti would love this apartment.* Patti rarely got any downtime.

She closed her eyes and again leaned into the folds of the couch, trying to relax, trying not to read too much into Brandon's e-mail.

But it was no use.

Next week couldn't come fast enough.

Chapter Three

CASSIDY SPENT THE next few days preparing for a keynote address she'd been asked to give at a women's conference in early November. She had sat on a handful of panels before, but those had been at smaller, writing-specific events. Standing on a stage alone in front of hundreds of strangers was light-years out of her comfort zone, and she'd almost turned down the invitation, but then she'd found out the conference was in San Jose, which meant a free plane trip home for Halloween, so she'd agreed—albeit with some reluctance. Whenever her nerves started to get the best of her, she reminded herself that she was going to be able to take Caroline and Courtney trick-or-treating. Though they were only five and seven, she was already dreading the day when they thought it wasn't cool to dress up for Halloween.

She was in the middle of reviewing her notes for the presentation when her editor called. She set down the pad of paper and picked up the phone.

"Hi, Nigel. How are you?"

"Hi, Cassidy, I'm good. Listen, I've got good news and bad news. Which do you want to hear first?"

She stiffened. No author ever wants to hear bad news from her publisher. "I guess the bad news. What is it?"

"I know we originally agreed on New Year's for you to turn in your new book, but now I'm going to need it by the first week of December."

"What? Why?" She knew from experience that the publishing industry often operated by the motto hurry up and wait, so she didn't want to rush without a legitimate reason.

"The marketing team wants more advance time to promote it before the launch. But look at it this way—you'll be able to enjoy the holidays without a deadline looming over your head."

She balled her hands into fists at the thought of the avalanche of stress she knew was coming her way. "OK, so you've just chopped a month off my deadline. What's the good news?"

"The good news is that Malcolm Lennox wants to include you in a short video he's presenting to the board."

"Malcolm Lennox wants *me* in a video?" Malcolm Lennox was the CEO of Rio Media, the holding company that published Cassidy's books and also had its fingers in many pies, including radio, television, and magazines, plus a number of Internet ventures.

"Indeed he does. He's giving a big shareholder presentation early next year, which will include a section on the publishing division, and he wants to feature three of our authors. You've been chosen as one of them."

"But why?"

Nigel chuckled. "Do you want me to go ask him?"

She chewed on her fingernail and laughed nervously. "Of course not. I'm just surprised, is all."

"Don't be. Your books are selling great, Cassidy. You should be thrilled."

"I am thrilled. I'm sorry, I'm just a little . . . stunned. When do they want to tape it?"

"We've rented a studio in Williamsburg for next Thursday. Are you free?"

She flipped the calendar on her desk to the following week. "All clear."

"Cool beans. Someone from the production team will be in touch about logistics. They'll send a car for you and take care of your hair and makeup, that sort of thing."

Cassidy raised her eyebrows. "They'll do my hair and makeup?" Her mind immediately turned to Brandon. He hadn't yet suggested a day for them to get together, but now she hoped it would be Thursday. What woman wouldn't want to be primped by a professional before meeting a handsome man for a drink?

"Of course. They'll make you look great, not that you need much help."

She glanced down at the faded sweatpants she was wearing. "Er, thanks, Nigel." *If you could only see me now.*

"So any ideas for your next book? This video won't be used for a few months, so that might be something worth mentioning in it."

Cassidy laughed. "Hello? I'm still working on this one. I don't even have a title yet."

"Work harder, dear. Your deadline is looming."

"Given what you just told me, *looming* is an understatement. I may need to become a hermit to finish on time."

"Well then, I'll let you get to it. Good luck at the taping next week, although you don't need it. I'm sure you'll shine, as always."

"Thanks, Nigel."

She hung up the phone and put her hand on the computer mouse, then opened the file to her manuscript. Her speech could wait. Right now she had to get her novel back on track. She wasn't sure how she'd lost her motivation to work on it, but she'd been trying to be patient. As she'd learned with her other books, the best way to write a good story was to let it unfold at its own pace. Forcing a plot didn't work, so when one spoke to her, she did her best to listen. But for some reason this one was staying rolled up in the corner of her imagination, and its stubbornness was beginning to concern her.

She also suspected the block was partly because the story wasn't exactly going in the direction she thought it would.

Or hoped it would.

She stared at the screen for a few minutes, then began to type.

Chapter Four

BRANDON E-MAILED CASSIDY again a couple of days later. As she clicked to open the message, she was surprised—and slightly embarrassed—to realize she was holding her breath.

> *Hi Cassidy, looks like next Wednesday is the only night that will work for me. Let me know if you're free. I'll be staying at the Standard in the Meatpacking District. I hope to see you.—Brandon*

She sent a quick reply, letting him know that worked for her, then leaned back against her chair.

Oh my gosh, this is really happening!

She chewed on her fingernail and wondered what it said about her that she was more excited about having a drink with Brandon on Wednesday than she was about the corporate video shoot for Rio Media the following day. Either she wasn't taking her career as seriously as she should be, or she was seriously starved for male company.

Or both.

She wasn't sure she wanted to know the answer to the question either way.

Besides, she didn't have time to ponder the inner workings of her mind—she had a book to write.

She shifted gears and got to work, but after an hour or so she hit a wall. As she always did when faced with a bout of writer's block, or confidence block—which was often the same thing— she read a few fan e-mails to give herself a little boost. She clicked open the folder of reader messages and scrolled through a few from recent weeks.

Dear Cassidy,
Although I have a passion for reading books, it has taken
a backseat to my busy life. I recently decided to dust off
the old Kindle and Montague Terrace *was just the thing*
to rekindle (no pun intended) my passion. I read it in a
weekend, and you can only imagine my excitement when
I found out that you had written a few other books. I love
your real-life perspective and sense of humor about it all.
Please continue to create. You have such a gift!

Several others were similar in spirit to what Cindy in Southern Ohio had to say. As usual, reading fan e-mails did the trick. With a smile on her face and a renewed sense of purpose, Cassidy got back to work.

After a late night at her desk, Cassidy wasn't exactly bursting with energy the next morning, so she opted to chop a mile off her regular run through the park. The shorter route avoided the dreaded Harlem Hill, which tended to make her feel like an old lady even when she wasn't a bit sluggish. And today she was already dragging enough. But she'd made a fair amount of progress on the novel the night before, so the lack of pep in her step was worth it.

After completing a four-mile loop at a leisurely pace, she stretched on a bench, then slowly walked over to a popular brunch spot called Good Enough to Eat on Columbus and Eighty-Fifth. She and her college friend Danielle tried to get together in some capacity every other weekend, although with Danielle's hectic work and travel schedule, it ended up being more like once a month, if that. Danielle was an ambitious sales rep for a pharmaceutical company and had more frequent-flier miles than anyone Cassidy had ever met.

When they were settled into a table in the back corner of the restaurant, they both ordered pancakes and coffee. Danielle poured a packet of sugar into her mug and stirred. "So what's new? I feel like I haven't seen you in forever. How's your book coming?"

"It's coming, but my deadline just got pushed up, so I'm a little stressed, to be honest."

"I hate deadlines. Have you decided what you're writing next?"

"Not a clue, but I'm not worrying about that right now. I need to finish this one first."

"I still think you should write about my life. I've got some great stories."

Cassidy narrowed her eyes. "You do realize that *everyone* tells me that, right?"

"Everyone tells you to write about me? How flattering." Danielle batted her eyelashes.

"Very funny."

The waiter refilled their coffee, and Cassidy cupped hers under her chin to warm herself up. "Where have you been since I last saw you? I'm almost afraid to ask."

Danielle paused to think, then held up one finger, then two, then three, then four. "Let me see . . . Zurich, Paris, London, and Atlanta."

"Good lord. All that in a month?"

"And you wonder why all I want to do is sit on my badonkadonk and *chill* when I'm in town." She gestured to Cassidy's workout gear. "There's no way I could do the running thing like you, especially later in the year, when it's freezing outside. I'd rather just embrace my lady curves." She took a sip of her coffee. "So tell me about the dreaded high-school reunion. You did muster up the courage to go, didn't you?"

"I did."

"Are you glad you did? Was it as wild as mine?" Danielle had gone to her twentieth reunion on Long Island over the summer and returned with multiple tales of drunken hookups between married former classmates . . . who weren't married to each other. She now referred to her alma mater as Infidelity High.

Cassidy shrugged. "It was pretty tame, actually, especially compared to yours. Nothing too scandalous, as far as I could tell."

They both paused as the waiter served them their pancakes. Danielle immediately smothered hers in syrup. "How did everyone look? Any surprises?"

"It was a mixed bag. Some had gotten a bit squidgy around the edges—while others still looked annoyingly fabulous."

"Was everyone married?" Danielle wasn't interested in settling down or having kids. She was quite happily married to her career.

Cassidy scratched her cheek. "Most, but not all. And a handful of people there were divorced, which was a little strange. I don't feel like we're old enough for that phase of life yet."

"Believe me, we're old enough. One of the girls from my high-school class is a grandmother."

Cassidy's eyes got big. "No way."

Danielle took a bite of pancake. "Oh yes. That's what happens when you get knocked up at sixteen."

Cassidy leaned toward Danielle and lowered her voice. "Actually, speaking of divorced people at my reunion, something sort of interesting did happen."

Danielle raised her eyebrows. "Is that so?"

Cassidy filled her in on the Brandon situation, then leaned back in her chair, an anxious expression on her face.

"So, what do you think? Am I foolish for being sort of excited about this?"

"Of course not. He sounds great."

"What if he's not interested?"

"What if *you're* not interested? It works both ways, you know."

"I'm just a little apprehensive, that's all."

"Why would you be apprehensive?"

"I don't know. After what happened with Dean, I guess I've sort of given up on the idea of romance, at least in my personal life." Her books were a different story.

"That's ridiculous. If anyone needs to believe in romance, it's you. Besides, Dean's ancient history. You can't let him affect your attitude like that."

"But—"

"But what? He's *gone*, Cassidy. You need to forget about him and move on. There are zillions of men out there who are way better than Dean. Maybe this Brandon is one of them."

Cassidy frowned. "Most of the dates I've had since Dean and I broke up have basically been a disaster. Remember that twitchy life-insurance salesman I met for coffee who put ten packets of sugar into his *sugar-free* vanilla latte? And the guy who showed up at the bar wearing a pair of high-waisted jeans—with his shirt tucked in?"

Danielle laughed. "I love that story."

"Which one?"

"Both."

Cassidy reached for her coffee. "And remember the cute doctor who said he was separated from his wife, but then admitted on our first date that he still lives with her . . . and their three kids? I'm not sure I even know what a good date is anymore."

Danielle smiled. "Well . . . maybe you'll soon find out. So you two are meeting on Wednesday?"

"Yes. But I'm not even sure it's a date."

"Where are you going?"

"I haven't picked a place yet. He's staying at the Standard. Any suggestions?"

Danielle pointed a forkful of pancake at her. "You should go to Diablo Royale in the West Village. Tristan and I went there a few weeks ago. Amazing margaritas. And if you decide to have dinner, the shrimp tacos are little bundles of heaven."

"You think he'll want to have dinner with me?"

"Why wouldn't he? He has to eat, right?"

"He might already have dinner plans."

Danielle poured more syrup on her pancakes. "If he's meeting you at seven, I highly doubt that. You should really try to have more self-confidence, Cassidy. Self-confidence is attractive to a man. Besides, you're a catch."

Cassidy smiled, grateful to have a friend like Danielle in her corner. "Thanks. Anyhow, enough about me. How are things going with you and young Tristan?"

"I think I'm going to end it."

"Why?"

"He told me he loves me."

Cassidy made a face. "Oh, jeez." Tristan was twenty-seven.

"I know. Not good."

"So you're still not into him?"

"I like him well enough."

"But you're not *in love* with him." It wasn't a question.

Danielle shook her head. "I'm not opposed to being in love with him, but unfortunately I'm just not feeling it."

"You probably should have broken up with him a while ago, don't you think?"

"Probably, but I do like hanging out with him, and the sex is off the hook. How can I let him down easy?"

Cassidy crinkled her nose. "Well . . . if you didn't tell him you love him back, he probably knows something's up, right?"

Danielle shook her head. "I don't think so. He's a sweet guy, and fireman-calendar hot, but he's not all that quick on the uptake."

"What exactly did he say?"

Danielle gave her a look. "Was I not clear? He said 'I love you.'"

"Smart-ass. What did you say back?"

"I said 'thank you.' Then we had sex."

"Danielle!"

She shrugged. "What was I supposed to do? He's hot."

"I don't know, maybe *not* sleep with him?"

"So says you."

"When was this?"

"Last night."

"Where is he now?"

Danielle cut another piece of pancake with her fork. "He's on a bike ride with a friend. We're supposed to get together later and go to a movie."

"You've got to end it."

"I know that. I even *said* that, if you were listening to me."

Cassidy laughed. "Don't get feisty, I'm just agreeing with you. You can't string the poor guy along anymore."

Danielle pretended to stab herself in the neck. "I've been thinking... maybe I could fake my own death?"

Cassidy laughed again. "Have mercy on the poor guy—he loves you! Plus that could get kinda messy, what with all the fake blood."

"Do you have a better idea?"

"Have you thought about... I don't know... telling him the truth?"

"Of course, but I don't know if I can stomach that. He's such a sweetheart."

Cassidy sipped her coffee. "I think honesty is always the best policy. That way he won't hold out hope that you'll change your mind. Think of how many times you've held out hope for a guy because he gave you some excuse for why he couldn't date you instead of just manning up and telling you he wasn't feeling it. It's a waste of time, right?"

Danielle gave her a blank look. "I've never been in that position."

Cassidy stared back. "You haven't?"

"No."

"You've never been dumped?"

"Not really, no."

Cassidy set down her mug and put her face in her hands. "You've lived a charmed life in the heartache department, my friend."

"It's possible. So you really think I should tell Tristan the truth?"

"I really do. If he's in love with you, it's not fair to lead him on, right?"

Danielle poured yet more syrup on her pancakes—the remaining bites were now like lily pads in a pond. "OK, I'll do it. I just wish the sex weren't so good. I hate to give that up."

"You're like a guy, the way you act with men. You realize that, right?"

"I'm aware. I'm just not cut out for relationships. I excel at flings, though."

The waiter returned to refill their coffees, and Cassidy again cupped her mug under her chin. "I wish I could be that casual about dating. Either I'm totally smitten by someone from the get-go or I have absolutely zero interest. There's never an in-between with me."

"So? What's wrong with that?"

"I just wish I could enjoy having fun without it always having to *mean* something. I've never been able to do that the way you can. Remember how many guys you were always juggling in college? It was like watching *The Bachelorette.*"

Danielle shrugged. "You and I are wired differently, that's all."

"I just wish I knew your secret. Men love you."

"Please. Men love you too. You get asked out all the time."

Cassidy frowned. "Only by guys I don't find appealing. A couple of weeks ago I got hit on by a man who must have been sixty years old. Do I look like I should be dating men in their sixties?"

Danielle shrugged again. "Some women like older men."

Cassidy set down her cup. "Please. He had one foot in the grave. I must be doing something wrong if that's what I'm attracting."

"Nonsense. It's not about doing the right thing or the wrong thing. It's about chemistry and timing and a bunch of other factors that are out of your control. So don't beat yourself up about where you are right now. Loads of people would cut off an arm to have your life."

Cassidy tilted her head to one side and smiled. "You're a good friend, do I tell you that enough?"

"As are you."

Cassidy lowered her voice and leaned forward again. "I know you're focused on your career right now, but do you ever worry . . . that you'll *never* find the right guy and have a family of your own?" she whispered.

Danielle answered without hesitation. "Nope."

"You're not?"

Danielle shook her head. "I'm perfectly fine by myself. Most of the time I prefer it, to be honest. I have zero interest in a life of car pools and trips to Costco."

Still leaning forward, Cassidy lowered her voice even further, to a near whisper. "Can I tell you something?"

"Of course."

"Sometimes, when I see happy couples all around me, I wonder if maybe . . . if maybe I don't have it."

"What do you mean?"

Cassidy swallowed. "I mean that maybe . . . maybe I just don't have *it*, that quality . . . or whatever you want to call it . . . that would make a man see me as, you know, *the one.*"

Danielle slowly shook her head. "Oh, hon, you can't think like that."

Cassidy made a sad face. "I know, but I can't help it sometimes."

"Cassidy, any man would be lucky to have you. Trust me on that. You can't let your mind play tricks on you. Hell, *I* would marry you."

Cassidy laughed weakly and picked up her coffee. "Thanks."

"You've got so much to offer. So much."

Cassidy sighed into her mug. "I know."

"Do you? Do you really? I mean, in addition to being smart, and kind, and witty, you're a *bestselling author*, for God's sake. Do you know how effing *cool* that is?"

"I do. Thanks, Danielle."

"You promise?"

Cassidy forced a smile. "Yes."

"Good. It's important to me that you realize that you have to be pretty freaking amazing to make it into my inner circle. My screening process is quite rigorous, if you haven't noticed."

Cassidy laughed. "I *have* noticed, and I'm honored to have been selected for membership in such an elite group."

"As you should be." Danielle tipped her head. "And for the record, you know there's no such thing as *the one*, anyway. Please. What if the one guy in the whole world for you happens to live in Germany? Or Ghana? How the hell are you supposed to meet him?"

"You make a good point. Funny how so many people seem to find their soul mate within a fifty-mile radius of where they live."

Danielle took another bite of pancake. "Now you're making more sense."

Cassidy leaned back against her chair, feeling much better. "I'm sorry for getting dramatic there. I know I tend to do that every once in a while."

Danielle shrugged. "Don't sweat it. You're entitled; you're an artist. You're supposed to be temperamental."

"You're always so even-keeled. Does *anything* rattle you?"

Danielle picked up the syrup and gestured toward the waiter. "It rattles me when they're out of this maple deliciousness."

After brunch Cassidy slowly ambled back to her apartment, knowing she needed to hunker down and get working on her novel, but not quite ready to give up the rest of her Saturday. Her eyes began to scan the storefronts along Amsterdam, searching for a practical excuse to postpone the tedious afternoon ahead.

Did she need anything from the grocery store? How about CVS? Maybe some shampoo? Toothpaste? Anything?

Finally, her eyes rested on a small nail and hair salon with a quaint wooden placard hanging above the door that said ANNABELLE'S in pretty blue lettering. Cassidy studied the sign. She'd walked down this block countless times but had never noticed this place before. Was it new? She peered through the spotless windows, which were framed by crisp white curtains dotted with blue and green flowers. She didn't see anyone inside, which was surprising, given that it was Saturday afternoon.

Cassidy glanced at her hands and wondered if she should get a manicure. When was the last time she'd done such a whimsical thing? She began to nibble on her thumbnail as she pondered the question, then yanked it away when she realized what she was doing. She held out both her hands in front of her with her fingers stretched wide, then raised her eyebrows. Maybe painting her nails would finally get her to stop biting them.

She doubted it.

She shrugged and decided to indulge herself anyway. It would be fun to be pampered for an hour or so, and it would offer a temporary reprieve from the hours at her desk that awaited her when she got home. She pushed open the door and was immediately greeted by the gentle sounds of ocean waves and the delicious smell of . . . cinnamon?

Is that cinnamon?

"I'll be right there!" called a voice from the back. A moment later a short, plump redhead who looked to be in her midfifties appeared from the back room. When she looked up and saw Cassidy standing there, she stopped walking.

"Oh, pardon me. I thought you were the deliveryman."

Cassidy smiled. "Nope, just a nail biter in desperate need of an intervention. Are you in charge here?" Was this Annabelle herself?

The woman put her hands on her hips and frowned. "I am indeed, but I'm sorry, love, we're not open for business yet."

"Got it. I was wondering how it was that I'd never noticed this place before." Cassidy looked around the salon, which featured a line of reclining black leather chairs for pedicures, as well as several pristine manicure stations. It was a small space, but it had character. The hardwood floors and light-blue walls were lined with leafy waist-high potted plants, which gave the room the pleasant feel of a sunny backyard deck. Unlike the countless generically sterile mani/pedi shops all over Manhattan, this one was clearly a labor of love. Cassidy found it extremely charming. "Did you design this place?"

The woman nodded. "I had a hand in it. What do you think?"

"I think it's beautiful."

"Well, I hope you'll come back, then. Can I make an appointment for you? Doors open on Monday. I'd love to have you as my first client."

Cassidy hesitated. She'd learned from experience that she couldn't commit to anything without first consulting her calendar. "I'll have to see what I have going on next week. I'm sorry."

"No worries, love, I hope to see you again. Have a nice day." The woman smiled politely and turned to return to the back room, clearly skeptical that she'd ever see Cassidy again. Cassidy couldn't blame her, though. In this city there was just so much going on all the time that people overscheduled themselves—and as a result, they tended to be less than reliable, if not outright flaky, when it came to making plans.

It was just how New York was.

Or perhaps it was just how New Yorkers were.

Hmm.

Cassidy looked up at the wooden sign as she walked outside, then during the slow walk home played what she called the character game, something she often did to spark ideas for her novels. She'd pose questions to herself about the people she encountered, then make up answers on the spot. Now she used Annabelle as a subject.

What's her full name? Annabelle Carmen Donnello.
Where does she live? Washington Heights.
Family situation? Married with three grown sons, all stand-up men with pretty young wives, two precious grandchildren, and another one on the way. Her husband, who was her high-school sweetheart, works at a tire factory in New Jersey.
Education? One year of Rutgers, then happily dropped out to get married.
Favorite food? Linguini with white clam sauce, her own recipe, of course.
Secret talent? Sings like an angel.
Biggest secret? Was a virgin on her wedding night.
Dream job? Raising kids, then opening up her own salon on the Upper West Side . . . called Annabelle's.

By the time she reached her building, Cassidy had Annabelle all figured out, or at least a fictional version of her.

Chapter Five

CASSIDY SPENT THE next few days hard at work on her book, and before she knew it, Wednesday had arrived.

Today was the day.

Drinks with Brandon Forrester.

A few hours before she was set to meet him, she decided to go for a run to clear her head. After spending all day cooped up in her apartment, she found the crisp air refreshing. She'd been staring at her computer screen, trying to figure out how to resolve a key issue between Emma, the protagonist, and Jeremy, her long-term boyfriend. The plot had finally begun to speak more clearly to her, but she still wasn't sure she was ready to hear what it had to say.

Despite the fact that it was the middle of the workday, the park was filled with people, some jogging, some walking, some just sitting and staring at the extraordinary human spectacle that was Central Park. That was what Cassidy loved most about the park, what she loved most about New York itself. The city was always buzzing, always bursting with energy, every street, every corner, every nook and cranny constantly offering a glimpse of life unlike anywhere else in the world. Where else would you see a tiny Ecuadorian grandmother merrily selling salted mango slices alongside a prepubescent hip-hop phenom hawking copies of his debut CD?

Cassidy played the character game as she ran, beginning with a pretty brunette dressed in a crisp black pantsuit and holding a briefcase. She appeared to be in a hurry.

What's that woman's name? Amber. Amber . . . Sullivan.
Where's she from? Philadelphia. No, Long Island.
What does she do? She's an architect. In Midtown.
What makes her angry? When people don't take her seriously because she's good-looking. She wasn't as attractive before she had her nose done. Was it worth it? She's not sure.
What makes her laugh? Anything her brother says makes her laugh. She wishes she were as funny as her brother. And as smart as her brother. At least in her dad's eyes.
Pet phrase? Suck it up, buttercup! Actually, her brother says that, but she loves it.
Dream job? Talk-show host.
Secret talent? She can do the splits.
Biggest secret? She spent years in competitive cheerleading.

Cassidy had come up with more than one idea for a character who wound up in her books during a run through the park.

Right now, however, she was thinking about something else.

Or someone else.

She hoped that when they met up in a few hours, Brandon wouldn't be able to see in her eyes just how much she'd been looking forward to tonight.

After her run Cassidy walked back to her apartment, stretching her arms above her head and trying to decide what to wear. Should she go subtle, with a nice pair of jeans and a cute top? Or glam it up a bit with a dress and heels? And what about makeup? On a recent excursion to Bloomingdale's, the friendly woman at the MAC counter had convinced Cassidy to buy some smoky shadow she said made the green in her eyes "pop." Cassidy had yet to open the box, doubtful she could successfully re-create the skilled work of the saleslady, and with no real reason for doing so. Maybe tonight was the perfect occasion?

Then she thought of something.

Annabelle's!

She'd completely forgotten about the quaint nail salon until just now, but it seemed like the perfect time to get a manicure. She'd have to hurry, though. She quickened her pace and headed upstairs to shower.

"Well, hello there; welcome back." The owner stood up from her desk and approached Cassidy as she gently shut the salon door behind her. "What was your name, love? I didn't catch it the other day." Soft music and the scent of cinnamon again filled the air. Or was it something else? Whatever it was, it made Cassidy crave a sugar cookie.

"I'm Cassidy. I'd love to get that manicure now, if you have time." She looked around the room. Only one of the pedicure chairs was occupied, by a young blonde reading a magazine as her feet were being worked on by an equally young brunette. She didn't see any other attendants.

The woman glanced at her watch. "We don't normally take walk-ins, but you're in luck. I had a facial scheduled, but it looks like she's stood me up."

"You do facials here too?"

"Yes, dear, in the back rooms." She reached toward a tin mailbox painted with daisies perched on the wall, then removed a crisp brochure and handed it to Cassidy. "Here's a list of all our services."

Cassidy glanced quickly at the offerings and blanched at the prices. No wonder they didn't take walk-ins. Half of them would probably walk out once they saw how expensive the place was.

The woman put a gentle hand on her arm. "We're worth it, love, I promise. Do you still want that manicure?"

Cassidy hesitated for a moment, then smiled. Why not treat herself for once? "I think so. Tonight's a bit of a special occasion, and as you can see, I need some help." She reluctantly held out her hands for inspection.

"Let's have a quick look." The owner reached for Cassidy's fingers and studied them. "Oh my, you weren't kidding. You're quite a squirrel, aren't you?"

Cassidy felt her cheeks get a bit warm. "I'm terrible." She debated whether to confess that she'd only begun to bite her nails on a daily basis after Dean broke up with her, worried that it might lead to a conversation about her personal insecurities that she wasn't ready to have. She'd done enough of her own amateur psychoanalysis, and it seemed pretty clear. Her fingers represented her biggest strength, but they were also evidence of her biggest weakness.

The woman pointed toward one of the manicure stations. "Well, you've come to the right place. Why don't you have a seat, and we'll do something about that, shall we?"

"Sounds good." Cassidy was halfway to the table when she heard the door open, then slam shut, followed by the sharp sound of a woman's voice—jarring the soft ambience of the salon.

"I'm sorry I'm late. You can't rely on *anyone* these days," the woman said with an audible sigh.

Cassidy turned around and saw a petite woman in the doorway, her hair an unnatural shade of black, her diminutive stature at odds with the scale of the disruption she'd just caused.

"Hello, Mrs. Polanski," the owner said with a pleasant smile.

Without smiling back, the tiny woman took off her fur jacket and laid it over her forearm. "After such a stressful day, I'm *so* looking forward to my facial."

Cassidy pointed toward the door and mouthed *I'll come back another time* as she held up the brochure in her hand. She'd call to make an appointment for next week, or at least try to remember to do so.

The owner smiled at Cassidy, clearly grateful for her discretion in not calling attention to the situation. "Please do."

As Cassidy quietly slipped outside, her thoughts turned back to Brandon, and before she even realized what she was doing, she was nibbling on her thumbnail again.

Wearing a sleeveless violet dress cut a couple of inches above the knee, Cassidy arrived at Diablo Royale seven minutes early. Suddenly feeling a bit like Patti and not wanting to look too eager, she strolled right past the entrance, hoping Brandon wasn't behind her to witness her ridiculousness. She headed toward the water on West Fourth and wandered around aimlessly for about ten minutes, taking deep breaths and telling herself to relax and get a grip.

At 7:05 on the dot she returned to the front of the restaurant. She smoothed her hair with her hands, checked her reflection in the window, then pushed the door open.

Brandon was sitting at the bar, facing away from her. Just seeing the back of his head—not to mention those broad shoulders—made her anxious. She hesitated for a moment, then tentatively approached him.

"Hi, Brandon." She gave him a nervous smile.

He stood up and offered his own easy smile back. "Hey, Cassidy, it's good to see you again."

Just being this close to him sent a little shiver down her back. *Wow, he* is *good-looking.*

They embraced in a quick hug, which felt a bit awkward to Cassidy given that—outside of their brief conversation at the reunion—they were virtual strangers, despite their shared history. Brandon gestured to a stool. "What can I get you?" A glass of water sat on the bar in front of him, and Cassidy was impressed that he'd waited for her to arrive before ordering himself a real drink.

"I hear the margaritas are pretty good here."

"Sounds great. How do you like yours?"

"Strong."

He laughed. "Got it. Anything else?"

"On the rocks, no salt, please."

"Coming right up." He turned toward the bartender and ordered two margaritas, and as he did so, she noticed the five o'clock shadow on his face. It was salt and pepper, like the thick hair on his head—and she couldn't help but wonder what it would feel like to touch it.

Just then Brandon looked at her and smiled, and she wondered if he'd caught her staring. She quickly looked down at her hands and wished her nails looked better. "So, what brings you to New York?"

"Nothing too exciting. A client is suing a company that infringed on one of its patents."

"I'm guessing that's about all you can say about it?"

He smiled. "Exactly. Sorry to be so secretive. Sort of comes with the territory."

The bartender set their margaritas in front of them, and Brandon handed Cassidy's drink to her. Again, she was impressed by his manners.

"Welcome to New York. I hope your secret mission was a success." She held up her margarita for a toast.

"It's nice to be here." He clinked his glass against hers. "To old friends who never actually knew each other."

She sipped her drink. "High school's strange that way, isn't it? I knew who you were, of course, but I don't think we ever met."

He nodded. "We met."

"We did? When?"

"Senior year I went to a party at Krista Nelson's house. You were there."

"You did? I was?"

He nodded again. "We talked for a minute or two, but then you took off."

She raised her eyebrows. "Are you sure?"

"I'm sure. You bolted like your hair was on fire. I may not have been the best student, but I have a really good memory."

"Then you're the exact opposite of me. We'd probably crush it on a game show."

He laughed. "Talking to you is a refreshing change from the deadly serious types I deal with at work all day long. One of the attorneys at my firm has been there for four years and I've never seen him crack a smile, much less a joke."

"Well, even though it was twenty years ago, I'm sorry I ditched you at that party. Will you accept an extremely belated apology?"

She certainly hoped she hadn't been rude. Knowing her, she'd probably bailed on their conversation because she got flustered, fretted briefly about how awkward and nervous she got around boys in social situations, then blocked out the entire experience and gone about her business getting straight As at school.

But still, how could she have done that to a boy who would one day grow up to look like the man sitting across from her now? She silently kicked her teenage self.

He winked at her. "It took a few therapy sessions, but I think I'm over it now."

She felt her cheeks flush. "I know I was on the timid side back then, but sometimes I also wonder if people thought I was a bit of a snob because I didn't know I needed glasses."

"What do you mean?"

"Krista once told me she thought I was rude because I never waved back at her from afar on campus, but then we realized that it was because I couldn't even see her. I got contact lenses soon after that."

"I wouldn't worry about it. You're clearly not rude. Famous, maybe, but definitely not rude."

"I'm hardly famous."

"You're a little famous." He half smiled, and it was all she could do to keep herself from staring at his lips.

"What about you? What were you like in high school?" She tried to maintain her focus on the conversation.

"Me? I was *clueless*. That pretty much sums it up."

She smiled. "I doubt that."

"I wasn't a jackass or anything, just a typical teenage guy. Too much gel in my hair, too little time spent on my homework, that sort of thing."

"Sounds like my brother. He put way more effort into his after-school activities than school itself. Total social butterfly, even joined the prom committee. My mom used to joke that she'd felt him fluttering in the womb."

"Who did you go to our prom with?" Brandon asked.

The question caught her off guard, and she froze. "I, uh, I didn't go to the prom."

He looked surprised. "Why not?"

She took a sip of her margarita and forced a smile. "If you think about it, you can probably figure it out. But just as well— this way I'm assured no embarrassing photos of me in an awful taffeta dress with crimped hair will pop up on the Internet." She cringed slightly. She was trying to act nonchalant about it, but she was mortified that her single biggest disappointment from high school had just been revealed.

Just then she heard a beeping coming from her purse. *Oh frick.* She reached inside and pulled out her phone to silence the alarm. She was grateful for the interruption but not thrilled that another of her shortcomings was on display so soon into the evening.

"Important call?" Brandon asked.

"Reminder alarm. I told you my memory sucks." She glanced at the display and saw *Send Dad birthday card!!* "I'm sorry about that."

He gave her a curious look, and she was afraid to know what he was thinking. She wracked her brain for something interesting to say, but before she could come up with anything he broke the silence.

"Do you like being a writer?" he asked.

She raised her eyebrows. "Honest answer?"

"Of course."

"Sometimes yes, sometimes no. I'm not sure how it is for other authors, but when I'm working on a book, I tend to suffer from low-grade anxiety throughout the entire process."

"What do you mean?"

She shifted on her stool. "I mean that until I get some positive feedback from my editor, I'm usually secretly afraid that what I've spent months writing might in fact be terrible."

He laughed. "Well, for what it's worth, I think you're a very good writer. I enjoyed your books, and I'm not just saying that."

"Thanks." She briefly cast her eyes downward before looking up and adding, "It's actually worth a lot to hear that—when I'm huddled in front of a computer screen by myself, it's easy for me to lose sight of the fact that I'm creating something I hope real people out there will enjoy."

"I know I'm not the target audience, but I found them quite entertaining. I mostly read nonfiction, so it's fun to get lost in a novel once in a while, especially ones with characters worth rooting for. It's nice to see good people win, especially when it comes to romance."

When he said the word *romance*, she flinched. She wanted to be honest with him about her writing, but the truth was that the romance in her books helped fill a void in her own love life, and that wasn't information she felt like sharing. After revealing the dating desert that had been high school, she hardly wanted to draw more attention to her personal life by confessing her pattern of literary wish fulfillment—much less the reasons behind it.

Perhaps sensing he'd struck a nerve, Brandon changed the subject. "You worked in advertising before you became a writer?"

She gave him a curious look.

He smiled. "It was on your website."

She felt her neck get warm. He'd read the bio on her website. He'd read all her books. He knew way more about her than she knew about him. All she knew about him was that he was a lawyer, and that he was divorced.

And that he was nice.

And funny.

And interesting.

And gorgeous.

He's so gorgeous.

She sipped her margarita and prayed he couldn't read her mind. "I wrote my first two novels while I was still working, but eventually I quit my job to focus full-time on writing."

"And it wasn't easy. Took a few years to get published, right?"

She smiled, the tequila beginning to calm her nerves. "*Also* in my bio. I see you did your homework."

"I always do my homework, at least now I do. As I mentioned, high school was another story. But back to you: I can't imagine writing an entire book; that's so impressive."

She shrugged. "Impressive is relative. I can't sing, and I draw stick people. I can barely keep myself alive in the deep end of a swimming pool, and I rarely remember what I ate for breakfast. The thought of arguing in court makes me want to throw up, and don't even get me started on the being a surgeon thing because I *have* fainted at the sight of blood. Should I go on?"

He laughed. "I'm serious. Writing an entire book is a huge accomplishment. How do you do it?"

"You mean how do I come up with the ideas? Or how do I make myself sit down to write that many pages?"

"Both."

She felt herself relax more as the conversation moved into territory she was comfortable discussing. "Well, to be honest, coming up with the initial idea is the hardest part, and I'm still not sure how that happens. It just . . . does. But before I get to that point, I always go through a bit of a freak-out period when I think I'll never come up with anything ever again and that I'm going to end up on the street, starving to death."

He raised an eyebrow. "Starving to death?"

"OK, it probably won't come to that, but you get the picture. Anyhow, I always worry for a while, but then eventually something occurs to me, and I think, *I could write a book about that.* And after that it's just a matter of sitting down at the computer every day and seeing what happens."

"You make it sound so easy."

"I'm serious. That's how it works. Although this time around..." Her voice trailed off.

"This time around what?"

She wondered how much to share, then decided to be forthright. "Well, this time around, as usual, the plot is unfolding in my head, but . . . it's not exactly unfolding the way I expected it to." *Or wanted it to.*

"Is that a bad thing?"

She took a sip of her margarita. "Well, I thought it would have a happy ending, because as you know, all my books have happy endings, but now I'm not so sure. Now I'm thinking maybe this one should end with something a bit more . . . realistic."

"And you're afraid your readers won't like that?"

"Yes . . . and . . ."

"And what?"

She considered just telling him the truth, that she wanted to write a happy ending for *herself.* There was something about the way he was looking at her that told her he wouldn't think any less of her for the admission. But then a completely separate thought came to her, a detail for a scene she'd been struggling with earlier that day. She held up a finger and reached for her purse. "I'm sorry, something just occurred to me for the chapter I'm working on right now." She fumbled around inside her bag and pulled out a small pack of sticky notes. "If I don't write it down, I'll never remember it."

He laughed. "You weren't kidding about that memory."

"It's really quite tragic. Hang on a sec." She jotted down a quick sentence, then tossed the sticky notes back into her purse. "I need to use every trick in the book, no pun intended."

He picked up his glass. "Give yourself some credit. Memory tricks are one thing, but there's also something to be said for a little thing called talent. I know a lot of people who talk about writing a book, but you're the only person I know who's ever actually *done* it."

"Thanks." She couldn't help but think how different Brandon was from buttoned-up Dean, an ambitious banker who had always made her feel a little irresponsible for having abandoned the security of her advertising job to pursue a living as an author. On the list of risky career choices, *novelist* had to be close to the top.

"What's the hardest part of the writing process?" Brandon asked.

She pushed a few strands of hair out of her eyes. "Again, I'm not sure how it is for other writers, but I always find that getting started is the hardest. Developing the characters, making them believable and sympathetic—or not—is challenging. But once I have that down, the characters begin to tell *me* the story, and then I sort of just listen to what they have to say."

"How do you get the ideas for the characters? Are they all based on people you know?"

"Some are, but some are completely made up. I've actually come up with a fun game to create them, or at least a way to generate some ideas for them."

He raised his eyebrows. "A game?"

She explained how the character game worked, then glanced over his shoulder and lowered her voice to a near whisper. "See that woman sitting alone over there?"

"Can I look without totally busting us?"

"Yes." She laughed and noted his discretion—more points in his favor.

He stole a quick peek at the woman, then turned back to Cassidy and smiled. "OK, now what?" His gray eyes were poking holes in her resolve not to get nervous around him, but she did her best to stay composed.

"What's her name?" Cassidy asked him.

He pointed to himself. "You want me to name her?"

"Yep. What's her name?"

"OK . . . Amanda. No, Audrey."

"Audrey what?"

"Audrey . . . Winston."

Cassidy nodded. "Audrey Winston, got it. Where's she from?"

"Um . . . Alabama."

"Nice. What does she do?"

"I say . . . lead dancer in a Broadway musical."

Cassidy smiled. "You're already good at this. OK, what makes her angry?"

He thought for a moment, then snapped his fingers and pointed at her. "When people ask her how old she is. That *really* ticks her off."

Cassidy laughed. "Nice. What makes her laugh?"

Brandon scratched his chin. "Hmm . . . I'd say . . . when people trip on the sidewalk."

"Oooh, so she's *mean*. I like it. What's her pet phrase?"

"Her pet phrase?"

"Yes. Something she says all the time, like the way Patti always says *stop it* to me, or the way my editor likes to say *cool beans*."

"Ah, got it." He paused to think, then snapped his fingers again. "How about she calls people *darling*?"

Cassidy nodded. "Nice. She really *does* sound like a bitch. OK, last one for you. What's her secret talent?"

"You mean besides keeping her age under wraps?"

"Yes, something totally random. For example, I can stand on one leg for like an hour."

He raised an eyebrow. "I'd like to see that. OK . . . how about . . . she can touch her nose with her tongue?"

Cassidy applauded. "I think *your* secret talent might be playing my character game. Well done, sir. Maybe you can help me with my next book."

"That sounds way more exciting than writing legal briefs, although then again, pretty much anything is more exciting than writing legal briefs. Except maybe reading legal briefs."

She held up her palms like the scales of justice. "I'd call it a tie. Equally boring."

He smiled and sipped his drink. "Do you like living in New York? I think it would be fun but exhausting."

"Fun but exhausting pretty much sums it up, actually. I love it, but yes, it can be draining. There's just so much going on all around, all the time, which can be a good thing and a bad thing."

"How so?"

She gestured around the bar, which was now nearly full. "When you feel like going out for a margarita on a Wednesday night, the energy buzzing every which way is great. But when you have to elbow your way through a sea of pedestrian traffic just to buy a carton of milk on a Sunday morning, it gets a little old. And then there's the subway, which is superconvenient but an absolute nightmare during rush hour. I mean, who wants to be forced to stare into a stranger's armpit on a hot summer day?"

He chuckled and picked up his glass. "Thanks for the visual. Would you ever move back to the Bay Area?"

"I know I will." She answered without hesitation, which surprised her. Would she?

"Why do you say that?"

"Because my parents are there, and my brother and his family. In the back of my head I know I'll end up there, it's just a matter of when." She wondered what had triggered the conviction in her voice, but regardless, they'd been talking about her long enough. "OK, that's more than too much about me, so I'm officially turning the tables. At the reunion you said you have two sons?"

"Yes, twins. Jack and Henry. They're five and a half." His eyes brightened when he said their names.

"Wow, twins. How do you get any sleep with twins? You must have been a zombie when they were babies."

"I'm still a bit of a zombie. You don't want to know how much money I spend on coffee."

She briefly wondered if she should play dumb about his marital status, then realized that would be . . . dumb. Instead she opted for a more mature approach to the topic, which was to be direct. "How long have you been divorced?"

"It was final about a year ago."

She stiffened. Only a year? Was he ready to be dating?

"Not that long, then," she said.

"Long enough." He held her gaze as he said the words, and she felt a little buzz somewhere deep inside her.

"OK," she said softly.

The bartender interrupted the moment, or whatever it was. "Would you two like another round?"

Cassidy looked at Brandon, determined to follow his lead.

He pointed toward the dining part of the restaurant. "Are you hungry? Can I buy you dinner?"

She smiled. "I hear the shrimp tacos here are really good."

Cassidy and Brandon followed the waiter through the brightly colored restaurant, which hummed with chatter and laughter from groups of friends and couples huddled at tables tucked close together. They settled into a two-top in a cozy back corner, and over yummy shrimp tacos and another round of margaritas shared stories of where life had taken them since their high-school days. Cassidy was surprised by how easily the conversation flowed. She knew that, as an attorney, Brandon must be intelligent, and that he took his work seriously, but she was pleased to discover that he had a playful side to him as well.

She dabbed her eyes with a napkin. "You didn't have a towel or *anything*?"

"I had *nothing*. And it was so hot that I was sweating buckets the whole bus ride, so when we finally got there, it looked like I'd literally peed all over the seat. You should have seen the look on the face of the woman who was sitting next to me when I stood up. I don't speak a word of Chinese and couldn't think of how to mime that it was only sweat, so I just gave her a sheepish look and got the hell out of there."

"That's hilarious. Gross—but hilarious."

He raised an eyebrow. "Tell that to that poor woman in the Chinese countryside."

She set down her napkin. "Hey, speaking of languages, what did you take at Paly?"

"Apparently I should have taken Chinese, but I took German. What about you?"

"I took *Español* with Señorita Azevedo. She was the best. Who was your favorite teacher?"

"Probably Mrs. Hori for biology. Did you have her?"

"Yep. She was one of my favorites too. Did you have Mr. Bakken for physics?"

He nodded. "Who didn't?"

"I still think about that man every time I hear the words *concave* or *convex*," Cassidy said.

He cleared his throat. "Nerd."

"I prefer the term *straight-A student*. I can't believe we never had a class together in four years."

He took a sip of water. "Six years, if you count junior high school. And you were in all the smart people classes, if I recall correctly. But to be honest, it's probably for the best that you didn't know me then. As you may or may not remember, I sported a serious bowl cut until the end of ninth grade."

She laughed as the waiter set a plate of flan between them. "You're pretty funny. Maybe you're the one who should be writing books."

"I'll leave that to you. I'd make a terrible writer."

"I don't know about that . . . you've got some pretty entertaining material to work with. I especially like that story about how you jumped off the roof of your fraternity using a parachute made out of bedsheets. What an idiot move."

He laughed. "I don't dispute that I was indeed an idiot, but that was a long time ago. Now that I've got the boys and the firm, there's a whole lot less time for getting into trouble. I'm sure these days your life is much more exciting than mine."

"I doubt that's true. And I think you have a mistaken impression of my not-so-glamorous life. I take a nap nearly every afternoon. People who need a nap every afternoon can't be all that exciting." *Oh dear.* Had she really just admitted that to him?

He gave her a look. "You take a nap every afternoon?"

"I can't believe I just told you that. I don't tell anyone that, except for Patti, of course. It's my guiltiest secret."

"Your secret is safe with me. In fact . . . I like that you told me. I can't remember the last time I took a nap. Between work and the twins, I never seem to get enough sleep."

She sensed a shift in energy—that they were on the verge of something more intimate than funny stories and general small talk. Even though tonight was only the second time they'd spoken to each other, she felt like she'd known him for much longer than that. Maybe that was due to their shared childhood experiences—but maybe it was something else.

As she watched him cut a piece of flan with his spoon, she wondered how many women were lining up to date him.

Women who didn't live three thousand miles away.

Before she realized what she was saying, Cassidy heard herself ask, "So what happened with you and your ex?" She balled her hands into fists, immediately regretting having posed such a probing question. Intimate was one thing, nosy was another. She quickly held up a hand. "I'm sorry, Brandon. You don't have to answer that." After they'd been getting along so well, she hoped she hadn't thrown cold water all over the evening.

He shrugged. "It's OK, I don't mind. It's not scandalous or anything. It just didn't work out, unfortunately."

She remained silent, not sure how to react. Though it was true she didn't have her own frame of reference, she wondered how he could be so detached about something so . . . significant.

"I wanted it to, but in hindsight I think I always knew we weren't right for each other," he added.

She paused before responding. "Then why did you get married?" It wasn't like her to be so direct with a person she barely knew, but something in his demeanor told her it was OK to ask.

He looked her straight in the eye. "Honest answer?"

"Of course."

He picked up his water glass. "Because we were both around thirty and we both wanted kids, and that's what couples do when they're around thirty and want to have kids. They get married."

His frankness startled her, but it also impressed her. It couldn't be easy to accept that he'd gone down that path with the wrong person, but he had clearly come to terms with it.

He's so grown-up.

She hated to admit it to herself, but she suddenly realized she'd never really dated a full-fledged adult before. Single men in New York—no matter what their age—tended to have a Peter Pan complex. All her friends said that, especially Danielle. Although Danielle sort of had a Peter Pan complex of her own.

She caught herself in midthought. *I've never dated a grown-up before?*

Is this a date?

This really feels like a date.

Or is that wishful thinking?

She blinked and forced her brain to return to the conversation. "Are you and she . . . friends?"

Brandon took a sip of water. "I wouldn't call us *friends*, but we get along OK. She's not a bitch or anything."

"My brother's wife is sort of a bitch." Cassidy's hand flew up and covered her mouth as soon as she'd uttered the words. "I can't believe I just said that. Can we pretend I didn't say that?"

He smiled. "It's OK. I like your honesty."

She cleared her throat and tried to get the conversation back on track. "*Anyhow*, it's good that you and she get along. I guess for the boys' sake you have to at least try, right?"

He nodded. "Exactly. We have our differences, but that's one thing we're completely in agreement about, putting the kids first."

"Do you split custody?"

"Yep, right down the middle."

"Have either of you been . . . dating?" She clenched her jaw. It was like her brain and mouth had lost contact. But once the question was out there, her mind started to race again.

Is this a date?

Are we on a date right now?

He didn't seem to mind her straightforwardness. "I think she's been seeing someone, but I couldn't say for sure. I've been on a few dates, nothing serious. It's hard to make the time. I have a pretty busy schedule, so dating hasn't been a priority. What about you? You seeing anyone?"

Oh.

That answered the question.

She felt slightly deflated but forced a slight smile. "Me? No, not really."

He cut another piece of flan with his spoon. "I find that hard to believe."

She smiled again and wondered if he was flirting with her or just making an observation—she hated that she couldn't differentiate between the two. She feigned confidence and replied, "It's true. I, um . . . I haven't been that lucky in love."

"Broken a few hearts, have you?"

"I wouldn't say I've broken any hearts, maybe bruised a few. And I've been burned myself a few times, but let's just leave it at that." She cursed herself for sharing too much—again. What was it about him that made her feel she could open up like this? Where was her aura of mystery? Everyone knew men loved an aura of mystery. Even her characters knew that.

"Have you ever been close to getting married?" he asked.

Cassidy felt a tiny pang at the memory of Dean. "I dated this one guy for about two and a half years, and I thought it was heading that way, but apparently he saw things differently." That was about the best way she could think of to sugarcoat the experience of having been unceremoniously dumped.

"I'm sorry to hear that."

"Thanks." She offered a weak smile and looked down, suddenly feeling undesirable. Thinking about Dean always made her feel that way. *Ugh.* She took a sip of water and wondered how this conversation had gotten so off track. An hour ago she'd been floating. And flirting.

Now she was flailing.

And failing.

She wished there were a school somewhere that could teach her how to talk to men she found attractive. Maybe that was how all the happy women out there found doting boyfriends and husbands. Had they all taken some secret class?

"When I saw you at the reunion, I was surprised to find out you weren't married."

She looked up at him. "Why?"

He laughed. "Please. You're beautiful and smart and funny. Who wouldn't want to marry you?"

She caught her breath and felt her stomach do a little flip-flop. The questions started bouncing around inside her head again, as if they were inside a pinball machine.

Are we on a date?

Is this a date?

She was beginning to feel as if she were engaged in two conversations at once.

Before she could respond to his compliment, the waiter appeared.

"Can I get you anything else?"

Brandon shook his head. "Just the check, please, thank you."

Cassidy reached for her purse and stood up. "I'll be right back. I'm just going to run to the ladies' room."

As best she could, she walked calmly across the room and pushed open the door to the restroom, trying to process what Brandon had just said to her.

You're beautiful and smart and funny. Who wouldn't want to marry you?

She washed her hands and saw the confused look on her own face in the mirror.

Is he interested in me?

He must be interested in me to say those things, right?

Or was he just saying them to be nice?

She pressed a palm against her forehead.

How can I be thirty-eight years old and still have absolutely no idea how to read men?

"Thanks so much for dinner, Brandon. I had a really nice time."

"It was my pleasure. Thanks for taking the time out of your busy schedule to see me."

Cassidy rolled her eyes. "I left my apartment for the first time at three o'clock today. My schedule is hardly busy."

He held the door open for her. "Did you skip your nap?"

She laughed. "I guess I did."

"Well then, let me rephrase it. I appreciate your skipping your nap to see me."

"No problem. Apparently I'll do anything for an old high-school friend, even one who never spoke to me."

He held up his palms. "Hey now, I think we established that you're the one who never spoke to *me*."

As they made their way toward the subway entrance a block away, she wished the sidewalk ahead of them would magically elongate to prolong their time together. She stole a glance up at him as they walked, imagining once again what it would feel like to touch the stubble on his face. At the reunion she'd found him physically attractive, but tonight she'd been surprised by his intelligence and sense of humor. More than anything, the playful banter that had sprung up between them had caught her off guard. There was something undeniably magnetic about being able to joke around with a man she also wanted to kiss, and she wanted more of whatever it was stirring up inside of her. She wanted to suggest they go for a stroll around the West Village, or stop for coffee, or grab another drink, anything to keep this night from ending.

But she couldn't bring herself to speak up and make it happen.

Then again, he wasn't making it happen either.

Maybe that was her answer. If she'd learned anything about men over the years, it was that when they were interested in a woman, they usually made it known.

But not always.

Which left her at square one.

Much to her chagrin, they reached the stairwell leading down to the subway. She stepped to one side so as not to block pedestrian traffic, then looked up at him to say good-bye.

They might as well have been standing in front of her high-school locker, given how nervous she was.

"Well, I guess this is where we part ways," she said with a shaky smile. "When do you fly out?"

"Tomorrow morning. I have to meet a client back in Palo Alto in the afternoon."

"Got it." *New York will miss you*, she thought.

She stood there for a moment, wishing he would do something, anything, to indicate that he was interested in her. She couldn't be the only one feeling all this chemistry, could she? Was that possible? She didn't believe in one-sided chemistry.

He put his hands in his pockets. "It was really good to catch up. Get home safely, OK? Watch out for those armpits on the subway."

She smiled and stood on her tiptoes to give him a brief hug. "I'll do my best. Have a good trip back to California."

"Thanks. I'll be in touch."

She waved a bit awkwardly, then turned and quickly descended into the subway without looking back.

She swiped her MetroCard at the turnstile and walked toward a bench flush along the wall facing the track. She plopped herself down with a sigh, and as she waited for the next uptown train to arrive, all she could think was one thing.

I'll be in touch?

What in God's name does that mean?

Twenty minutes later Cassidy exited the subway at Seventy-Second Street and walked slowly toward her building. The entire ride uptown she'd been replaying the night's events in her head, reliving the conversation, trying to figure out what it all meant, if anything.

Date or no date, after spending two hours with Brandon she was certain of one thing: she liked him.

Liked him liked him, high-school style.

She balled her hands into fists. *Damn it.*

This is not convenient.

She was half a block from her building when she heard a man's voice. "Hey, Cassidy."

She looked up and saw her neighbor walking toward her. "Hi, Harper. Where are you off to?"

"Headed to the Ale House for a beer. Don't *you* look nice tonight. Are you coming from a hot date?"

She laughed weakly. "I'm not sure."

"Say what?"

"We went to high school together. He was in town for work and asked me out for a drink, so I think *maybe* it was a date, but to be honest, I don't really know." She frowned. "I'm so stupid about men."

Harper held out his arms. "Does Cassidy need a hug?"

She put her hands on her waist. "Don't tempt me. You know how much I love your hugs."

He put his arms around her and squeezed her tight. "Want to come have a brew with me? It's still early."

She thought about it for a moment, then looked up at him and nodded. "Sure, why not? It's not all that often I'm wearing a dress, much less on a Wednesday night, right?"

"That's the spirit."

They turned back on Seventy-Third toward the Amsterdam Ale House, the closest thing Cassidy had to a regular watering hole, which for her meant dropping by once or twice a month. Harper was in there all the time, but he was only twenty-nine. She still enjoyed going out for drinks on occasion, but most days she'd gladly take a coffeehouse over an alehouse.

They sat down at the bar, and Harper ordered them each a hefeweizen. He lifted his glass to hers for a toast. "I have some news."

She clinked her glass against his and took a sip. "Good news, I hope?"

"I think so. I've decided to apply to business school."

"No way. For next fall?"

"Yes."

"Where are you applying? You realize that's actually *bad* news if it means you're leaving town, right?" Despite their age difference, she and Harper had been close friends since the day they'd met in the elevator nearly three years ago. She loved having a male friend, especially one who was still in his twenties. It secretly made her feel cool that he wanted to hang out with her so much, although she'd never admit that to him.

"Well, NYU and Columbia are two of the schools I'm applying to, so if I get in to one of them, I may stick around. Will you help with my essays? I could use a professional opinion."

"Of course, although I'm not sure how much help I'll be. It's been quite a while since I've seen a school essay of any kind."

He gave her a look. "Cassidy, you write books for a living. I stare at spreadsheets. Believe me, I need some assistance."

She laughed. "OK, I'll help. Why do you want to go back to school anyway? Don't you already make like a zillion dollars a year?" He also had an enormous trust fund.

He shrugged. "I guess I'm a little bored."

"You're bored by making a zillion dollars a year?"

"When you put it *that* way . . . but seriously, I need a change, and going back to school seems like a good way to make that happen."

She held up her glass to his for another toast. "I'm all for change. I'm living proof of change."

"Cheers to that. So are you coming to my birthday party tomorrow? You didn't respond."

She put a hand over her mouth. "I'm sorry, I totally forgot. When's the party again?"

"Tomorrow night in SoHo."

The thought of attending a *thirtieth* birthday party at all was scary enough, and of doing so alone was unbearable. "Can I invite my friend Danielle?"

"Of course, the more the merrier. I rented out the upstairs at Novecento."

"Must be nice having money to burn."

He put a hand on her shoulder. "Does it bother you that I insist on paying for everything when we go out? If so, I can put a stop to that right now."

She patted his hand and smiled. "Let's not be too hasty, Mr. Moneybags. I can't believe you're finally turning thirty. I never thought it would happen."

"You and me both. I've come to terms with it, though."

"You'll make a good addition to the club. Is that girl you told me about going to be at the party? What was her name? Valerie?"

"Vanessa. And yes, she'll be there."

"Then I'm in. I want to meet any woman who can capture the interest of the elusive Harper Gold."

On their way home, Cassidy pulled her cell phone out of her purse to check the time. When she looked at the screen, she noticed a new text message.

She caught her breath.

It was from Brandon.

Had a great time catching up, was sorry to see you get on that subway.

She stopped walking. "Oh my God."

"Is everything OK?" Harper asked.

She showed him the text. "What do you think?"

He studied the screen. "This is from the guy you were with earlier tonight?"

"Yes."

He handed her the phone back. "Well, there's your answer about whether or not it was a date."

"Should I reply?"

Harper laughed. "I know he's from your high school, but you're not *in* high school anymore, Cassidy. Of course you should reply."

"What should I say?" She began to chew on her fingernail, then pulled it away from her mouth. *I need to get that manicure.*

"You're asking *me*?"

"You're a guy. I value your opinion."

"You're a *writer*, Cassidy. I'm sure you can come up with something. Just send him a nice note back."

"But should I reply now, or should I wait until tomorrow? I don't want to make the wrong move."

He shrugged. "I say reply now. You know I'm not into playing games."

She smiled at him. "I love that about you. Have I ever told you that?"

"Many times. You love me, you love me, you love me. Now text him back." He pointed to her phone.

She studied the screen for a moment, then typed a response she hoped would indicate the appropriate level of interest.

It was nice seeing you too. Regret is mutual. Have a safe trip home.

As soon as she hit send, she showed the phone to Harper. "How about that?"

He rolled his eyes. "I can't believe we're doing this. You're acting like you're sixteen, do you realize that?"

"I *feel* like I'm sixteen right now. Was that a good reply?" She pushed the phone at him.

He read the message and nodded. "It's good."

She exhaled. "This is exhausting. Fun but exhausting."

"As life should be," Harper said. "Otherwise what's the point?"

Cassidy smiled at him. "I like that. I might have to use it in a book."

Chapter Six

THE NEXT AFTERNOON Cassidy paced the lobby of her building, phone in hand, waiting for the car service that would ferry her to Brooklyn for the video shoot. The weather had taken a severe turn, and it was too cold and windy outside to stand on the sidewalk. She wondered if she had time to run back upstairs and tuck an umbrella into her purse, just in case. Getting stuck in the rain was no joke in New York; out of nowhere it could start pouring *hard*. She'd gotten soaked to the skin more times than she cared to admit.

Just as she took a step in the direction of the elevator, she heard the chime of her cell. The driver had arrived.

I guess that answers the umbrella question.

She gave the doorman a polite wave good-bye before ducking into the black sedan double-parked outside. The driver shut the door behind her, and soon they were on their way.

Before they'd driven a block, it started raining.

Well done, Cassidy.

Twenty-five minutes later they entered a remote corner of Williamsburg. As the car began to slow down, Cassidy wondered if they were in the right place. The area looked like something out of a movie. A scary movie. Maybe a movie about a crack dealer. When the chauffeur pulled to a stop in front of a run-down building with a broken window and peeling yellow paint, the sidewalk littered with trash, her mind began to race with thoughts along the lines of *There has to be some mistake. This can't be the right address. Please, Mr. Driver, don't make me get out of the car.* The driver apparently thought otherwise, because he exited the car and held up a large umbrella for Cassidy as he opened the back door and gestured to the entrance.

"We're here?" she asked.

"Yes, ma'am." He gave her a polite nod.

OK then, we're here.

She stepped out of the car and tentatively approached the building, looking to her left and right as she walked next to the chauffeur. There wasn't a soul in sight. She'd never been to a real studio before, but somehow she'd expected more than . . . *this.* A sign on the outside of the building, for example.

She rang the doorbell and was soon greeted by a short blonde woman carrying a clipboard and wearing a headset. "Cassidy Lane?"

Cassidy smiled. "That's me."

The woman extended her free hand. "I'm Diane French, the production assistant for the shoot. It's so nice to meet you. Please, come inside."

Cassidy followed her into the building and her jaw dropped.

The place was beautiful.

Stunning.

She looked around the cavernous studio. The entire left side of the room was staged to look like a plush living room; all the décor and furniture was white, with ivory vases filled with white flowers everywhere, and the entire scene was gently bathed by soft light. Even the brick walls were painted white. To the right was a bunch of camera and lighting equipment, behind which sat a long table covered with platters of cheese, crackers, sandwiches, fruit, and cookies.

Diane pointed to the table. "Can I get you something to eat or drink? Hair and makeup will be ready for you in a few minutes."

"Water would be great, thank you. Will this outfit work? I wasn't sure how fancy to go." Cassidy opened her coat to reveal the solid navy-blue dress underneath, a single strand of pearls around her neck.

Diane nodded. "It's perfect. I'll be right back with that water." She turned on her heel and walked away.

Just then Cassidy heard the chime of her phone. She pulled it out of her purse and smiled.

A text from Brandon.

> Just landed. Won't miss the screaming baby in the seat behind me. Might miss you, though. On my way to meet my client, hope your video shoot goes well.

She let out a little gasp, unable to contain her delight.

He might miss me!

She typed a quick reply, then silenced her phone and tossed it into her purse as Diane returned with her water.

Diane handed her the glass and gestured toward the makeup table. "You ready?"

Cassidy smiled, already feeling prettier than she had in a long time. "Let's do it."

"Look at you, picking me up in a town car. I could get on board with this celebrity thing."

Cassidy scooted over as the driver shut the car behind Danielle. "I'm hardly a celebrity. Do you think I have too much makeup on? I'm afraid I look like a prostitute."

Danielle waved a hand in front of her. "Nonsense. You look hot."

"Are you sure? I'm feeling really self-conscious right now. I didn't expect them to cake it on me like that, though at least they covered that annoying scrape on my nose."

Danielle gave her a look. "How does a grown woman scrape her nose anyway? Sounds very suspicious, if you ask me. I'm not sure I want to know."

"Don't get all excited. I think I must have scratched myself when I was sleeping."

"Well, scratch or no scratch, trust me, you look hot. So where's this party again?"

"An Argentinian restaurant called Novecento, on West Broadway and Grand. Have you been there?"

"Multiple times, I love that place."

"Harper rented the upstairs."

"I can't believe I'm finally going to meet this Harper you're always talking about." She gave her a sideways glance. "Are you sure you don't have a thing for him? Or vice versa?"

Cassidy rolled her eyes. "Give me a break. He's like my little brother."

"I'm just saying, you never know whence romance might spring."

"Have you already forgotten about Brandon?"

"Is Brandon the high-school guy?"

"Yes."

"I guess I have. Did you see him? How did it go?"

As the car drove them downtown—in traffic, but under clear skies after the earlier rainfall—Cassidy provided a summary of her evening. When she was done, she gave Danielle an expectant look. "What do you think?"

"He kept his hands in his pockets?"

"Yes."

"Hmm."

Cassidy held up her phone. "But he's definitely been flirting over text, so maybe he was just being shy?"

Danielle shrugged and leaned back into the folds of the town car.

"What?" Cassidy said.

"I didn't say anything."

"Exactly, and that says something. What is it?"

Danielle shrugged again. "I just think if he was truly interested, he would have tried to kiss you, at least on the cheek."

Cassidy's face fell, and she began to nibble on her fingernail. "You think so?"

"I'm just going from my own experience. Did you tell him you'd be out there for Halloween?"

Cassidy shook her head. "I didn't know how to work it into the conversation without sounding, I don't know, *obvious*."

"Obvious about what?"

"Obvious that I would want to see him while I was out there."

Before Danielle could reply, Cassidy's phone chimed:

My crazy client dragged me to happy hour at the Old Pro, already bought us tequila shots. This could get interesting. When was the last time you did tequila shots? Would be way more fun if you were here.

"Oh my God! Look!" She showed the phone to Danielle.

Danielle read the text and smiled. "OK, I take it back. He's definitely interested."

When they arrived at the restaurant, the private room upstairs was packed—and loud. As they wandered through the crowd, Cassidy wondered if she'd ever find Harper.

Danielle pointed toward the bar. "Let's get a drink. What's your poison?"

Cassidy scratched her cheek. "Hmm, given that we're in the Malbec Room, how about a glass of that?"

"I'm on it."

As Danielle waited to order their wine, Cassidy surveyed the party landscape. Most of the guests looked around Harper's age, although there were several who appeared to be in their forties or even older. Cassidy loved that about New York. No matter where she went, she never felt old. She could only imagine what it would be like to be thirty-eight and single at a bar in Kansas City. Or Omaha. Or most of the United States, now that she thought about it.

Danielle handed her the drink. "You see him anywhere?"

"Not yet."

"Do you know anyone else here?

"I highly doubt it. My world doesn't really intersect with the banker crowd."

"Tristan's in finance too. Did I ever tell you that?"

"Not that I remember, which probably means yes. Have you ended things with him yet?"

Danielle shook her head. "It's on my to-do list, though. I

promise. Unless he randomly shows up at this party, in which case I'll probably go home with him."

Cassidy laughed. "I'm so glad you're around this week. I don't know if I could have made myself come to this thing alone."

Danielle sipped her wine. "I know what you mean. I don't have a problem going out for a drink by myself when I'm on the road, but doing it in my own city would be another story."

"Cassidy!" The sound of a male voice made them both turn their heads. Harper emerged from the crowd, a tipsy grin on his face. "I'm glad you made it."

"Wouldn't have missed it." Cassidy set her drink on the bar and gave him a hug. "Harper Gold, this is my friend, Danielle Thompson."

"It's nice to meet you, Danielle." He offered his hand.

Danielle smiled at him. "Likewise. Happy birthday."

Cassidy glanced around the room. "This place is packed, Harper. Who knew you were so popular?"

"It's easy to be popular when you pay for the drinks."

Danielle laughed. "That sounds like something I would say. Do you work with most of these people?"

"Some of them. Others I know from college, a few from my basketball league. Some are complete strangers, probably friends of friends or freeloaders or both."

Cassidy held her glass up high. "What's a party without freeloaders?"

The three of them toasted, and Cassidy tugged on Harper's arm. "Is Vanessa here?"

"She just walked in. Directly behind you, red dress."

"Who's Vanessa?" Danielle asked.

"New crush." Cassidy mouthed the words.

Danielle nodded. "Ah, got it."

Harper lowered his voice. "I think she's coming over here."

"Hey Harper, happy birthday," Vanessa said as she walked up, then stood on her tiptoes and gave him a hug. As she did so, Danielle and Cassidy exchanged a look. Vanessa's dress was indeed red, but that wasn't the first word Cassidy would have chosen to describe it. An array of other adjectives popped into her head. Topping the list were *low-cut*, *tight*, and *inappropriate*.

She tried to mask the look of surprise she knew was on her face.

This is the girl Harper likes?

Classy, conservative Harper?

Vanessa broke the embrace and turned toward Cassidy and Danielle with a smile. "Hi, I'm Vanessa." She looked friendly enough, but it was hard to get past her outfit.

They all shook hands, and then Danielle grabbed Cassidy's arm. "We were just going to mingle, so we'll catch you two later." She quickly pulled Cassidy toward the other side of the room. "Yowsa, that was a lot of boobage," she whispered as they walked away.

Cassidy nodded. "She's the opposite of what I'd expect for him. I wonder what's going on there."

"To each his own. Maybe underneath that slutty outfit, she's a peach." Danielle looked up at the ornate ceiling. "I forgot what a great space this is. I haven't been here in ages."

Cassidy's eyes followed hers. "I've never been here before. I love that about New York. There's an endless supply of fun new spots to go have a drink. In Palo Alto there are like three bars, and it seems like everyone's in college."

Danielle sipped her wine. "I remember exactly the last time I was here. It was a couple years ago, for a coworker's going-away party. I got schnockered and ended up going home with this random guy who lived in White Plains."

Cassidy stared at her. "White Plains? As in it-takes-an-hour-to-get-there White Plains?"

"The one and only. Mind you, I was hardly in a state of mind to be thinking rationally. So I went home with him, and the next morning we took the train to Grand Central together. It was beyond awkward."

"He came back into the city with you?'

Danielle nodded. "The party was on a Thursday, so we both had to go to work the next day. It was the longest train ride of my life."

"Did you ever see him again?"

She waved a hand in front of her. "Oh God no. I think he was as mortified as I was. I can only imagine what the people around us were thinking. There I was, still in my going-out dress and rat's-nest hair. I'm sure it was superobvious that we had hooked up the night before."

"I love it! You totally took a train ride of shame."

Danielle nodded. "I did indeed. I also took a nap on the couch in our employee lounge that day. It wasn't one of my finer moments."

Cassidy sipped her wine. "I've taken the subway ride of shame, but I haven't reached train-ride status yet."

"It's an elite club. We take our membership seriously."

Cassidy laughed. "I should put that story into one of my books."

Danielle grabbed her arm. "If you do, be a dear and call me Elena, will you? I've always loved that name."

"Deal." Cassidy looked around the room, which was growing more crowded by the minute. "I wonder how many of these people will be doing the subway ride of shame tomorrow."

"I'd say about a baker's dozen. Or given how many finance types are here, perhaps a banker's dozen. Want another drink?"

Cassidy looked at her half-full wineglass and shrugged. "Sure, why not?"

On the way to the bar they were stopped by two men wearing suits and ties. Both had baby faces and looked like poster boys for a fraternity's young alumni organization.

"Hey now, slow down," the taller of the two said with a grin. "What's the rush?"

Danielle pointed to her empty glass, then to the bar. "Do I need to explain further?"

The shorter of the two put a hand on his chest. "This round's on me. What are you drinking? I'm Evan, by the way." He smiled at Danielle and appeared to be a bit smitten.

Danielle squinted at him. "You realize it's an open bar, right?"

Evan laughed but was clearly nervous. "Uh, yeah, that was supposed to be a joke."

Danielle shrugged. "OK, not bad, not bad. I'll have a gin and tonic. I'm Danielle."

Cassidy pointed to her glass. "Another Malbec would be nice. I'm Cassidy."

"One gin and tonic, one Malbec, coming right up. Stay right here." Evan pointed to the spot where they were standing, then turned and squeezed through the crowd toward the bar.

His friend held out a hand. "I'm Conner."

Danielle shook it. "Hi, Conner, it's nice to meet you." By the way Danielle was looking at him, Cassidy could tell she was sizing him up for a potential smooch. There was no denying he was cute, despite appearing so young. But given how Evan had just been ogling Danielle, Cassidy suspected an awkward love triangle was about to unfold.

"Do you work with Harper?" Danielle asked him.

He glanced down at his outfit. "That obvious?"

She smiled. "The banker uniform sort of gives it away."

He laughed. "Busted. What about you two? How do you know the birthday boy?"

Cassidy gestured to herself, then to Danielle. "I live in his building, and Danielle's a good friend of mine."

Connor nodded. "Cool. It's nice to see some older women here."

Danielle coughed. "Come again?"

Connor's face turned red. "Um, I didn't mean . . . I meant . . ."

"You didn't mean what?" Evan reappeared and handed Cassidy and Danielle their drinks.

"He didn't mean to say we're old." Danielle took a sip of her drink.

Evan flashed Connor an irritated look. "Dude, I was gone for like two minutes. What is wrong with you?"

"Uh . . ." was all Connor could come up with in response.

Danielle grabbed Cassidy's arm and pulled her away. "It was lovely chatting with you two, but we've got to run along to bed now, advanced age and all, you know how it is. Thanks for the drinks."

As they blended into the crowd, Cassidy leaned toward Danielle's ear and borrowed one of Patti's favorite lines. "We must never speak of that again."

Danielle laughed. "Holy frick. Maybe you can use *that* in one of your books."

Despite the evening's inauspicious beginning, Cassidy and Danielle ended up having a great time at the party and were two of the last people to leave. After Connor's candid admission, they'd retreated briefly to a corner to lick their wounds and considered going home, but then the DJ, who they jokingly decided must be from their generation, started playing a lot of early nineties music, and they hit the dance floor with a vengeance. Sometimes with a partner, but just as often without, they danced and danced and didn't stop until the DJ packed it in.

"Wow, you two seriously rallied." Harper came up to them as they were in line to retrieve their coats. Vanessa was on his arm and appeared quite drunk, as did many of the guests still milling about. Cassidy, who had cut herself off at two drinks hours ago, took a look around the room and thought *I remember those days*. Somehow it seemed like a lifetime ago and not long ago at all. One thing she remembered clearly from those days: most of these people were going to be hurting at work tomorrow morning.

Danielle smoothed her hair with one hand. "I haven't danced that much since my clubbing days. It's sad to say, but I bet my legs are going to hate me tomorrow."

Cassidy buttoned up her coat. "And I'm sad to say I never had *clubbing days* at all."

"I could really use a slice of pizza right about now. Interested?" Danielle looked at her.

Cassidy nodded. "I'm in. Harper? Vanessa? You guys hungry?"

Harper adjusted his scarf and tilted his head toward Vanessa, who was staring off into space. "I think I've got to put this one to bed and get some sleep myself, but thanks for the offer."

Cassidy gave him a look of feigned sympathy. "I understand. Now that you're thirty, you need to get to bed early."

Vanessa wrapped her arms around him and slurred, "You ready, old man?"

"Sure thing, just need to settle up with the manager." He pointed toward the front of the room. "Thanks again for coming, Cassidy. And Danielle, it was really nice to meet you."

"Likewise. Happy birthday, Harper."

As she watched Harper guide a wobbly Vanessa in the other direction, Cassidy wondered what it would be like to be twenty-five again. If she were to do it all over, knowing what she did now, would her life turn out differently?

The real question was, would she want it to?

She felt a rush of happiness as she realized that the answer was no.

Despite the occasional bout of self-doubt, her life was pretty good just as it was.

Cassidy was just about to bite into her second piece of pizza when she heard her phone chime. She set the slice down and began digging around in her purse.

Danielle gave her a look. "You're not going to eat this cheesy deliciousness while it's hot?"

"I just want to see who the text is from."

"You mean you want to see if high-school guy texted you."

Cassidy smiled as she dug. "Perhaps."

Danielle kept eating her pizza. "It would have to be a pretty steamy text to pull me away from this greasy slice of heaven right now."

Cassidy looked at her phone and let out a tiny squeal. "Three text messages in a row! All from him!"

"What do they say?"

"The first one says, 'Four tequila shots and counting.' The second one says, 'I'm hammered. Have I told you I think ur beautiful?' And the third one says, 'Ur so pretty. So so pretty.'"

"No way."

Cassidy showed her the phone. "Read for yourself."

Danielle looked at the screen and nodded. "He's definitely into you."

Cassidy pressed the phone against her heart. "Brandon Forrester likes me," she whispered.

Danielle gave her a look. "What is this—math class? You do realize you're not actually *in* high school anymore, right?

"I sort of feel like it right now."

"You think he's going to ask you to the prom?"

Cassidy smiled and fluttered her eyelashes. "Maybe."

Chapter Seven

THE NEXT MORNING Cassidy called to make an appointment for a manicure at Annabelle's, then spent a few hours working on her novel. After lunch she was on her way out the door to the salon when her phone rang. She smiled when she saw the name on the display.

Brandon!

She locked her front door and tossed the keys into her purse. "Well, hello there, Mr. Multiple Tequila Shots, how are we feeling today?"

"Not well. Did I wake you up from your nap?"

She laughed. "You're good. Way to deflect the heckling."

"I'm an attorney. It's all about diversion and plausible denial. So did I wake you?"

"For the record, it's not three o'clock yet, so no, you didn't. What happened last night? By the way, I'm about to get into an elevator right now, so if I lose you, don't think I hung up on you."

"If I tell you about last night, I fear you *may* hang up on me, then possibly delete me from your phone."

"Oh, really? Now you must tell me. Getting in the elevator right now."

"I rode the bull at the Old Pro."

Her jaw dropped as she pressed the button for the lobby. "No way."

"It's true."

She covered her mouth with her hand. "I can't believe it." Much to the chagrin of many a well-heeled Palo Alto resident, the Old Pro sports bar featured a mechanical bull in a back corner.

"I bet it's been a while since a gray-haired father of two has been on that thing."

She felt her face contort a bit. "I can't even imagine what that looked like."

"Please don't try to. It wasn't a pretty sight."

"I would have paid to see it. Did anyone take a video?"

"Oh God, let's hope not. That could put my firm out of business. Is it too early to order Chinese food?"

She stepped out of the elevator and glanced at the big clock mounted on the lobby wall. It was five minutes before one o'clock, at least on the East Coast. "Are Chinese restaurants open at ten in the morning?"

"I sure hope so. This hangover might kill me if I don't eat something greasy soon."

"I'm liking this side of you. At dinner the other night, you seemed to have it so together. Stepping outside now, so if I lose you it's because I got hit by a car."

"Thanks for the play-by-play. I hardly have it all together, as you could probably tell by my drunken confessional text messages."

She felt her cheeks get warm and paused.

"Did you get hit by a car?" he asked. "Are you still alive?"

She swallowed and finally replied. "Still alive. And actually

. . . I liked your text messages," she said softly.

"You did?"

"Very much." *I loved them!*

"I'm glad to hear that. I was a little worried when you didn't respond."

"I'm sorry. I wasn't sure whether it was, you know, just drunken chatter that you were going to . . . regret."

"No, can't claim it was just drunken chatter."

"So no plausible denial?"

"In this case, no."

Another silence followed.

It was delicious.

After a few seconds, Brandon spoke. "Thank God I don't have the boys this weekend. I'm going to be asleep by eight tonight."

"I take it you don't normally drink that much?"

"Not since I had kids, no way. It's just too hard. Now I only drink at all once in a blue moon, although that blue moon usually rises when this particular client is in town. He's nuts, and he likes to schedule late meetings so he can drag me out on the town afterward. It's usually a lot of fun, but I end up paying for it big-time. I just can't drink like that anymore and function like a productive human being the next day, much less a responsible father."

"I hear you. I had two glasses of wine last night and I can feel it today. How sad."

"Maybe for Halloween this year we should both go as old people. Then we wouldn't have to dress up."

She laughed. "I'm actually coming home for Halloween."

"You are? For book stuff?"

"Technically I'll be out there to speak at a conference, but to be honest, I agreed to do it because I want to take my nieces trick-or-treating."

"How long will you be in town?"

"About a week." *Please ask me on a date.*

"A whole week, eh?"

"Yes." *Please ask me on a date.*

"Why didn't you mention that the other night?"

She hesitated before responding. "Honest answer?"

"Of course."

She bit her lip. "Because I was too nervous."

He laughed. "I make you nervous?"

"Maybe."

"Am I making you nervous now?"

"Honest answer?"

"Yes."

She chewed on her thumbnail. "Maybe."

"I like when you're honest. I think it's attractive. I think *you're* very attractive."

She felt her neck getting hot. "Um, thanks." *Please ask me on a date.* She was just steps away from the salon now and would have to hang up in a moment.

She looked up at the friendly sign that said ANNABELLE'S.

It was time to go.

Damn.

She began to speak. "Listen—"

He interrupted her. "So . . . maybe you and I could try dinner again when you're out here?"

She exhaled and smiled into the phone. "I'd like that."

"Well, hello there. We meet again. Can I take your coat?" The owner approached Cassidy with a warm smile and gestured to the manicure table. "Please, have a seat. Would you like some tea?"

"Thanks, that would be nice." Cassidy removed her coat and glanced around the quiet salon, which was about half full and smelled like fresh pine needles. She took a seat at the table on the far side of the room and interlaced her hands in her lap, enjoying the classical music playing in the background. She could still hear the street traffic outside, but there was no denying the soothing ambience of Annabelle's. Cassidy had just arrived and already she felt more relaxed.

A few moments later, the woman set a steaming cup of tea on the table, then placed a warm wrap around Cassidy's neck before taking a seat across from her.

"That feels wonderful," Cassidy said.

The woman winked and held out her hands. "Now let's have another look at those mittens of yours, shall we?" She kept her voice low, which Cassidy liked.

"Do I have to show you?"

The woman laughed. "Believe me, I've seen worse than yours. Now hand them over."

Cassidy relented. "How is business going so far?"

"Pretty well, I must say. Our evening schedule is already booked up this week, as is Saturday. Sunday we have just a few appointments left."

"Already? That's impressive."

"It's mostly Annabelle's friends, but she has a lot of friends."

"Annabelle?"

"The woman who was in here the other day, the one I thought was missing her appointment? She owns this place."

Cassidy could feel the confusion spread over her face. "You're not Annabelle?"

"Oh no, love. I'm Darlene."

"This isn't your shop?"

Darlene shook her head. "Oh, how I wish it were, but no.

Annabelle Polanski owns it. Or she and her husband do, I should say. I'm just the manager, love."

"I'm sorry, I just assumed . . . because you were here the other day."

Darlene squeezed her hands. "Don't worry. I care about this place as if it were my own. That's enough for me. Now let's do something about these nails."

Cassidy closed her eyes and spent the entire manicure reliving the conversation with Brandon in her head.

Several hours later Cassidy was still at her desk when she heard the chime of her phone. She picked it up and smiled at the sight of Brandon's name:

Just wanted to repeat that I find you very attractive.

The rest of the conversation was threaded throughout the afternoon and evening:

You do?

Yes. There's something in your eyes. It's sexy.

MY eyes? Do you own a mirror?

I like yours. The green is . . . alluring.

Yours are beyond cool. They remind me of a wolf's.

You're telling me I look like a wolf?

Ha. Just the eyes, silly. You definitely do not have a
wolf face.

Glad to hear it. I'm already looking forward to our date.
T-minus three weeks, and believe me, I'm counting.

Brandon texted her again the next morning to say hi, as well as
the morning after that, and before she knew it, they were texting
back and forth regularly, each day sprinkled with a steady stream
of flirtatious banter combined with regular conversation that left
her with a permanent half smile on her face. In addition to the text
messages, every few nights he'd call her on the phone, and they'd
chat for an hour or two, the time whipping by until a weary Cassidy
finally had to force herself to go to bed. Between talk about family,
friends, his kids, her books, his work, and their favorite movies,
there seemed to be no lack of topics of conversation.

They even covered their favorite foods.

"Marshmallows? For real?" Brandon said one Tuesday night
after his kids had gone to sleep. "I thought it was just your favorite
dessert, not your favorite *food*. Is that even a food?"

Cassidy curled her legs up against her chest. "You sound like
Patti, and I already know where this conversation is going. Let's
just agree to disagree, OK?"

"Disagreement agreed. How's the book coming along?"

"It's coming. I still need to come up with a good name for one
of the characters. Hey, want to help?" She reached for the note-
book on her nightstand.

"Sure. Who is it?"

"It's a tall, skinny woman in her late forties, American, sort of
bitchy. She runs a Pilates studio in San Francisco."

"A bitchy Pilates instructor? I don't do Pilates, but isn't that
sort of an oxymoron?"

Cassidy shrugged. "Perhaps, but not this time. So what do you think? It's always hard for me to name characters because I always associate them with people I know in real life. And when the character isn't a fan favorite, it's especially hard because I don't want to offend anyone."

He laughed. "You know that many people?"

"Hey now, it's harder than it sounds. So what have you got?"

He paused for a moment. "How about Liza?"

"Nope. There was a Liza in my sorority. What if I run into her at a reunion or something? You know how people run into each other at reunions . . ."

"I *do* know how people run into each other at reunions. What about Simone?"

"No way. A Simone works for my publisher. She'd hate me."

"Brenda?"

She chewed on her pencil. "My aunt's name is Brenda. Plus there's the whole *Beverly Hills 90210* thing. Who could forget *that* bitch?"

"Man, you weren't joking about this not being easy."

"I told you! Welcome to my world, Wolf Eyes."

"What about Crystal?"

"No can do. Remember Crystal Hightower from high school? She's a huge fan of my books. I could never do that to her."

"OK, how about Blair?"

Cassidy raised her eyebrows. "Oooh, Blair is good. I don't know anyone named Blair, but it sure sounds bitchy."

"Blair definitely sounds bitchy."

Cassidy jotted the name down on her notepad. "OK, I'm going with Blair. Well done, kind sir. Thank you very much."

"You're welcome. That was quite a change from prepping a witness for a deposition."

"It's hard work, but someone has to do it. I may have to put you in the acknowledgments for your help."

He lowered his voice. "I can think of other ways you can thank me."

She caught her breath, unprepared for the sudden change in tone. "Is that so?"

"It is so. Now get to bed and dream about *that*."

She smiled. "I'll do my best; good night."

The calls and texts kept coming, and soon Cassidy felt as though she'd been close to Brandon for years. She had more energy during her runs than she could ever remember, wanted to smile for no reason, and felt a light buzzing sensation deep inside herself at all times, as if the energy between them was constantly flowing, even when they weren't actually in contact. To pass the time on the subway, she'd often scroll through her phone and reread her favorite parts of their ongoing conversation, some of which made her stomach do a little flip-flop at the promise of what this might be turning into.

Monday afternoon:

I'm so glad you went to the reunion.

I'm glad you're glad. You didn't seem all that interested. Too many girls swarming around you, I suppose . . .

Are you joking?

Krista Nelson wouldn't shut up about you. Had you opened the door even a smidge, I think she would have kicked poor Andre to the curb.

You were the prettiest girl there.

Liar.

It's true. Did you tell Krista we've been texting like teenagers?

Ha. We ARE texting like teenagers. What is wrong with us?

I'm serious, btw. You were the talk of the reunion, at least as far as the guys were concerned.

I don't believe that for a second. You weren't even looking at me.

I didn't want to stare. I'm a gentleman.

You're making me blush.

I want to do more than make you blush.

Oh, do you?

I'm a gentleman, but I never said I was a Boy Scout.

And Tuesday morning:

I woke up thinking about you today.

You did? What were you thinking?

I'll wait to tell you in person.

You're mean.

You're sexy.

There are a lot of girls who live way closer to you than I do. Why are you so interested in me?

There are pretty girls out here, but they're usually dumb as rocks. You're beautiful AND smart. Do you realize how hard that is to find?

I could say the same thing about you.

Plus you're funny. Sexy and smart and funny. A triple threat. I was an idiot for not trying to kiss you when I was in New York.

You're making me blush again.

And Tuesday afternoon:

Did you talk to Kevin Tyson at the reunion?

Oh God, don't remind me. I'd nearly purged that experience from my memory.

I ran into him at Home Depot yesterday.

Let me guess. He complained about his arthritis?

Bingo.

It's like he's eighty years old.

Exactly. Sort of sad. I don't ever want to be like that.

Who would? To think, I used to have a crush on him in high school. So scary.

I like that we went to high school together.

Me too. It's like you're already vetted.

Me? I was thinking the same thing about you.

Be careful now, or I may delete you from my phone. I know how to do that, you know. I took a technology class at a local community college.

You're funny.

I'm glad you think so.

But you're right, I'm the lucky one here.

And later Tuesday afternoon:

Do you like Greek food?

I like all food.

I'm trying to figure out where to take you on our date.

You're already planning that far ahead? I'm flattered.

I'm organized. Some may use less flattering adjectives.

Ha. You would freak if you saw my desk.

If that means I get to see your apartment, I'll manage.

Somebody's flirting. They say it may snow here this weekend. Do you like snow?

I love snow, get up to Tahoe whenever I can. Maybe that's where we should go on our date. My friends have a great place I can use whenever I want.

That's like a four-hour drive. You'd want to spend that much time with me on our first official date?

Yes, shocking.

What if you hate me after we've been in the car for only twenty minutes? It would be a little awkward if you ditched me at a gas station or something.

LOL. Good point.

Maybe we should stick with dinner for now, then see

how it goes? That way if things go downhill fast I won't
be alone on the side of the road.

Ha. Sounds good.

Interspersed with the banter were more serious phone conversations hinting that there was more than just flirting going on.
They talked about his firm, her progress on her book, what they
liked and disliked most about their careers. When Cassidy thought
about how nervous she'd been when they'd met in New York, how
reserved he'd been when they'd said good-bye at the subway, she
was surprised at how far they'd come in such a short time.

What really told Cassidy that Brandon trusted her was when
he talked about his boys . . . including one evening in which he
confided that Jack was being teased at school because of his lisp.

For Cassidy, that was when they crossed a line.

That's when things began to feel real.

From then on, their communication grew even more intimate.

Wednesday evening:

Tough day at work today. Contentious client. Sigh . . .

Can you talk about it, or is it confidential?

Unfortunately, I can't really get into it. Just
complicated.

It must be exhausting to deal with conflict all day long.

It will be fine. I'm just venting.

Not every client's going to take you out for tequila shots, Wolf Eyes.

And thank God for that. My liver couldn't handle it.

And Thursday afternoon:

Another tough day at work. Client X is really getting under my skin.

Clients can really suck. I remember when I worked in advertising, I hated having to be nice to clients no matter how awful they were to us. I don't miss that at all. Who has the nerve to keep bothering you?

Just a high-ranking executive who won't admit he made a mistake early on. Life would be so much easier if people just admitted their mistakes.

The desire to save face can be strong.

I like your face.

Ha! You just changed the subject on me.

I like this subject better.

And you say you're not a good writer. Look at you, with all the wordplay.

Do you prefer clean-shaven or scruffy?

You're already thinking about that?

T-minus two weeks and counting. So clean-shaven or scruffy?

Surprise me. Actually, scratch that, pun intended. Clean-shaven.

Done. Or should I say scratched?

Even though he had yet to kiss her, she knew without a doubt that Brandon Forrester liked her. He really liked her.

It was almost excruciating to think that she had to wait another two weeks before California.

Chapter Eight

"HEY, HOW'S IT going, Cassi—Travis Bramble Baker! If you don't put that down *right now*, you'll be *sorry!*"

"Patti?"

"Hang on a minute, Cassidy. *Travis!!* I'm *serious!*"

Cassidy heard a crash in the background, then feet stomping, then silence.

"Patti?"

"Hey, I'm back. Roy's taking care of it. Sorry about that; we just had a bit of a situation."

"What happened?"

"Travis was chewing on the lamp cord again. I swear to God, my children will eat anything but their own dinner. How are you?"

Cassidy laughed. "I'm good; on my way to meet Danielle for a leisurely brunch. Do you remember what a leisurely brunch is?"

"Vaguely. I can't remember my own birthday anymore. What's up?"

"I wanted to touch base about Halloween. You still want to take the kids out together?"

"Wouldn't miss it. Although I can't promise Jason won't try to eat one of your nieces. When do you get in?"

"The thirtieth."

"Nice. How's the prep for your speech coming?"

"Pretty good. I think it will be fine, because I'm supposed to talk about myself, and how hard can that be, right? I mean, it's not like I can forget the material. Or so I'm telling myself. Actually, to be honest, I'm sort of nervous about speaking in front of all those women. OK, who am I kidding? I'm totally praying I don't choke."

"Wow, that was quite a fall from grace, and all in like ten seconds."

"I'm serious, Patti. What if I fall on my figurative face?"

"Stop it. You'll be great."

"Are you sure?"

"I'm sure. I'm changing the subject now. What's on the docket with Brandon while you're here?"

"He's taking me to dinner the night I get in."

"The same day?"

"Yes, ma'am. To say I'm not already watching the clock would be grossly inaccurate."

"Not wasting any time there, are we now? How many text messages are you two up to? Is your phone still counting them for you?"

"Yesterday we passed two thousand."

"*Two thousand?* Good lord, Cassidy! I get like ten text messages a year from Roy."

"I know, I know. It's sort of crazy. But it's fun. My phone's chime is my favorite sound these days. I love the flirting. I love the banter. I love it all. He's so much wittier than I first thought. And he's really nice too."

"It's like you're back in olden times, writing love letters from afar, only with your thumbs."

Cassidy smiled into the phone. "I know it's unconventional, but I'm really enjoying getting to know him this way. The distance has forced us to become *friends*, you know? And I really like him as a person."

"That's great, Cassidy, being friends is important. Without that, you're doomed."

"Not that I'm not dying to kiss him."

Patti laughed. "As you should be. That man is gorgeous, and I say that as a happily married woman. I'm excited for you too; you deserve some attention like this. Where are you going to dinner?"

"I'm not sure yet."

"Is he picking you up at your parents' house?"

"Yes. Don't laugh."

Patti laughed. "That's awesome. Do you think he'll bring you a corsage?

"I'll tell you on Halloween. Are you dressing up?"

"I may just wear my standard witch costume, which is appropriate, given how I spend most of my time these days yelling at my bratty children."

"It's just a phase. I'm sure they'll grow out of it by the time they leave for college."

"I hope you're right, or I may end up flying away on my broomstick and leaving Roy to deal with them. It would suck for him, but he probably wouldn't blame me."

"I just got to the restaurant. I'll be in touch about Halloween, OK?"

"Sounds good. Talk soon."

Cassidy took one look at the bags under Danielle's eyes and put a hand on her arm. "Hey, are you OK? You don't look too good." Despite her hectic work and travel schedule, Danielle somehow always managed to look put together.

But not today.

Danielle sighed as they sat down at a table. "Can I get a Bloody Mary first?"

"Sure. I need to write today, though, so I can only have coffee."

"Suit yourself."

A few minutes later, the waiter set Danielle's Bloody Mary down in front of her. As soon as he did so, she picked it up and took a huge gulp.

Cassidy gave her a look. "What is going on with you?"

Danielle closed her eyes and took a deep breath.

"Danielle?"

Danielle opened her eyes and took another sip of her drink, then slowly set it down.

"This past week I was in Baltimore at a conference with a bunch of our senior executives," she said.

"OK."

"And . . . there were a lot of social events happening each night, all of them involving alcohol."

"OK."

"And . . ." She closed her eyes again briefly. "Something happened with one of the executives."

"What do you mean?"

Danielle took another sip of her drink and muttered to herself, "I'm *Catholic*, for chrissake. I'm supposed to be against this sort of thing."

"Against *what* sort of thing?"

Danielle continued to avert her eyes. "It had been building up between us for a while, and I didn't want it to happen, but one night, after dinner and bar hopping and a *lot* of drinking, it just . . . did."

Cassidy caught her breath. "You slept with one of your executives?"

Danielle nodded slowly. "The CFO."

"And you feel guilty about it because you're *Catholic*?"

Danielle nodded again.

Cassidy looked at her, not understanding what she meant. Then it slowly clicked.

Is that why she's never been in love?

Have I been blind to this since college?

Has she been afraid to tell me before now?

The waiter interrupted them. "Here you go, two veggie scrambles." He set down the plates and promptly disappeared.

Cassidy picked up a fork, then chose her words carefully as she looked at her friend. "Danielle, is your CFO a woman?"

Danielle laughed weakly and poured hot sauce over her eggs, still avoiding eye contact.

Cassidy reached across the table and put a hand on her arm. "It's OK. Who cares what the stupid church says? The heart wants what the heart wants, right?"

Danielle set down her glass and pressed her palms against her eyes for a moment. Then she removed them and slowly shook her head.

"Our CFO isn't a woman, Cassidy. And I'm not a lesbian."

"Oh." Now Cassidy felt foolish. "I'm sorry for jumping to conclusions. I just—"

"He's *married*." Danielle finally looked her in the eye.

Cassidy caught her breath. Despite her liberated attitude about her sexual partners, Danielle had steadfastly refused to cross the line into adultery—and took great pride in that resolve. Both she and Cassidy had had their opportunities with married men over the years, but they'd heard enough horror stories from friends who had gone down that thorn-laced path to steer clear.

Until now, apparently.

"I'm so disappointed in myself," Danielle whispered, her shoulders slumping, her skin a little ashen. "I can't believe I did it."

Cassidy had never seen her this way.

Danielle had always been so strong, so confident. But right now she looked . . . frayed.

Cassidy leaned over again and squeezed her shoulder. "Try not to beat yourself up. *You're* not the one who cheated, right? You never took any vows, right?"

Danielle scooped up a forkful of eggs and tried to laugh. "You sound like a defense attorney."

"Are you going to see him again?"

She wiped a small tear from the corner of her eye. "Definitely not. I don't ever want to feel like this again. I feel awful."

"Will you run into him at the office?"

"Not if I can help it."

"Want me to go down there and tell him to stay away from you?"

Now Danielle laughed for real. "Now that would be quite a sight. You're a good friend, Cassidy. Thanks for not judging me. Now can we please change the subject? What's going on with you?"

"I'm good, still chipping away at the book."

"How's it coming?"

"It's coming. I've been tearing my hair out a bit since my editor moved up the deadline, but I think I can finish it on time. I just hope it's not awful."

"I'm not worried. You say the same thing with every book. You know that, right?"

"I am aware of that, yes."

"You said the same thing with every paper you wrote in college. You know *that* too, right?"

Cassidy shrugged. "Old habits die hard."

"Speaking of the old days, how's it going with high-school guy?"

Cassidy smiled. "Actually, it's going really well. He texts me all the time now. I mean *all the time*. And he calls me too. It's so fun having a guy call me."

"That's old school. No one calls anymore."

"I know. Isn't it crazy how much the world has changed? Remember when we didn't even have cell phones to call?"

"Are you going to see him when you go home for Halloween?"

"Yep. He's taking me to dinner."

"Nice, a dinner date. Another throwback to the olden days."

Cassidy lowered her voice. "I really like him, Danielle. Is that bad?"

"Why would it be bad?"

"Well, for one thing, he lives in California."

"So?"

"And he has two kids."

"So? You like kids. Plus it's not like you're marrying the guy. I think it's great that there's a new man in your life. Anyone who will get you over Dean has my vote."

Cassidy gave her a look. "Hey now, I'm over Dean."

"You're over *him*, but you're not over the damage your relationship with him did to your self-esteem. Am I right? I think I'm right."

Cassidy sighed. "OK, you're right."

Danielle pointed a fork at her. "As I always am."

"As you always are."

"Just want to be clear about that."

Cassidy laughed. "We're clear."

Danielle held up her coffee mug for a toast. "Well, whatever it is that's going on with you and high-school guy, I'm all for it, and I think you should just enjoy it. I'm happy for you, Cassidy."

Cassidy smiled and clinked her mug against Danielle's mug. "Thanks. I'm happy for me too."

After brunch Cassidy hugged Danielle good-bye, then stopped at the grocery store on the way back to her building. As she browsed the vegetable aisle, she heard her phone chime. She smiled when she saw the text message on the screen:

I just bought a rake. I told you your life is more exciting than mine.

Depends on what you're planning to do with the rake.

This is true. How is your Saturday going so far?

So far, so good. The police still don't know it was me last night, but it's probably only a matter of time.

Someone is a little feisty today.

Ha. I think I drank too much coffee at brunch.

Did you get pancakes? You talk about pancakes a lot.

Veggie scramble today. My friend Danielle just told me she slept with a married man from her office.

Oh boy.

I know. She feels terrible.

I see that all the time.

Life isn't always so black and white, is it?

Definitely not.

Cassidy spent the entire afternoon and most of Sunday working on her novel, which was barely inching along thanks to her
recent lack of focus. Her trip home was less than two weeks away
now, and while she loved the daily interaction with Brandon, she
was becoming anxious about seeing him in person. It had been
a long time since she'd been caught up in the swirl of romance,
and while she was thoroughly enjoying the feelings stirring inside
her, she was a bit concerned by just how disruptive those feelings
were proving to be. The evidence was staring her in the face on her
computer monitor. There was no denying that if Brandon hadn't
entered the picture, she'd have written significantly more by now.

Plus she was running the risk of getting hurt again. It had
taken her a long time to get over her breakup with Dean, but
she'd finally done it, and she liked feeling independent and strong
and happy again. Now she was undeniably smitten, and it was
delightful. But truth be told, she felt a bit captive—however will-
ingly—to the next chime of her phone. She knew from experience
that one day those chimes could stop, though for some reason she

didn't think that was going to happen this time. Or was that just wishful thinking?

Late Sunday afternoon she stretched her arms over her head and decided to go for a run before it got dark outside. Her novel could wait, but the lovely fall sunset would not.

After doing a five-mile loop, Cassidy walked slowly back to her building, enjoying the bright colors of the leaves now covering the trees and occasionally swirling in the air. As she entered her building, she ran into Harper, who was also dressed in workout gear, in the lobby.

"Hey, Harper, haven't seen you in a while. How are the application essays going?"

He scratched the back of his head as they stepped into the elevator. "Not as well as I'd hoped, although I should have known better. I'm quite the procrastinator. I just took a Zumba class, Cassidy. A *Zumba* class. I was the only guy in there."

"Have you even started?"

"Not a word. This is exactly how I was in college. I practically majored in pulling all-nighters."

Cassidy laughed. "No wonder you can handle the pressure of banking. Need some help getting started? I could ask some questions to get the creative juices flowing."

Harper pressed his palms together and grinned. "Would you really? I'll buy dinner."

"You mean tonight?"

"Are you free?"

"But it's still the weekend. Are you sure you don't want to go enjoy the rest of Sunday Funday playing flip cup at a bar or something?"

He gave her a look. "I hate to break it to you, Cassidy, but you know you're getting old when you associate being thirty with the shenanigans of a college student. I have a job, you know. I even have a few people who work for me."

"Oh my God, you're right. I sound like an old lady."

"I won't tell anyone if you won't. So will tonight work then? I really need a kick in the pants or I'm going to run smack into the deadlines and screw myself."

She nodded as the elevator opened to her floor. "Just let me take a quick shower and finish a few things first. Meet you at your place in about an hour?"

"Deal. Thai sound good?"

She stepped out into the hall and waved good-bye. "Perfect. See you soon."

Before she jumped into the shower, Cassidy checked her phone in hopes of seeing a new text message from Brandon.

She wasn't disappointed.

I'm at Toys "R" Us now with the boys, picking out gifts for a classmate's birthday party. Toys "R" Us on a Sunday afternoon. Kill. Me. Now.

After they'd spent two straight hours brainstorming and jotting down notes for his essays, Harper stood up and put his hands on his head. "I'm fried. Want a glass of wine and some dark chocolate?" He picked up the empty Thai food cartons and walked into the kitchen. Cassidy held up a thumb. "Sounds delicious. I think you may be the only guy I know who likes chocolate."

"*Dark* chocolate. It must be dark chocolate or it's not worth it." He opened up the cupboard and pulled down two large goblets.

"That is such a girly thing to say. You know, now that I think about it, you may also be the most metrosexual guy I know," she called into the kitchen. "Your taste in clothes, your immaculate apartment, your perfectly coiffed hair. It's all textbook."

"I'll take that as a compliment," he called back.

Cassidy left the couch and took a seat on a bar stool at the island separating the living room from the kitchen. "Trust me, it's a compliment. So whatever happened with Vanessa? Are you still seeing her? You haven't mentioned her all night."

He shrugged and opened a bottle of wine. "We've been hanging out."

"Is it serious?"

He began pouring. "Not really."

"She doesn't really seem like your type."

He handed Cassidy a glass. "And that would be . . . ?"

She looked across the spacious living room and gazed out the window. Harper lived in a two-bedroom on the twenty-eighth floor, so his apartment was not only nearly twice the size of Cassidy's but also had a spectacular view. "I don't know. Despite your fancy job, I just picture you with someone a little less . . . *flashy.*"

"Is that a writer's way of saying you don't like the way she dresses?"

Cassidy laughed and took a sip of her wine, then stood up and walked back into the living room. "Perhaps. How old is she? Twenty-five?"

Harper followed her. "Twenty-six."

"What does she do?"

"She's a nanny for a family here on the Upper West Side."

Cassidy sipped her wine slowly. "Let me guess. She wants to be an actress."

Harper laughed. "It's possible. What's with the third degree?"

"I'm sorry, just being a little protective of you. There are a lot of gold diggers out there, looking for eligible bankers like you to take care of them."

"Vanessa's not like that. At least I don't think she is."

Cassidy smiled. "Then good. Let's forget I brought it up. I shouldn't have said anything."

They sat down on his matching large black leather couches, and Harper propped his feet up on the coffee table. "What about you, are you seeing anyone these days?"

Cassidy tipped her glass toward him. "Now that, my friend, is a good question."

"What kind of answer is that?"

"Now that would be . . . a true one."

He looked at her sideways. "Are you OK? You're acting weird."

She set down her wine and leaned back against the couch. "I know. I'm sorry. I'm just a little . . . anxious." She stared at the ceiling.

"Anxious about what?"

"Remember that time you asked if I'd been on a date . . . and I said I wasn't sure?"

"Of course."

"I think I was."

"Nice. So what's the scoop?"

"You really want to know?"

"Are you really asking me that? Of course I do."

She took a deep breath. "So I went to my high-school reunion . . ."

"Damn, Cassidy." Harper picked up the bottle and topped off her wine after she was done telling him about Brandon. "Two *thousand* text messages?"

She gave him a sheepish look. "Am I crazy? Is he crazy? I feel sort of silly for getting so wrapped up in this, but I can't help myself."

"I don't think it's crazy at all. I love that story. It's very romantic. And modern, when you think about it."

She nibbled on her thumbnail. "You sure it's not weird? I don't want to turn into one of those freaks who have horrible social skills because all their interactions with other people are online."

"Shut up, you know you're great with people. I can't wait to hear what happens when you see him in person."

"I'm almost afraid of that, to be honest. Part of me thinks he might be too good to be true."

Harper patted his chest. "Don't say that. *I'm* not too good to be true, am I?"

"Definitely not. If you weren't set on marrying a Jewish girl, I might throw my hat in the ring—despite my advanced age."

"See? Good guys exist, at least for Jewish girls. And from what you've told me, Brandon sounds like a stand-up guy too."

Cassidy twirled the stem of her wineglass between her fingers. "I think he is too. I think he's the real deal."

"And he'd be lucky to have you. Remember that when you're in California, OK? Promise?"

"You sound like Danielle."

"Well, Danielle is clearly one smart woman. I know that douche bag Dean really messed with your head."

"He wasn't exactly a douche bag. He just wasn't . . . in love with me." She frowned.

"Well, regardless, he didn't treat you very well in the end, and there's no excuse for that."

She narrowed her eyes at him. "Are you sure you're only thirty years old? You sound like my dad right now."

"I know we always joke about it, but thirty isn't that young, Cassidy. Maybe in New York City it is, but not in the rest of the world."

She sighed. "I guess you're right. I remember when I was in junior high school, thirty might as well have been fifty it seemed so old to me."

"Well, I may be a few years younger than he is, but this guy Brandon had better treat you right. Otherwise he'll have to answer to *me*." He patted his chest.

She smiled and sipped her wine. "Thanks, Harper. And I hope Vanessa's as nice as you say she is, because if not, she's going to have to answer to *me*."

Chapter Nine

HER TRIP TO California was finally here.

Almost.

The day before her flight, Darlene took Cassidy by the arm and gently led her to a manicure table. "Welcome back, love. Can I get you some tea?"

"That would be nice, thanks." Cassidy took a seat, then closed her eyes and inhaled deeply. The salon once again smelled of cinnamon.

Darlene returned with the tea and a heated wrap, then sat down across from Cassidy after she'd secured it around her neck. She reached for her hands. "Have you been nibbling since I last saw you?"

Cassidy bit her lip. "A little, but I'm trying, I promise."

"No need to make me any promises, love. Sometimes trying is all we can do."

Cassidy thought the comment was a bit odd and wondered what Darlene meant by it. She noticed that the woman looked tired today, with small dark circles under her eyes. She wanted to ask if anything was wrong but remained silent, unsure whether that was an appropriate question.

A few minutes into the manicure, she decided to speak up.

"Are you OK?" she asked quietly.

Darlene nodded without looking up. "Don't worry about me, love. I'll be fine."

"Are you sure?"

She kept her eyes focused on Cassidy's hands. "Yes, love. Now please, let's not talk about me. Are *you* having a nice day?"

Cassidy hesitated for a moment, then smiled. "I am, actually. I'm off to California in the morning, for a week." Cassidy said it casually, but the truth was she'd been thinking of practically nothing else and felt as if tomorrow would never come.

"Is that so? You going for work?"

"A little work, a little pleasure, I guess."

"Sounds nice, love. I've never been."

Cassidy wondered how much traveling Darlene had done in her life. She remembered how she'd played the character game after first meeting her. That day she'd painted a vivid picture of who Darlene was, a depiction that still held true in her mind, incorrect though it must be. *Loving wife, mother, and grand-mother, talented singer and cook.* Was any of it real? All she knew for sure was that Darlene had a warm, gentle way about her that immediately put her at ease. Darlene was also clearly a private person, so Cassidy didn't want to pry with questions about her personal life. At least not today. Right now she was content to enjoy the moment, simply letting her mind wander to what lay ahead.

She reached for the teacup with her free hand as Darlene worked on her nails, humming softly as she filed.

As Cassidy sipped the tea, she felt her lips curl into a shy smile.

That night she could barely sleep, but as she finally drifted into slumber, her thoughts were consumed by a single thought.

Brandon Forrester is going to kiss me tomorrow.

"Do you live in San Francisco?" The young woman seated next to Cassidy asked over the din of the flight attendant's announcements before takeoff.

Cassidy adjusted the buckle of her seat belt. "I'm from there, but I live here now. What about you?"

The woman pointed to the floor of the plane. "Born and raised in Westchester, live in the West Village now."

"Are you going out there for work?"

The woman shook her head as the plane slowly rolled toward the runway. "A wedding. Although I'm a bridesmaid, so I guess technically that means I'll be working too."

"That should be fun. I haven't been to a wedding in quite a while."

"To be honest, I'm really getting sick of them. This is the *tenth* one I've gone to this year, and the third time I've been in one. I'm going broke!"

Cassidy smiled. "I remember those days. Let me guess: are you in your late twenties?"

"I'm twenty-eight."

"The year I was twenty-seven, I went to *thirteen* weddings."

The woman's eyes got big. "No way."

"Yep. Two of them were even at the same church *and* reception hall, on back-to-back weekends. I even wore the same dress. It was totally different crowds, so I figured why not? I called them the Groundhog Day weddings."

The woman laughed. "I like your attitude. Are you married now?"

Cassidy tensed a bit as she realized she was a full decade older than the woman. "No, still haven't met the right guy yet." She wondered what she must be thinking. *Does she find it sad that I'm not married? Or do I seem independent and cool?* Cassidy hoped it was the latter, but she knew if their roles were reversed, she'd probably be thinking the former. When Cassidy was twenty-eight, it hadn't occurred to her that she'd still be sitting at the singles table ten years later. At least there weren't any weddings to attend in her near future.

"What about you? Are you going to the Bay Area to visit your family?" the young woman asked.

"More or less. A little bit of work, but I hope not too much."

"What do you do?"

"I'm an author."

"For real? I've never met an author before."

Cassidy smiled and half shook her head. "Meeting me is not that exciting, trust me."

"What do you write?"

"I guess you could call it women's fiction, with a hint of romance. But definitely not like those romance novels that have heaving bosoms on the cover. And definitely no corsets."

The woman reached for her purse. "What's your name? I'm totally going to read your books."

"Cassidy Lane."

"Molly Benson. It's so nice to meet you." She jotted down Cassidy's name on a piece of scrap paper and tucked it into her wallet.

"What about you? What do you do?" Cassidy asked.

"I'm in my first year of business school at Columbia."

"One of my good friends is applying there. How do you like it?"

"It's kind of a grind, but it's also fun being back in school. Sort of a trade-off, I guess."

"What were you doing before?"

"I worked at an advertising agency. Sounds glamorous, but I hated it."

Cassidy gave her a knowing smile. "I used to work in advertising. I hated it too."

Molly leaned toward her and lowered her voice. "I think everyone who works in advertising hates it, at least secretly. That's just my opinion, of course, but I'm pretty sure I'm right."

Cassidy laughed and reached for her own purse. "Do you mind if I write that down? My new book is about a woman who works in advertising, so I may have to use that line."

Molly put a hand on her heart. "You'd quote me in a book? What an honor."

Cassidy scribbled on her pad of sticky notes, then tossed it into her purse. "Sure. I have to get my material from somewhere, right?"

Molly rubbed her hands together. "This is so cool. Now I'm even more excited to read your books. I love a good romance, and God knows I could use some in my own life."

I could too, Cassidy thought.

After they'd chatted for a bit longer, Molly drifted off to sleep. Cassidy felt a pang of envy as she watched her lean against the window, her breathing even. Despite Cassidy's normal aptitude for napping, she knew there was no way she'd be able to get any shut-eye right now. She'd barely been able to fall asleep last night and had awoken bright and early this morning, so giddy with anticipation she almost felt as though she'd had a couple of drinks.

She booted up her laptop and set it on the tray in front of her, planning to work on her book as a way to pass the time. But her brain had other ideas, and she ended up staring at the same sentence over and over, not registering or writing a word. No matter how hard she tried to focus, her mind remained fixated on a text

Brandon had sent her shortly before she'd gone to bed:

Soon I'll be able to kiss you good night for real.

She smiled at the thought of what the message meant, feeling a bit silly but unable to stop herself. She'd read the text over and over in the cab on the way to the airport, and now it was burned into her memory.

Maybe it really is my turn.

She silently willed the pilot to fly faster.

Eventually she gave up hope of getting any real writing done and shut down her laptop. She decided to watch a movie, hoping that might keep her distracted—as well as help the flight go by more quickly. They were due to land at three thirty, and Brandon was picking her up from her parents' house at seven. She planned to go for a run in between, knowing from years of experience that exercise would help calm her nerves. She doubted it would clear her head, however. Her every thought was permeated with visions of their first kiss.

He's really going to kiss me!

As she navigated the buttons on the video screen mounted on the seat in front of her, she replayed what she could remember of last night's conversation with Brandon before he'd sent her that playful text message. He'd called to get her parents' address, and they'd ended up talking for an hour. The details were fuzzy now, but one thing he'd said as they were getting ready to hang up burned brightly in her memory: *I can't wait to see you.*

It was such an earnest comment that it made her cover her mouth with her hand, even though she hadn't said a word. She'd never dated a man who was as unguarded as Brandon was being with her. He always told her what he was thinking, and how he was *feeling*, straight up, with no pretense whatsoever. With other men she always had the feeling they were putting their best foot forward, that they were playing it cool, that she'd never really know what was going on inside their heads unless the relationship became serious, which it never did. But from day one it had been different with Brandon. He made her feel special, included, interesting, *important*. Maybe he was like that with everyone in his life, which only made her admire that quality in him more. He was open, and sincere, and *real*, and she wanted to pinch herself when she realized that in a few hours he'd be standing right in front of her.

As she scrolled through the video options, several of which were romances, she couldn't help but smile. She felt like she was starring in one of her own, and she couldn't wait to see what happened next.

It wasn't until after she'd landed in San Francisco and said good-bye to Molly that Cassidy realized she hadn't mentioned anything about her date with Brandon to her parents.

"Can we take you out to dinner tonight?" her mother asked as her dad unloaded her suitcase from the back of his SUV. Her dad always insisted on carrying her suitcase for her, just as he always insisted on parking the car and meeting her outside security instead of just picking her up at the curb. "Your father and I were thinking we could go to Sundance. We know how much you love the salmon there."

Cassidy shut the back door. "Actually, I sort of have plans. Is Tyler here?" She pointed to a silver Lexus sedan parked across the street.

Her dad nodded. "He mentioned he might stop by to borrow a power drill. Jessica's got him building her another closet."

"Another one? Doesn't she have enough clothes?" Cassidy headed toward the front steps of the two-story brick house. The white trim looked recently painted, and a bed of yellow and white chrysanthemums lined the walkway.

"I don't ask questions like that," her dad said with a chuckle.

"Do you have plans with Patti tonight?" her mom asked as she unlocked the door, the disappointment of not being able to spend the evening with her daughter written all over her face. Cassidy realized how similar she was to her mom in that regard. The Lane women would make terrible poker players.

Cassidy hesitated, suddenly feeling sixteen years old again. She stepped into the foyer and glanced around for her brother, hoping for a temporary reprieve before having to explain the Brandon situation. "Tyler? Are you here?"

"It depends who's asking," called a deep voice from the kitchen.

"It's your favorite sister," Cassidy called back.

Tyler appeared, a toolbox in one hand. "You're my *only* sister."

Cassidy put her hands on her hips and frowned. "Mean brother. Mean, mean brother."

He set down the toolbox and embraced her in a bear hug that lifted her off the ground. "Welcome home, little sis. The girls can't stop talking about going trick-or-treating with Auntie Cassie tomorrow. I hope you're ready for them."

"I'm excited too, even have my costume all ready. Are you dressing up?"

He patted his expensive tie. "Of course. I'm going as a businessman. My getup is very similar to what I have on now."

"Ah, just like last year."

"And next year. You catch on fast."

"Are you sure you and Jessica won't come trick-or-treating with us?"

Tyler shrugged. "You know I'd love to, but unfortunately I'm not in charge." He reached down and picked up the toolbox. "I'm sorry to run, but I've got a meeting with a new client in twenty minutes. Welcome home, and see you tomorrow, OK?" he called over his shoulder as he walked toward his car.

"Sounds good," Cassidy said.

"Bye, son." Their father waved after him.

Cassidy looked at her mom and lowered her voice. "How can Jessica want to skip Halloween with her kids? Isn't that why people *have* kids?"

Her mom closed the door and sighed. "I like Jessica, but I don't understand why she feels the need to walk all over him sometimes, or why he lets her do it."

Cassidy shrugged. "Everyone knows pretty women, especially blondes, have special powers over men, especially pretty blondes who are . . . um . . . *strong willed*."

Her mom smiled and gave her a knowing look. "Very diplomatic word choice. So you were saying you have plans tonight? With Patti?"

Cassidy hesitated. "Um, not with Patti."

"Oh?"

Cassidy swallowed.

"Honey?"

Out of stalling options, Cassidy finally replied. "Actually, um, I have a date."

Her mother's eyes flickered with curiosity. "A date?"

"I'll put this in your room, kiddo." Her dad pointed down the hall to the guest room, then promptly disappeared, obviously uncomfortable with the topic. Cassidy smiled as she watched him go. *Ah, Dad.* Some things never changed. His daughter was approaching forty, but he still got flustered at the thought of her out with a member of the opposite sex. Cassidy and her mom shared the lack of a poker face, but she'd clearly inherited the easily-rattled-by-the-simple-idea-of-going-on-a-date gene from her dad.

After he was gone, her mom crossed her arms in front of her and smiled. "You have a date?"

Cassidy took off her coat and tried to act nonchalant. The last thing she wanted was for her mother to know how anxious she was about tonight. It would only make her more nervous.

"It's no big deal. I ran into a guy from high school at the reunion, and we've sort of been . . . in touch since then." Talk about an understatement. She could only imagine what her mom would think if she knew how many text messages she and Brandon had exchanged since that night, the extent to which her thoughts had been consumed by their date tonight.

"Do I know him?"

Cassidy shook her head. "I doubt it. He and I didn't really know each other in high school. His name is Brandon Forrester."

"Where are you going?"

"I'm not sure. He's taking me to dinner."

"Is he picking you up?"

"Yes, at seven."

Her mom clasped her hands together, clearly delighted. "Well, I look forward to meeting him."

"He's nice, you'll see." Cassidy turned toward the guest room. "I want to go for a run before he comes, so I'd better get a move on."

Her mom shooed her away. "Of course, go, go. I don't want you to be rushing."

Cassidy headed toward the guest room, and as she changed into her running clothes, she realized this would be the first time a date had come to pick her up at her parents' house.

Throughout all four years of high school, no one had ever asked her out.

Not once.

Maybe that was why her dad was so flustered.

At 6:45, Cassidy stood in front of a full-length mirror in the bedroom, hands on her waist. She tilted her head to one side, grading her appearance. *Not bad.* Her loose hair and light makeup looked pretty good, and she could barely see that pesky scab on her nose. She'd found a sleeveless scoop-neck dress in a deep blue that was figure flattering and comfortable but not too dressy, which she'd paired with the small diamond necklace and matching earrings her parents had given her for her thirtieth birthday. She ran her fingers over the pendant and took a deep breath, trying to relax.

Chill out.

It didn't work.

By 6:55, she was a nervous wreck. She glanced at herself in the mirror again. Outwardly she looked normal, but on the inside she felt nauseated. She could only hope Brandon wouldn't realize how unnerved she was. Happy to see him was one thing. About to vomit up her lunch was another.

She walked to the window and peered out the white plantation blinds, waiting for him to arrive.

I can't believe this is finally happening.

At 7:02 he pulled up in front of the house in a pristine black Mercedes SUV. A moment later he exited the car, and Cassidy caught her breath. Dressed in dark jeans and a crisp lavender button-down , he was even more attractive than she remembered.

Oh my God.

He's so handsome.

She quickly closed the blinds just as he turned to face the front walkway. The last thing she needed right now was to be caught spying on him. She hurried over to the bed and sat on her hands to stop herself from chewing her thumbnail as she waited for the doorbell to ring. Darlene would be so proud.

She heard the chime a few seconds later, then a door opening, then her mother's voice, then Brandon's. She waited a few moments, her eyes closed.

It's just dinner.

Don't freak out.

Just have fun.

Finally, she stood up, smoothed her hands down the front of her dress, and took a deep breath. As calmly as she could manage, she slowly walked down the hall toward the foyer, where Brandon was standing with her parents. Cassidy cringed slightly as she approached them, the inherent awkwardness of the situation impossible to overlook.

I'm thirty-eight years old, and this beautiful man is picking me up for our first official date at my mom and dad's house.

"Hi, Brandon," she said with a shaky smile.

Brandon turned to face her, not looking nervous at all, which somehow made her even more anxious. "Hi, stranger. Thanks for not giving me a fake address. That would have been a little awkward."

She laughed and gave him a quick hug, then stepped away, not sure how familiar to act with him, especially in front of her parents, who were unaware of the thousands of text messages they'd exchanged. She gestured to her mom and dad. "I see you've met my parents?"

"Yes, we were just chatting about high school."

Her mom put her hands on her waist. "Seems silly that you two didn't know each other, doesn't it?

Cassidy swallowed. "It was a big school." *And I wasn't popular.*

"Cassidy was too popular to pay me any attention," Brandon said.

"Yeah, right." Cassidy lightly pushed his arm, and as she did so she felt the ice between them crack a little bit. She also felt a little spark of electricity run down her own arm at the contact.

Cassidy's father put his arm around her. "Brandon said he's taking you to Baumé. That's quite a nice place, kiddo. Have you ever been?" He looked impressed.

She looked up at her dad. "Baumé? I don't think so."

"It's on California. It's my favorite restaurant, actually," Brandon said, then glanced at his watch. "Speaking of which, we should probably get going so we're not late for our reservation."

"Sure, just let me get my coat." Cassidy turned and darted back into the guest room. As she opened the closet, she had a flashback to the dread she'd felt as she dressed for the Paly reunion, and how in the end she'd gone only because Patti had guilted her into it.

Now she didn't feel any dread at all.

She felt the opposite of dread, whatever that word was.

Anticipation?

Excitement?

Eagerness?

Right now she was feeling them all.

Thank God for Patti.

"Looks like you decided to go for scruff?" Cassidy glanced over at Brandon as they walked toward his car. She remembered his question about her preference in facial hair, and was pretty sure she'd told him clean-shaven. Or had she? For a moment she was tempted to dig out her phone to relive the text conversation, then realized she was actually *with* him now and didn't need her phone to feel close to him. Their relationship had finally entered a new dimension, one based in reality, or at least physical reality. The heart palpitations she was currently experiencing told her this had been real in a different way long before tonight.

He ran a hand over his chin. "I meant to shave but didn't have time. Plus I'll have a full beard in two days. It's ridiculous how fast this thing grows."

She stole another glance at him. He looked happy, but he also seemed a bit tired. She didn't remember him appearing that way in New York. Then again, his sons hadn't been with him. Her friends who were working parents often told her they slept better on business trips than at home. That was probably the case with him.

She pointed to the thick locks on his head. "Better too much hair than not enough, right? Some of those guys at the reunion were looking a little thin up top. That's got to be rough."

"That's for sure." He clicked his key fob to unlock the car, then opened the door for her. As she climbed inside, she watched him move around to the driver's side, running a hand through his salt-and-pepper hair as he walked.

I want to do that, she thought.

Brandon pulled to a stop in front of the restaurant and looked over at Cassidy as he turned off the ignition. "Hey, I forgot to ask, did you get a nap on the plane? I'd hate to think the flight interrupted your schedule."

She gave him a mock look of shock before exiting the car. "Are you making fun of me?"

"Of course I am. So did you get a nap?"

"Actually, if you must know, I did *not* sleep on the plane." *If you only knew why.*

"Poor thing, I'm sorry to hear that. I promise not to keep you out too late tonight then." He handed the keys to the valet, then held the door to the restaurant open for her. The moment they walked inside they were greeted by the owner, a short, rotund man with thick gray hair, a matching mustache, and an infectious smile.

"Brandon, hello and welcome. I saw you were coming in tonight. Your favorite table will be ready in just a few minutes."

"Thank you, Stefan." Brandon turned toward Cassidy. "This is Cassidy Lane, a bestselling author. We went to high school together."

Stefan reached for Cassidy's hand and kissed it. "An author? My, what a pleasure. What do you write?"

She smiled politely. "Contemporary fiction, nothing too serious."

"She's being modest. Her books are really good," Brandon said.

Stefan winked at her. "Well then, if Brandon says so, it must be true. He's one of my best customers, you see."

"Thank you, Stefan. Should we get a glass of wine at the bar?" Brandon briefly placed his hand on Cassidy's lower back, and she felt a jolt of heat shoot through her spine.

"Sure, sounds good." She hoped her face hadn't turned red. *Oh my God, he touched me.*

The bartender waved as they approached the bar. "Hey, Brandon. Welcome back. Can I get you the usual?"

"Sounds good, Peter." Brandon looked at Cassidy. "What would you like to drink?"

"A glass of sauvignon blanc would be nice," she said with a shy smile.

"Sauvignon blanc and a vodka martini, coming right up," Peter said.

As Peter poured their drinks, Cassidy glanced over her shoulder to take in the scene around them. The restaurant was bustling, the tables filled with well-heeled couples and groups engaged in lively conversation. The muted color palette of the room was punctuated by oversized vases of fresh flowers, and classical music played softly in the background.

She turned back to Brandon just as he handed her a glass of wine. "Nice place, isn't it?"

Cassidy nodded. "It's gorgeous. My dad was right."

Stefan returned and led them to their table, whose location in the center of the room somehow made Cassidy feel welcome and special. Seconds after he left, a crisply dressed waiter appeared in his place.

"Brandon, it's nice to see you again. I'll be right back with some water," the waiter said.

"Thanks, Pierre."

Cassidy tilted her head toward Brandon as Pierre slipped away. "Are you on a first-name basis with *everyone* here?"

He laughed. "I told you this is my favorite restaurant. I used to come here three times a week."

"Three times a week? That's more than most people exercise. Why did you come here so often?"

He shrugged. "When Juliette and I first split up, I moved into an apartment right around the corner from here. Cooking for one after cooking for a family of four was a little depressing, so for a while I just avoided the kitchen altogether."

She felt her cheeks flush and regretted having asked the question. "Oh. I'm sorry. I was just . . . I was just curious."

He smiled. "Don't apologize. The food here is amazing. You'll love it."

"So how's the book coming?" Brandon asked.

Cassidy stabbed a brussels sprout with her fork. "It's coming. I'm struggling a bit to stay focused, but it's getting there." She didn't tell him *he* was the main reason for her lack of concentration. She wanted to be open and honest with him, but that was one piece of information she was determined to keep to herself. At least for now.

"Are you ever going to tell me what it's about? I am paying for this dinner, you know."

She laughed. "OK, fine. It's about an ambitious young advertising executive whose professional life is on track, but her personal life is falling off the rails a bit."

"Advertising, you say?"

"Yes."

"Didn't you use to work in advertising?"

"I did. First in San Francisco and then in New York."

"But you quit the New York job to become a writer, correct?"

She nodded. "Eventually."

He scratched his chin. "So how much of the book is autobiographical?"

She took a sip of water. "To be honest, not all that much."

"You sure about that? I promise I won't tell anyone."

She smiled. "I've found that yes, when I write a book it always begins with a small piece of me and my life, but then once I get into the story, it starts to take on a life of its own, and it usually evolves into something I'd never imagined at the outset. Plus things pop up in my own life along the way, and they sometimes have an impact too."

"Like what?"

"For example, on the plane today I met a young woman who used to work in advertising but hated it, and I know our conversation will end up leaving a footprint on the book in some way or another. I can just tell."

"What did she say?"

"I can't remember exactly, but I wrote it down."

"Ah, yes, the sticky notes."

She pointed at him. "Yes, the sticky notes. Thank God for the sticky notes. Anyhow, when one of my books is finally signed, sealed, and delivered, I'm always amazed that I actually wrote it, because I have no idea where a lot of it came from."

"That must be a strange feeling."

"Yep, it's very strange, but it's happened several times now. Anyhow, I know that was a roundabout way of answering your question of how much my books are autobiographical, I guess you could say they are about my life . . . if my life were much more exciting."

He picked up his glass. "We've been over this. Your life is very exciting."

"Says you. I disagree."

"Then we'll have to agree to disagree."

She held up her glass as if in a toast. "Agreed. And what did you say when you were in New York? That you liked watching good people win? Here's to that, in books and in real life too."

He smiled at her. "I *did* say that I like watching good people win. Your memory is better than you think."

"My memory has a mind of its own. I can remember the name of my second-grade teacher, but not where I parked the car."

He scratched his chin again. "For what it's worth, I wasn't kidding. Your life seems very glamorous, at least to me it does."

She tilted her head to one side. "Says the man who just asked me if I took a nap today."

He chuckled. "I like that you make me laugh. Have I ever told you that?"

She speared another brussels sprout and pointed it at him. "You may have, but with my memory, I probably forgot."

"I like that you make me laugh. Have I ever told you that?"

"Now you're making *me* laugh. Actually, I'm glad that I can make you laugh in person. As you've probably noticed, I'm much better with the written word than in real-life conversations."

"I wouldn't say that at all. I think you're pretty great in both."

She smiled and put a hand to her cheek, which felt a bit warm. "Now you're making me laugh *and* blush. If you think I'm funny, you should meet my brother. Once, in high school, we went to Denny's, and he made Patti laugh so hard she passed out."

"She really passed out?"

Cassidy nodded and picked up her water glass. "Right there on the floor. It was amazing. We had to call the paramedics."

"Laughter is good. I went a long time there without laughing." A shadow flickered across his eyes, and she was startled by the sudden shift in his tone.

She didn't respond immediately, not sure how to do so. She assumed he was referring to his marriage, but she didn't know what the appropriate reaction was. Or was he referring to something else?

Should she ask him?

She took a long sip of water, looking down, staring at nothing, saying nothing. Though the room was buzzing with lively chatter all around them, at that moment she felt as if the two of them were in a vacuum.

After an extended and undeniably awkward pause, she lifted her gaze and regained eye contact with him.

"I'm sorry, Brandon," she said in a near whisper.

As if sensing the awkwardness between them, Pierre appeared out of nowhere to refill their water glasses. The interruption served its purpose, and Brandon seemed to recover from his momentary dip in mood.

"What's your middle name?" he asked.

She was surprised by the question, which, after his dark comment, seemed more than a bit out of left field. But at least they were on a new subject, and she felt herself begin to relax.

"Leigh. It's my mother's maiden name. What about you?"

"Dean."

She tensed.

"Are you OK?"

She took a sip of water. "I'm fine, I swear. It's just that Dean was the name of my ex-boyfriend, so that caught me a little off guard. It's not often you hear that name." She forced a smile.

"Dean's the guy you told me about in New York?"

She nodded.

"I have to wonder what he was thinking, letting you go like that."

She smiled and set her water on the table. "Thanks."

"I'm just being honest."

"I could wonder the same thing about your ex."

"I have my flaws, believe me. Divorced men aren't easy."

She wondered what flaws could offset being so nice . . . and smart . . . and attractive. But instead of asking him to elaborate, she decided to take the conversation in a less hazardous direction. "I haven't dated many divorced guys, but at our age I think meeting *anyone* to date is hard. Especially in New York City."

"Why is that? I would think it would be easy, given how many people live there."

"I think part of it is because of my profession, which is about as solitary as it gets, but also I think meeting people is hard because everyone's so busy, like ordering-their-groceries-online busy, or taking-a-week-to-reply-to-an-e-mail busy. Have *you* ever ordered your groceries online?"

"I didn't even know you could do that."

She tapped her palm on the table. "Well, there you go. You probably meet more women than I do men simply because you shop at Whole Foods."

"Maybe, but when I meet women at Whole Foods, they're usually wearing workout clothes. I'm not a fan of that."

She gave him a puzzled look. "You don't like it when women work out?"

He shook his head. "I don't like it when women who *don't* work out wear expensive workout gear as regular clothes. It's like false advertising."

She smiled, relieved that the conversation had turned playful again. "Ah . . . I see what you're saying. So it bugs you when women wear yoga pants to a nice dinner, for example?"

"Exactly. What is that all about?"

She shrugged. "I have no idea. I love my sweatpants dearly, but I don't wear them to dinner. Unless it's at my brother's house, of course." She'd actually worn sweatpants on the plane ride earlier today, but that was another piece of information she'd keep to herself. For now.

He picked up his glass. "So what about you? Do you have a pet peeve about men?"

"You mean something that isn't an indicator of intelligence or character yet might in fact preclude me from dating that person?"

He laughed. "Well put."

She sat up straight. "Well, along that vein, I'd have to say grammar, particularly the misuse of pronouns. I know I'm super-picky because I'm a writer, but I can't stand it when a man says something like 'let's keep this between you and *I*.' Or 'this is a great opportunity for you and *I*.' Why do people do that? Why?"

"I might be in trouble. My grammar's terrible."

"No it's not!" She realized she'd practically shouted and lowered her voice. "Believe me, after all those text messages, I would know. I've been paying attention." In fact, she could tell by Brandon's text messages how smart he was, and that just made him more attractive to her.

"I'm glad to hear I passed the test. Were you an English major in college?"

"Yep. What about you?"

"Economics. You know, I had a crush on you in high school."

The non sequitur caught Cassidy off guard, and she felt her neck get hot. Was he always like this in person, changing the subject between playful and serious on a dime? Before she could respond, Pierre came to clear their plates.

"How were your meals?" he asked with a polite smile.

"Delicious, as always. Thanks, Pierre," Brandon said.

Cassidy leaned back in her seat and put a hand on her stomach. "Unbelievable. But *oh my God*, I'm stuffed."

Brandon shook his head. "You can't be stuffed. We have to split the chocolate fondant. You've never tasted anything like it."

"That good?"

"Better. If it's not rocky road ice cream, I rarely eat dessert. But here? Always."

"Rocky road ice cream?"

"It's my one vice when it comes to sweets. When I start eating it, I can't stop."

She laughed. "I'm like that with marshmallows. I completely lose control."

"Losing control can sometimes be a good thing." He held her gaze, and she practically stopped breathing.

"So . . . are you interested?" he asked, still maintaining eye contact.

"Interested in what?" It came out as a near squeak.

He pointed to the dessert menu. "The fondant."

She blinked and sat up straight. "Oh, of course. Sure, I'm in, but you may have to wheel me out of here."

He gestured for Pierre. "It would be my pleasure."

As they waited for the valet to bring around Brandon's car, Cassidy gave him a curious look. He and the driver had engaged in a brief conversation when Brandon handed him his ticket.

"You know the valet too?"

"Yep."

"So you basically know everyone here."

He laughed. "Yep."

She put a hand on her hip. "I need to ask you something."

"Shoot."

She swallowed. "OK, this may be a little out of line, but do you bring a lot of women here?" Truth be told, despite the attention heaped on them, she was beginning to wonder if maybe tonight hadn't been as special as she'd initially thought, if maybe the staff was so nice to her only because Brandon was such a good customer. Could it be that she was the flavor of the month? Had she misread his intentions all this time?

He quickly shook his head. "I've never brought a date here."

"You haven't?"

He paused briefly, then gave her a half smile. "Cassidy, you don't bring just any woman to your home base."

"Oh," she whispered. "Good to know."

The closer they got to Cassidy's parents' house, the more anxious she got.

And excited.

And nervous.

She began to nibble on her thumbnail, than yanked it away and interlaced her hands on her lap.

Oh my God.

I can't believe this moment is finally here.

He's really going to kiss me.

Brandon pulled up in front of the driveway and put the car in park. "Here we are," he said.

She nodded and looked over at him. "Casa Lane. Do you . . . want to come inside for a bit?" She could feel her heart beating and willed it to slow down.

"I'd love to, but I can't."

Her face fell. "Oh."

He squeezed the steering wheel. "I have a meeting with a new client tomorrow morning that I haven't prepped enough for because we've been swamped with other cases, and I've had the boys the last two nights. If I want to keep from making a total ass of myself, I need to be up by five to do some reading before I get the boys ready for school."

A tiny alarm bell rang in a far corner of her brain, but she did her best to ignore it and forced a smile. "Got it."

"I'm sorry, Cassidy. Things have just been really crazy lately."

"Don't worry about it. I like that you take your job seriously." She glanced at the blinking lights all over the dashboard. "You apparently take your cars seriously too. I feel like I'm in the cockpit of a seven-forty-seven right now."

He laughed. "I do like my gadgets. Can I walk you to the door?"

"Sure."

They exited the car and slowly began walking toward the front steps of the house. She tried to think of something to say but couldn't come up with a single word, so she remained quiet and kept her gaze fixed on the pavement.

The silence was palpable.

When they reached the door, Brandon cleared his throat and looked at her.

"I had a really nice time tonight."

She smiled. "Me too. Thanks so much for dinner, and dessert. You were right, it was out of this world."

"I'm glad we finally got to spend some time together in person."

"Me too. After all those text messages and phone calls, in a way it's like I know you so well, but at the same time I don't really know you at all," she said.

He didn't respond right away, and she looked at the ground, wondering if it had been a mistake to say that. His demeanor was almost businesslike, not at all what she'd expected given everything he'd said to her in texts and on the phone, as recently as last night. And now that she thought about it, except for when he'd briefly put his hand on her lower back, he hadn't touched her all evening, not even an accidentally-on-purpose arm brush. Had she done something wrong? She wondered if maybe he was less comfortable expressing his feelings in person. She certainly was.

"Did I tell you how pretty you look tonight?"

She looked up and smiled, his comment silencing the chatter in her brain, the doubt retreating as quickly as it had appeared. "I don't think so. But then again, maybe I forgot."

"You're an extremely attractive woman, Cassidy Leigh Lane."

"Thank you, Brandon Dean Forrester."

She stood there on the step, waiting for him to say something.

Or, better yet, *do* something.

Now was the time.

But he didn't say anything.

And he didn't do anything.

He just stood there, his hands in his pockets, looking at her.

The nerves came back once again, and she cast her gaze downward.

Why is this so awkward?

After a few more excruciating seconds, she cracked. She took a deep breath and raised her eyes. "Are you *ever* going to kiss me?" she whispered.

He smiled slightly, then took a step toward her. He put his arms around her lower back and gently pulled her close, then slowly leaned down.

"I thought you'd never ask," he whispered into her ear.

Then he kissed her.

His lips were warm and soft, and she felt her body melting against his. He pulled her closer, and the heat quickly spread throughout her body, even reaching her fingertips, which gently stroked the back of his neck. She'd never experienced a kiss like this, and she began to feel a little dizzy.

She felt like she was . . . floating.

Wow.

After a bit they finally broke apart.

She looked up at him and smiled. "What took you so long?"

He smiled back. "What can I say? I'm conservative."

"*Clearly.* But that was definitely worth the wait."

"Agreed."

"And I don't just mean tonight."

"Agreed." He gently brushed a strand of hair out of her eyes, his touch igniting another spark down her neck and spine. Then he leaned close again and lowered his voice. "You smell really good."

She nodded toward the house. "You *sure* you don't want to come in for a while?"

"I do, but I really can't. Plus it's your parents' house. I wouldn't feel right."

She laughed. "We're in our thirties now, Brandon." *Late thirties, yikes.*

He shrugged. "I know, I know. But I just told you, I'm conservative."

"I thought you said you weren't a Boy Scout."

He put his hand on her neck, then leaned down and kissed her again. "I'm not," he whispered.

"You're not?" she whispered back.

"No, but let's wait for that until Friday." Friday was when they'd scheduled their next date, when he wouldn't have work the next morning or the boys to take care of.

She rolled her eyes in a playful manner. "All right, if you *insist.*"

"It's a date." He kissed her again and turned to leave but hesitated for a moment, his eyes suggesting he had more to say.

She looked at him, doe-eyed.

He smiled at her. "I'm . . . really glad our paths crossed again, Cassidy."

She smiled back. "Me too."

Chapter Ten

"HAPPY HALLOWEEN!" PATTI opened the door to greet Cassidy and her nieces, who were both dressed as princesses. Patti kneeled down and gave each girl a hug. "Hi, Princess Courtney; hi, Princess Caroline. Don't you two look pretty tonight?" Then she stood up and looked at Cassidy. "Wow, they're really getting tall. Little WNBA players in the house."

Cassidy's eyes got big as she ushered the girls inside. "Tell me about it. Total bean sprouts. It's sort of freaking me out."

Patti showed the girls to the playroom, then turned her full attention on Cassidy. "*So*... how was the big date? I can't wait to hear about it. Hilarious costume, by the way."

Cassidy put her hands on her waist and did a little twirl. "You like my cone? Keeps me from scratching after a visit to the vet." She was dressed as a cat but had fastened a large piece of plastic around her neck, funnel style.

"Very clever, much more creative than my witch costume. Now let's get this show on the road so you can tell me all about last night. My kids have been going nuts waiting to hit the candy circuit. I hope the pot of mini Kit Kats I'm leaving on our front step doesn't get swiped in the first ten minutes we're gone."

"I'm sorry we're late. After Tyler and Jessica dropped off the girls, I had to wait for my mom to get home from the supermarket so she could see them in their princess costumes."

"Are Tyler and Jessica staying home to give out candy? I figured they would be with you."

Cassidy waved a paw. "They're having a date night: dinner and a movie. They went to the girls' parade at school earlier, so Jessica said they'd put in their time. She never gives out candy because she doesn't want it in her house. It's a miracle she lets Courtney and Caroline keep their loot."

Patti adjusted her black hat. "Jessica's not very warm and fuzzy in the parenting department, is she." It wasn't a question.

Cassidy shrugged. "To be honest, she's not warm and fuzzy in any department."

Wearing a cowboy hat and his standard plaid flannel shirt, Roy appeared with Jason and Travis, who were both dressed as Power Rangers, and little Anna, who was also a princess. Cassidy collected her nieces from the playroom, and the eight of them set out trick-or-treating. The streets were filled with delighted children running about, followed by their harried parents trying to keep up with them. Watching the chaos swirl around her, Cassidy couldn't imagine a worse nightmare for Danielle. Danielle was probably at an adult Halloween party right now, most likely at a bar, and certainly far removed from anything remotely resembling suburbia or parenthood.

"Look at those cool jack-o'-lanterns!" Jason darted up a driveway, Travis and the three princesses fast on his heels. As Cowboy Roy shuffled to keep up with them, Cassidy and Patti lagged behind so Cassidy could continue sharing the details of her date with Brandon.

"He really took you to his favorite restaurant and told you he'd never been there before with anyone else?"

"It was so nice, Patti. Everyone there knows him, and they treated us like royalty. I've never had anyone fold my napkin for me while I was in the ladies' room. I thought they only did that in the movies."

Patti held up her broomstick in one hand and lightly pounded her chest with the other. "In man code, that's sort of a big deal that he took you there. You realize that, right?"

Cassidy remembered how she'd briefly thought the exact opposite. "I understand that . . . now. But it took me a while. I was a little flustered the entire evening, to be honest. I think he was too, actually."

"Sounds like someone's a little smitten."

"Are you talking about me or about him?"

"It could be that I'm talking about both of you."

As they wandered through the neighborhood, Cassidy finished recounting the story, then looked at Patti. She held up a hand to nibble on her thumbnail, then let it drop to her side when she realized it was covered by a paw—and obstructed by the cone.

"What do you think?"

"What do I *think*? I think it sounds like it went great."

"So you don't think it's a big deal that he didn't want to come inside?"

Patti half laughed. "Come inside your *parents'* house? Definitely not. If anything it's the opposite."

"How so?"

"Think about it, Cassidy. The guy clearly likes you, and he obviously respects you. He's read your *books*, for frick's sake. He even respects your parents too much to put the moves on you under their roof. Those are all really good signs."

"What about the fact that I basically had to ask him to kiss me? That was a little embarrassing."

Patti shook her head. "Same deal. I'm telling you, Cassidy: he was a nice guy in high school, and it sounds like he still is. He's just a gentleman, and a shy one at that."

Cassidy adjusted her cone. "He told me he had a crush on me at Paly."

"That's not surprising. I bet a lot of guys did but were too chicken to do anything about it."

"I doubt that. Did I tell you he suggested we go to Tahoe sometime?"

"Jason! Stop kicking that pumpkin NOW! Stop it! Roy, get him!"

Roy ran over and scooped up Jason, then together he and Patti made the boy apologize to the woman whose pumpkin he'd just dented with his tiny Power Ranger foot.

"Auntie Cassie, see what we got!"

Cassidy turned and looked down at her nieces, who were staring up at her with big grins. They held up fun-size Snickers bars.

"Mmm, yummy," she said, rubbing her belly with a paw.

"Halloween is the *best*!" They turned and ran ahead to the next house with Travis and Anna, while Roy and Patti scolded Jason for kicking the pumpkin. As Cassidy watched her nieces scamper along, she felt a rush of love and wondered—as she did from time to time—what it would be like if they were her daughters.

Would I be a good mother?

Her thoughts turned to her date last night.

Would I be a good stepmother?

She knew she was getting way ahead of herself and was grateful to be distracted from such big questions when Patti rejoined her, followed by Roy and a contrite Jason.

Patti put a hand on her shoulder. "I'm sorry. It's never ending. What were you saying about Tahoe?"

"A couple of weeks ago, when Brandon was planning what we should do on our first official date, he asked if I wanted to go to Tahoe with him."

"For real?"

"Yes. He said his friends have a cabin they don't use very often."

"Wow, talk about a full-court press. He must be really into you to bring up Tahoe already."

"That's what I thought too, which is why it sort of threw me when he didn't make a move to even kiss me last night. After all that buildup, it made me wonder if maybe . . . maybe I inadvertently did something to turn him off." She felt her cat shoulders droop.

Patti waved a dismissive hand. "I highly doubt that. So was the kiss good?"

Cassidy put a paw over her heart. "*So* good. Like *amazing* good."

"Awesome. Then stop worrying about it."

Cassidy gave her a hopeful look. "Just as he was leaving, he *did* say he's glad our paths crossed again."

"As he should be. When are you seeing him next?"

"He's with his kids tonight, so we're going out tomorrow. I bought a new dress this afternoon."

"A new dress? I like it. What are you doing?"

"He's taking me to the Rosewood for a drink, and then we're going to the Los Altos Grill for dinner."

"Both excellent choices. Well done, Brandon Forrester. That man has good taste in more than just clothes and women."

Cassidy lowered her voice to a near whisper. "I really like him, Patti. It kind of scares me a little."

Patti put a hand on her shoulder. "Don't be scared. Try to just enjoy it, Cassidy. God knows, you of all people deserve this."

Chapter Eleven

CASSIDY WOKE UP early the next morning, still on New York time and too excited about her date with Brandon to sleep in anyway. She changed into shorts and a long-sleeved T-shirt and headed out for a run, not sure which route she'd take but well aware that it would bring back childhood memories no matter which direction she ran. Practically every block had a house where she'd attended either a slumber party, a Girl Scout troop meeting, or a study group of one sort or another.

As she made her way through the streets of her youth, she forced herself to stop thinking about Brandon and went over her keynote address in her head, something she'd done many times over the weeks leading up to Monday's conference. The topic they'd asked her to speak about was following your dreams, something she knew quite a bit about, given her bumpy road to becoming a full-time author.

If you aren't happy, do something about it.

When you know what you want, don't give up until you get it.

Only you know which path in life is best for you.

Her parents were in the kitchen pouring coffee when she returned to the house nearly an hour later.

"Looks like someone got an early start today," her mom said. "We thought you were still sleeping."

Cassidy retrieved a large plastic tumbler from the cupboard and filled it with water. "If I were at my apartment, I would be. I love the three-hour time difference. I never wake up this early in New York."

"Did you have a nice jog?" her dad asked.

Cassidy finished her water and set the glass on the counter with a nod. "I ran over to the creek and back. I'd forgotten how pretty it is over there."

"How'd the trick-or-treating go last night?" her mother asked.

"We had a blast. Caroline and Courtney scored enough candy to last them through Easter. Jessica's not going to be happy."

"Sounds like things went splendidly." Her dad gave her a wink. "Who cares about calories, much less cavities, at that age?"

Cassidy pointed at him. "You are a smart man. Did you get a lot of kids here?"

"Not as many as last year. We put the leftover candy in the fridge if you're hungry," he said.

Cassidy glanced toward it. "Ooh. I'll have to remember that."

"What's on your schedule for today?" her mom asked, handing her a mug of coffee.

Cassidy held the steaming cup under her chin. "Nothing too exciting. I'm pretty set on my speech, so I'll probably spend most of the day working on the book."

"You seeing Brandon again tonight?"

Cassidy took a sip of coffee. "Yes."

"He seems like a nice guy."

"He is."

Her parents knew her well enough to leave it at that, so her mom stopped asking questions and her dad changed the subject to one of his, and every father's, favorites: the weather. "It's supposed to rain cats and dogs today, kiddo. You may have gotten your run in just in time."

"It is?" She took a peek out of the window. The sky was already looking a bit darker.

He stood up and folded the newspaper under his arm. "If you go back out today, be sure to take an umbrella just in case."

"Will do." She took another sip of coffee and hoped the turn in the weather wasn't an omen.

After breakfast Cassidy enjoyed a long, hot shower, then changed into jeans and a sweatshirt and took her laptop into the kitchen. She loved working at the kitchen table at her parents' house. It reminded her of being in school, when she'd come home and spread out her books and binders in front of her on that same table every day. When it was cold outside, her mom would light a fire and make her a mug of hot chocolate with tiny marshmallows before preparing dinner. Tyler usually did his homework in his bedroom, but for some reason Cassidy had always liked working at the kitchen table, smack in the middle of everything.

She took a seat, then glanced around the room and felt the memories, good and bad, begin to float up and around her.

The time Tyler broke his arm skateboarding.

The day she mustered the courage to call Jimmy Hanson about the Sadie Hawkins dance—and he turned her down.

The day she got her braces off.

The afternoon she received her acceptance letter to Yale.

The evening of the prom, which she'd spent making cookies with her mom.

The time Patti showed up in tears and said her parents were fighting... again.

As it did on every visit, sitting here as an adult made her remember what life had felt like as a teenager. Though there hadn't been cell phones, e-mail, or Facebook back then, she imagined the fundamental essence of the teenage experience was still the same: angst.

As though reading her mind, her phone chimed with a text message.

Brandon!

But the message was from Patti. It was a close-up photo of them in their Halloween costumes with the caption:

Don't sweat the wrinkles. In ten years we will kill puppies to look this young.

She smiled. *Ah, Patti.*

The text snapped her back into the present, as well as the reality of her adult responsibilities. She set down the phone and got to work on her book, specifically a pivotal scene in which Emma, the ambitious young heroine, begins to realize that despite how hard she's working to climb the corporate ladder, a career in advertising isn't making her happy. What does being happy mean? Emma is almost too afraid to ask herself the question because she doesn't want to know the answer.

About an hour later, her phone beeped with an alarm. Startled, she picked it up.

E-mail Nigel feedback on cover design

Even though she loved helping choose the covers of her books, for the time being it could wait, and she was annoyed at the break in her concentration. She silently cursed herself for needing reminder alarms going off at all hours to keep her life on track. She'd been on a roll with the novel, the first time in a while that she'd been in such a groove, and hated to have it interrupted. She dismissed the alarm but kept the phone in her hand for a moment, realizing she still hadn't heard from Brandon.

It was after noon. Until today he'd always reached out to her with a friendly and/or flirty greeting by now, literally every single day for weeks.

Should I text him?

Would that be weird?

She put the phone down on the table, deciding not to do anything. She had enough drama to deal with on the screen in front of her, so she'd do her best to refocus her mental energy on that. She was sure she'd hear from Brandon eventually. He was probably just busy with work.

Cassidy finally received a text message from Brandon at four o'clock. It made her gasp.

> **Need to postpone our dinner. My mother had a major stroke last night. I'm at the hospital.**

She stared at the phone.

Oh my God.

"Honey, are you OK?"

At the sound of a voice, Cassidy glanced up to see her mom standing in the doorway. "You look like you've just seen a ghost."

Cassidy held up her phone. "It's Brandon. His mother had a stroke."

Her mom walked toward her, then put a hand on Cassidy's shoulder. "Oh, Cassidy, that's terrible."

"He's at the hospital. Do you think I should call him? Texting in response to news like that seems sort of, I don't know, impersonal, don't you think?"

Would he want me to call him? Would he want me to go see him?

It stung a bit to realize she didn't know him well enough to answer those basic questions, but she tried not to think about that. She had more important things to think about.

Her mom squeezed her shoulder. "I would call. You can never go wrong by reaching out to someone who's having a rough time."

Cassidy strummed her fingers against the table. Brandon hadn't talked about his parents much, but she knew they were divorced, and that his dad now lived down in Carmel with his second wife. His mother hadn't remarried and still lived in the house he grew up in.

"I think I'm going to run to the supermarket. Can I get you anything?"

"I'm good, thanks, Mom." She doubted her mother really needed anything at the store and was grateful to her for giving her space.

Her mom reached for her purse and car keys. "I'll pick up some marshmallows, just in case."

As her mom slipped out the door, Cassidy dialed Brandon's number. It went straight to voice mail, so she left a message.

"Brandon, it's Cassidy. I just got your text. I'm so sorry. Are you OK? Is your mom going to be OK? Is there anything I can do? I feel terrible for you. Please let me know if you need anything at all, and of course don't worry about tonight. Sending you lots of good thoughts and a big hug."

She hung up the phone, then sat at the kitchen table in silence.

Two hours later she hadn't heard back from Brandon, so she called Patti.

"What's up, hot potato?"

"Hi, Patti."

"Oh no, what's wrong?" Patti was crazy perceptive.

"Brandon's mother's had a stroke."

"Oh Jesus, is she OK?"

"I don't know. I haven't spoken to him. He just sent me a brief text this afternoon saying he was at the hospital. I left him a voice mail a couple of hours ago, but I haven't heard back."

"That's awful."

"I know, I feel terrible for him, but I don't know what to do."

"I guess that means no date for you tonight."

"I guess not. I feel like a horrible person for being a little disappointed about it, but I am."

"Do you want me to replace him? Roy's still at work, but I'm expecting him any minute. He can watch the kids."

"You'd really do that for me?"

"Stop it. Of course I would. Plus God knows I could use a night out."

"You're the best, Patti. I mean that."

"Tell that to my offspring. When I picked them up at school today, Travis asked if he could go live at his little friend Timmy's house. Apparently little Timmy's mommy is a much better cook than I am. Ungrateful little punk. "

Cassidy laughed. "Call me when you're ready to meet."

"OK, so tell me what you know." Patti dipped a fry in ketchup.

Cassidy spread spicy mustard on her chicken sandwich. "I don't know anything. I still haven't heard back from him."

"Did he say how serious it was?"

"He said *major*, and I know that's no joke. Danielle's dad had a major stroke when we were in college. He was never the same after that. Actually, she was never quite the same after that either."

"Not quite the same how?"

"It really messed her up for a while after it happened. If she weren't so crazy smart, she might have flunked out of school. Maybe that's why she lives such a carefree lifestyle now. I mean, she works hard at her job, but she rarely lets anything bother her. I've always admired that about her."

"I'd like to meet her someday. After all these years of hearing you talk about her, I sort of feel as if I already know her."

"She'd like to meet you too. I think you'd get along really well, even though you're leading completely opposite lives."

"Not *entirely* opposite. Maybe if my family and I were living on a farm in Nebraska." Patti looked around the crowded restaurant. "I haven't been to Gordon Biersch in ages. Given the rapid-fire turnover in downtown Palo Alto, I'm surprised this place is still here."

Cassidy dipped her knife into the mustard jar. "I bet Gordon Biersch will outlive all of us. No matter what happens in the world, there will always be demand for beer and french fries."

"I wonder if we'll run into anyone from Paly here." They were seated at a high table in the bar area.

"Maybe we'll run into that Trent guy from the reunion. Think we can score some weed off him?"

Patti held up her palms. "Oh my God, if he shows up, I will leave. I swear on my children's lives, I will just up and walk right out of the restaurant without saying a word."

Cassidy laughed and spread more mustard on her sandwich. "Why don't you tell me how you really feel?"

Patti set her hands back on the table. "I'm officially changing the subject. Have you thought about calling Brandon again?"

"You think I should? I don't want to push."

Patti picked up her beer and took a sip. "It's hardly pushing to let a guy you care about know you're thinking about him."

"OK, maybe I'll call him again after dinner."

"Patti Bramble, is that you?"

Cassidy and Patti turned their heads to see a much older woman approaching their table.

"Mrs. Stephens?" Patti set down her beer and stood up.

"Hello, dear, how wonderful to see you." The woman gave her a warm embrace.

Patti hugged her back, then gestured to Cassidy. This is my best friend, Cassidy Lane. We went to high school together. Actually, junior high too."

"It's nice to meet you," Cassidy said.

"You two probably met at some point," Patti said to Cassidy. "The Stephens family lived right across the street from us growing up. Their sons were several years ahead of us in school."

Mrs. Stephens put her hand on Patti's shoulder and gave her a knowing squeeze. "How are your parents?"

"My mom's remarried and lives up in Marin. My dad moved to Florida a few years ago." Cassidy couldn't help but notice that Patti kept it brief and didn't mention that she hadn't spoken to either of her parents in ages. She couldn't imagine what that would feel like.

"I'm glad to hear they're doing well. What about *you*, dear? What have you been up to since I last saw you?"

"Not much since I got out of jail."

Mrs. Stephens put a hand over her heart. "You always did make me laugh."

"Actually, my life's been pretty vanilla since college, to be honest. I worked in software sales for a few years, then got married, and now I'm a full-time mom to three kids who never listen to me. I'm Patti Baker now. My husband, Roy, and I live in San Carlos."

Mrs. Stephens smiled. "I'm so glad to hear you have a family of your own. Is Roy a good man?"

Patti sat back down with a shrug. "I think I'll keep him. Maybe."

Cassidy reached across the table and gently pushed Patti's shoulder. "Give me a break. Don't listen to her, Mrs. Stephens. Roy's a *great* man."

"I'm glad to hear it." Mrs. Stephens looked at Cassidy. "What about you, dear? Are you married?"

"Me? No, not yet. Maybe someday."

"Do you have a special someone?"

"Oh, um, not really."

Mrs. Stephens patted her on the arm. "That's too bad. But you're still young. You'll find him if you look hard enough."

"Cassidy's too busy to date," Patti said. "She's an author, and I'm the proud president of her fan club."

Mrs. Stephens clasped her hands in front of her. "Is that so? Have you written anything I might know?"

Cassidy gave Patti a grateful glance before listing her novels: *Gretel Court*, *Nisqually Drive*, *Montague Terrace*, *Cambridge Avenue*, and *Hanover Square*.

Mrs. Stephens shook her head. "I'm afraid none of them ring a bell, though I do like those titles. Are they all street names?"

Cassidy nodded. "I'm not sure why I started that, but now it's become a bit of a tradition."

Mrs. Stephens pointed toward the far side of the restaurant. "I'll be sure to look them up. I see Harry just parked the car. Patti, it was *delightful* running into you. Cassidy, it was lovely to meet you, and don't give up on finding love yet. I'm sure the right man will come along soon." She gave Patti a quick hug, and then she was gone.

Cassidy picked up her beer. "Did you see her face when she found out I'm not married? Sheer pity."

"Stop it. She's just from a different generation."

"I know, but as you mentioned only a few minutes ago, this is Silicon Valley, not Nebraska. Women are supposed to be different here. It shouldn't be such a big deal to be single at our age."

Patti shrugged. "She's old-school. Always has been, always will be. But she's a great lady. I remember running across the street to her house many times when my parents were fighting, or drinking, or both. I'm sure it was inconvenient for her when I'd just show up out of the blue at dinnertime—which happened way too often—but she always invited me in with a smile. I think she just wants everyone to have a happy family, but she doesn't realize that you don't *have* to have a family to be happy. Besides, the family you have right now is pretty damn cool."

Cassidy smiled. "OK, now I feel better. Thanks."

"Just doing my job as president of your fan club." She pointed to Cassidy's plate. "Now can you please get a move on with that sandwich? I need to get going soon."

After dinner they parted ways at the restaurant entrance. As Cassidy walked toward her car, she dug her phone out of her purse to call Brandon again. There was a new text message from him.

My mom's not doing well. I'm still at the hospital.

She stopped walking and decided to call him right there from the sidewalk. She didn't expect to reach him, but she wanted him to know how much she was thinking about him.

Surprisingly, he answered on the third ring

"Hey." He sounded tired.

"Oh my gosh, Brandon, how are you?"

"I've been better. I just got home from the hospital, but I plan to head back after I take a shower."

"How is she?"

"The same. Pretty unresponsive."

"I . . . I don't know what to say, Brandon. I'm so sorry."

"Thank you. My brother's with her now; he flew down from Portland this afternoon."

"I'm so sorry." She reached for something to say other than *I'm sorry*. "Is there anything I can do?"

"No, but thanks for asking."

"Are you sure?"

"Yes."

"OK." She stared at a crack in the sidewalk and felt a tiny one forming somewhere else.

"Listen, I'll probably be at the hospital all day tomorrow, but maybe we could meet up for coffee at some point? I'd really like to see you," he said.

"You would?" She felt the corners of her mouth turn up.

"Of course I would. Why wouldn't I? Listen, that's my brother calling on the other line. I'll be in touch tomorrow, OK?"

"OK. Hang in there. If you need anything at all, just let me know."

"I will, thanks."

"I wish . . . I wish I could give you a hug right now."

"I'd love that. I'm sorry, but I've really got to go now. Good night, Cassidy."

"Good night." She hung up the phone and stared at it for a moment, then was struck by an idea. She did a quick Internet search and dialed the number of a local business she'd read about that offered what it called Emergency Care Packages to be delivered around the clock. It was designed with college students in mind, but who said she couldn't give it a try?

She put in an order for a small cooler of rocky road ice cream to be delivered ASAP to Mrs. Forrester's room at the hospital.

Chapter Twelve

THE NEXT AFTERNOON Cassidy ordered a large coffee and took a seat at a table by the window, watching the cars drive by on Ramona Street. She glanced at the clock on the wall to check the time, then looked around the bustling café. She'd spent several days there over the summer, working on the earliest pages of her current novel, drinking coffee and debating whether to set the story in San Francisco or New York. That had only been a few months ago, but it seemed like much longer, given how much had happened since then—in both the novel and her personal life. She found it interesting how some Palo Alto locations triggered memories of her adult life, while others brought her back to her teenage years, or even earlier. She peered out the window again. Coupa Café inevitably took her for a stroll down the adult version of memory lane, but the Stanford Theatre, barely a block away, brought her all the way back to age sixteen.

"Hi there, pretty girl. I made it."

She turned and saw Brandon standing there, looking a bit haggard yet still undeniably handsome. His stubble from the other night was much thicker now, and there were crinkles at the corners of his eyes that she hadn't previously noticed. He'd texted her earlier, suggesting they get together for coffee, but hadn't been sure he'd be able to swing it.

Before she realized what she was doing, she jumped up and threw her arms around him. "I'm so sorry," she whispered into his chest. "I'm so, so sorry."

He held her tight, then released the embrace and pointed toward the counter with a weary smile. "I'm going to grab a cappuccino. Can I get you anything?"

She picked up her coffee. "I'm good, thanks."

"OK, I'll be right back. And hey, thanks for the ice cream last night. That was really thoughtful of you."

She gave him a sympathetic smile. "You're welcome. Fitting that your favorite flavor is *rocky road*, don't you think?"

"You're not kidding. My life is anything but smooth right now."

As he turned and walked toward the counter to place his order, she tried to imagine how she would feel if *her* mother were lying comatose in a hospital bed right now. Her sweet, kind mother, who was always there for her, who believed in her more than she believed in herself, who had never shown her anything but love.

Just the thought made her want to cry.

"What happens now?" Cassidy asked.

Brandon took a sip of his cappuccino. "We just wait and hope she wakes up."

"Do they know if there's been any brain damage?"

"They're hopeful that there hasn't been, but it's too early to tell right now."

"Have you talked to your dad?"

"I called him yesterday. He and my mom aren't too close, though. They split up a long time ago."

She reached across the table for his hand. "This must be so hard on you, and on your brother too."

He gave her hand a squeeze, then began to rub his thumb over her fingers. "He hasn't slept a wink since he got here."

"Have *you* slept a wink?"

"Barely. Can't you tell by the bags under my eyes?"

She smiled. "I think they're handsome."

They sat there in silence for a few moments, holding hands across the table.

Finally, Brandon pulled his hand away. "I'd better get moving. I don't want to be away for too long."

Cassidy nodded and reached for her purse. "Of course. I'm glad you were able to come by at all."

As they walked toward the exit, Brandon put his arm around her. "Pretty horrible timing for your visit."

She leaned her head against him and sighed. "Ya think?"

He gave her shoulder a squeeze. "I'll be in touch about rescheduling our dinner before you head back to New York. I wish I could tell you more than that, but I just have no idea what's going to happen. Plus I've got to coordinate the boys' schedule with Juliette, which now includes speech therapy twice a week for Jack's lisp . . ." She could see the strain on his face as his thoughts began to drift.

She adjusted her purse strap over her free shoulder and turned to face him as they stood on the sidewalk. "I understand, really. Don't worry."

"When do you leave town again?"

"Tuesday afternoon. My keynote is Monday morning."

"I'm sure you'll crush it." He smiled, but she could tell he wasn't thinking about her speech. Or about their date. Or about the two of them at all. In a way it was as if he weren't even there anymore.

He was already back at the hospital.

Or making arrangements with his ex-wife.

Or being Daddy.

No matter how predestined their encounter at the reunion may have seemed, how magical their long-distance communication had been, at that moment it became crystal clear to Cassidy that dating a grown-up was nothing like high school. In adulthood, romance had to fight for time with real concerns and responsibilities: work and exes and caring for children—and sick parents.

He gave her a quick kiss on the lips before heading to his car. She watched him for a few moments, then turned and looked across the street at the Old Pro sports bar. Through the window she could see the mechanical bull in a back corner, the one he'd ridden the night of the tequila shots. She remembered how much he'd made her laugh while recounting the drunken evening over the phone, not to mention the flirtatious text messages he'd sent her while still under the influence. Just thinking about those texts still made her feel warm inside.

She glanced back at him, his broad shoulders slumping slightly as he walked along the sidewalk.

He was like a different person now, and her heart hurt for him.

And loathe though she was to admit it, it hurt for her a little bit as well.

The next morning Cassidy laced up her running shoes and went for a run in the direction of Jordan Middle School, where she'd once been a proud Jaguar. When she reached the main entrance she put her hands on her waist and slowed to a walk, her neck suddenly on a swivel. As she set out to explore the outdoor areas of campus, memories from those two years of budding adolescence began to hit her from every direction.

There's where my locker was in seventh grade.

There's the water fountain where Kevin Tyson once said hi to me.

There's the patch of grass where the popular kids used to eat lunch.

There's the bench where Patti and I used to eat lunch.

There's where they sold coffee cake and buttered French bread at the midmorning "brunch" break. I wonder if other schools called it brunch?

There's where I had Spanish class both years. I wonder what happened to Mr. Bernal?

There's where I tripped running to math and cut my lip. And no one stopped to help me.

It's all so familiar, yet unfamiliar.

It was a shapeless blur of random recollections, but when she reached the science buildings, one specific memory from seventh grade catapulted itself high above the others:

The frog.

It was in Mr. Faulder's science class that she'd first met Patti. The first week of school they were paired up to dissect a frog, but the moment the jars were unscrewed, Cassidy nearly passed out from the pungent odor of formaldehyde that quickly invaded her olfactory system. Patti had skillfully completed the dissection while Cassidy spent the entire class period with her nose covered by a napkin, trying not to gag, embarrassed by her weak constitution and hoping no one would notice she wasn't doing any actual work. Patti never let on to Mr. Faulder what had happened, and a lifelong friendship was born.

When she'd had enough of adolescence alley, she headed back toward her parents' house. Once she reached the busy intersection of Middlefield and Embarcadero, she trotted in place, waiting for the light to change. Red finally gave way to green, and as it did so the honk of an impatient driver's horn startled her. She jumped high off the sidewalk into the crosswalk, and as she landed she felt a slight sting in the lower part of her left leg.

She kept up her pace, but the sting slowly grew into a sharp pain, and soon she was practically walking. She knew what the problem was, but she didn't want to accept it because she'd had this injury before: Achilles tendinitis. For a runner it could be debilitating. Ice and ibuprofen could help, but the only surefire way to make it go away was to do the one thing a runner hates to do: stop running.

Damn it.

Cassidy's parents were reading the newspaper at the kitchen table when she opened the front door. Her dad took off his reading glasses and set them down. "Why, good morning. How was your run? You were gone quite a while."

She frowned and pointed to her lower leg, then opened up the freezer to get an ice pack. "It was good until I strained my Achilles."

"Oh, sweetheart." Her mother gave her a sympathetic look. She knew how much Cassidy hated being injured. "I'm so sorry."

"I'll live." Cassidy pulled an ACE bandage from a drawer, then sat down at the table and wrapped the ice pack around her leg. "I just need to give up running for a few weeks."

"Can I make you some pancakes?" Her mother also knew how much Cassidy loved pancakes.

Cassidy smiled at her. "Of course. I will never say no to your pancakes. And could you get me a glass of water, please?"

Her mother jumped up and practically ran to the cupboard, clearly excited for the chance to reprise the role of Mom. "Of course. Have you picked out your outfit for your speech tomorrow? I was thinking of heading over to Stanford Shopping Center this afternoon, if you'd like to join me." She filled up a glass and handed it to Cassidy.

Cassidy took a big gulp of water. "I have a dress already, but I'd be up for a little shopping." Just a few days ago she'd hoped to be spending at least some of today with Brandon, but that clearly wasn't going to happen. Maybe she could buy him a Christmas present? The holidays weren't all that far off now.

As if reading her mind, her mother asked, "Any word from Brandon?"

Her dad glanced up from the newspaper but didn't say anything.

"Not since yesterday. I guess that means no change. Although I haven't checked my phone since before I left on my run."

Her mom poured Cassidy a mug of coffee and handed it to her. "Do you want me to get it for you, sweetheart?"

"I'm fine, thanks, Mom." She always felt a bit silly being addressed the same way she often addressed her nieces, but she would never let her mom know that.

"It's such a shame what's happened to his mother. Just awful," her dad said.

Cassidy nodded in agreement, and the three of them absorbed the silence. Cassidy wondered what was going through her parents' minds. They were both healthy, but it had to rattle them that someone their own age had fallen so ill so quickly. It had certainly disturbed her in a way she hadn't expected. Yet another reason not to ask her mom to stop calling her *sweetheart* or *angel*. Or to ask her dad to retire *kiddo*, his perennial favorite. What would be the point of that? Her parents' happiness was more important than her own hang-ups.

After a few moments, her mom broke the silence with a change of subject, much to Cassidy's relief. "Maybe Patti would want to come with us today? I always enjoy seeing her."

"Great idea. Let me finish icing my leg, then I'll see if she can get away."

Cassidy gave Patti a hug. "Thanks for coming. Does Roy hate me? This makes twice in one weekend that I've taken you away from him."

Patti waved a dismissive hand. "Oh God no. He loves hanging out with the kids on the weekends. He's taking them bowling, his favorite sport. No one can hear them screaming in there, so when one of them has a tantrum, he says it's like the tree-falling-in-the-woods thing."

Cassidy laughed. "You chose well with that man. I hope you realize that."

"I know, I know." Patti turned and hugged Cassidy's mom. "It's great to see you, Mrs. Lane."

"Patti, dear, you *must* start calling me Iris. I've known you more than half your life!"

Patti waved her hands in front of her. "No can do. That would be like calling one of my elementary-school teachers by their first name. I just couldn't do it, even now. I'm sorry, Mrs. Lane, but it just *has* to be this way."

Cassidy's mom laughed. "You may change your tune about that when you're my age."

"Maybe, but I still can't do it."

Cassidy smiled at the irony. This was just like the way she felt about the nicknames her mother called her. Or was it the reverse? She knew it was something, and whatever it was, it made her grateful that her mother was standing there right then.

Cassidy pointed to the Starbucks entrance. "As long as we're here, anyone want a coffee?"

"That is a question you *never* have to ask me," Patti said as she opened the door. "Mrs. Lane, you order first." When Cassidy's mom stepped up to the register, Patti poked Cassidy in the side.

"Any word from him?" she whispered.

"He texted me right before we left the house. No change," Cassidy whispered back.

Patti shook her head. "Brutal."

Coffees in hand a few minutes later, the three of them set out to explore the mall. "Is there something specific we're trying to find, or are we just wandering?" Patti asked Cassidy. "Just point me in a direction and I'm good. Being here without the kids is like a vacation, so I'd literally be happy strolling through the parking lot."

Cassidy looked at her mom. "Anything in particular we're looking for?"

"I need to buy a gift for Mary Freeman's daughter. She's throwing a baby shower for her next weekend. I also need to pick up some socks for your father."

Cassidy sipped her coffee. "Mom, that sounds absolutely *thrilling*, but I think I'll opt for the parking lot over baby clothes and socks. And of course I have to stop by See's Candies at some point. I love those chocolate lollipops."

Patti gave her a look. "Are you joking? The butterscotch kicks the chocolate's *ass.*"

Cassidy's mom looked at her watch. "How about we meet at See's at three o'clock? The lollipops will be my treat."

"Deal," Cassidy said.

As Cassidy's mom turned to go, Patti put a hand on her arm. "Mrs. Lane, may I ask you a question?"

"Why, of course you can, Patti. What it is?"

"Are you interested in adopting a thirty-eight-year-old woman?"

She laughed, then pointed at Cassidy. "Did you hear that, my dear daughter? You might soon have some competition, so watch that attitude of yours." She playfully flung her purse over her shoulder and strutted away.

"Your mom is so cool," Patti said.

Cassidy smiled as she watched her mom blend into the other shoppers. "I know."

"I wish my mom were a fraction of that," Patti said.

Cassidy reached over and squeezed her friend's shoulder. "I know."

They headed over to Banana Republic, and as they were sifting through the sale rack, Cassidy remembered the other reason she'd wanted to come to the mall. "Hey, Patti, I was thinking I'd like to get Brandon something for Christmas. Do you have any ideas?" She tried not to feel anxious at the thought of him, but she couldn't help it.

"He's sort of a fancy guy, right?"

"*Fancy*? That doesn't sound like a compliment."

"I mean he cares more about his appearance than, say, my husband does."

"Oh, yes, definitely. Except for your wedding day, I don't think I've ever seen Roy wear anything but a flannel shirt, jeans, and sneakers."

Patti pressed a palm over her eyes. "I know, and God help him. Anyhow, maybe ask that banker friend of yours for ideas. What's his name, Hollis? Hanover?"

"You mean Harper?"

Patti snapped her fingers. "Yes, Harper. Ask him. He sounds fancy too."

"Good thought. Harper always looks put together. I bet he'll have some good ideas."

"I'd love to help, but I have zero experience shopping for men who actually care what they look like. Roy's entire wardrobe is basically variations on the same order from the Columbia catalog."

Cassidy nibbled on her thumbnail. "I'm not used to shopping for men at all."

Patti turned back to the rack. "Call it a hunch, but something tells me you'd better get used to it."

That evening, after practicing her keynote address one last time, Cassidy curled up on the couch and watched a movie with her mom. Just before bed she thought about sending another message to Brandon, who hadn't texted her back since that morning. She reached for her phone, then changed her mind.

It was late, and he was probably exhausted.

Chapter Thirteen

AFTER THE KEYNOTE the next morning, Cassidy did her best to hold her smile as she signed books for the handful of women in line.

But she didn't feel like smiling.

She felt like crying.

How had she gone off the rails like that?

Her speech hadn't been a complete disaster—far from it—but it certainly hadn't gone as well as she'd hoped. She'd wanted to inspire the women in the audience to pursue their passion, but she hadn't sounded passionate herself.

She'd been distracted, a bit scattered, and very nervous.

Why was I so afraid to open up?

She'd planned to include elements of her personal story in her speech, to share the pain of the countless rejections she'd suffered while trying to get published. But when she'd looked out at the audience of strangers, she'd suddenly felt gripped by fear. If she told the truth—if she revealed how her self-esteem had nearly been shattered by the rejections and had in fact never completely recovered—if they knew how insecure she still was deep down, despite her outward appearance of success, would they think she was a fraud?

Would they stop believing in her talent?

Would *she*?

The fear had taken over, and almost without realizing it, she'd stripped down her speech and focused on the basic outline.

Find what makes you happy.

Go for it.

Don't give up until you succeed.

She had sprinkled in a few personal anecdotes, but she'd stuck to the positives, not the negatives, nervously holding her true feelings close to her chest as she encouraged the audience to pursue their dreams.

Not revealing how scared she still was that her next book would be a failure.

That people would say she had no business trying to make up stories for a living.

That she'd never be taken seriously as a novelist.

That she needed to grow up and get a real job.

Although the speech had been perfectly acceptable, she'd kept to generalities, and as a result, in her opinion, it had come across as a bit . . . generic.

A bit bland.

A bit boring.

Because she was afraid to open up, she'd let herself down.

She forced a smile as she handed a signed copy of *Montague Terrace* to the last woman in line, who didn't appear to notice, or care, that Cassidy had delivered a keynote address that was mediocre at best.

"Thanks for the inspiration," the woman said with a smile.

Cassidy smiled back. "You're welcome. I hope you enjoy the book."

Afterward Cassidy sighed and began to collect her things. She just wanted to get out of there, to stop thinking about how she could have done better, and put it behind her.

"Hi, angel."

Cassidy looked up and saw her parents approaching the table. She felt her jaw drop a bit. "Mom? Dad? What are you doing here?"

"We couldn't miss your first keynote address," her mom said.

"But I thought you had some important meeting with your insurance agent this morning."

Her mom held up her palms. "What can I say? We canceled. We thought it would be best not to tell you, so you could focus on the audience, not us."

Cassidy pressed her palms against her cheeks. "I was terrible. I'm so embarrassed."

Her dad shook his head. "Hey now, kiddo, that's not true at all. I was proud to see you up there." She noticed a small tear in the corner of his eye, which he quickly wiped away with a handkerchief. She'd never seen him do that before.

Cassidy frowned. "I didn't expect to be so nervous. I felt frozen up there."

"You did look a bit uncomfortable, but you still did a good job, honey," her mom said.

Cassidy shook her head. "Not good enough."

"Don't be so hard on yourself, kiddo. We're proud of you," her dad said.

Cassidy stood up and forced a smile. "I know you're trying to be nice, and I love you for it, but it's OK. I know I wasn't very good."

Her mom gave her a sympathetic smile. She knew. "Can we take you out to breakfast?"

Cassidy raised her eyebrows. "Pancakes at Stacks?" If anything could cheer her up, pancakes at Stacks was high on the list of potential candidates.

"Anything you want," her dad said.

She nodded. "OK, let me go get my coat and say good-bye to the program coordinator. I'll meet you there."

She picked up her purse and headed down the hallway, the strain in her lower leg still slightly painful.

At least I didn't break it.

For the first time in weeks, she felt motivated to finish her novel. It was time to snap out of her funk and just get to work. She'd been approaching the process as a burden as opposed to a privilege, but this morning's subpar performance had reminded her that it *was* a privilege. *I'm one of the lucky ones who get paid to write books. I can't take that for granted.* She certainly wasn't going to make a living as a keynote speaker, that was for sure.

Despite how hard she'd worked to get here, sometimes she lost sight of how fortunate she was to be in this position, and she was grateful for the wake-up call.

As she walked she pulled out her phone to check the time.

She had four new text messages:

From Danielle: When are you back? I'm in some trouble. Not with the law, though. Come back! Did you rock your keynote? Of course you did.

From Patti: How did it go? I'm sure you were amazing. Love you lots.

From Tyler: Did you stink it up? Just kidding. I bet you knocked it out of the park.

From Brandon: Sorry for not getting back to you yesterday, was with my mom most of the day. I know you leave tomorrow, but unfortunately I have the boys tonight and have to work late in addition to everything else that's going on, so I can't do dinner. Will coffee in the morning work?

She smiled at the screen, grateful to have such good friends in her life to cheer her up. She was also happy to hear from Brandon, even though his message was laced with stress and sadness. Just seeing his name on the display made her stomach flutter.

She replied to all the messages and tossed the phone into her purse, then bade a quick good-bye to the program coordinator. As she made her way through the hallway toward the exit, waving here and there at conference attendees passing by, she tried to tell herself that it didn't matter that her speech hadn't gone so great.

She also rationally knew that she shouldn't expect Brandon to think about something so trivial as a keynote address when his mom lay in the hospital, but she couldn't help but wish that their timing weren't so . . . crummy.

Chapter Fourteen

"SHE'S ALERT?"

Brandon nodded. "Looks like she's out of the woods."

"And no brain damage?"

"They don't think so."

Cassidy smiled and reached for his hand. "That's wonderful news. You must be so relieved." They were seated at an outdoor table at Mayfield Bakery, located at the bustling Town & Country shopping center, directly across the street from Palo Alto High School.

He took her hand and squeezed it briefly, then released it and picked up his cappuccino. "Unfortunately, she's paralyzed on the left side of her body."

Cassidy's face fell. "Oh my God. The entire left side?"

"Pretty much."

"Is it permanent?"

"They think it will go away, but she's going to need extensive therapy, both physical and speech."

Cassidy put a hand over her mouth. "You mean . . . to learn to talk?"

"Yes." His demeanor was matter-of-fact, more hardened than he'd been on Saturday. He still looked exhausted.

"I'm so sorry," Cassidy whispered.

"Thanks."

"Will she stay in the hospital?"

He shook his head. "We need to get her into a rehab facility. Finding a good one is our top priority right now."

"Is your brother going to stick around to help you?"

"Unfortunately, he can't. He's headed back up to Portland tomorrow. His wife's about to have a baby, their third."

"Oh, wow, not the best timing." As soon as the words left her mouth, she stiffened, remembering how she'd thought the same thing about their budding romance.

"Terrible timing. And we just got two new clients, so things are about to get crazy at work."

She nodded but didn't reply. What could she say?

They sat in silence for a few moments, sipping their drinks. Then he reached for her hand again, and she felt her whole body relax.

"Thanks for being so supportive." He stroked his thumb over her fingers. "You've really been great."

"Oh, gosh, of course."

"It means a lot to me."

She squeezed his hand. "*You* mean a lot to me."

"You mean a lot to me too."

She considering bringing up her keynote, then decided against it. Although she would have liked to share her disappointment in her performance with him, he had enough on his mind.

He glanced at his watch. "What time do you leave for the airport?"

"In about an hour."

"You all packed?"

"Yes, sir. I couldn't go for a run this morning, so I packed instead."

"Why couldn't you go for a run?"

"Achilles tendinitis. It should be fine, but I need to rest it, which means no running for a few weeks."

"I need to *start* running. I haven't worked out in ages. I'm getting soft."

She gave him the up and down with her eyes. "You look pretty good to me."

He laughed. "I think you need to get your eyes checked." He stood up without letting go of her hand, then gave it a squeeze. "We'd better get a move on. You need to get to the airport, and I need to stop by the office on my way back to the hospital."

He walked her to her car, and when she stopped and reached for her keys, he released her hand and gently touched her cheek. His fingers were warm and soft, and she felt her knees wobble slightly at the contact.

"You've been really good to me, Cassidy. I know I've been distracted, and you've been so patient. I want you to know how much I appreciate it."

She smiled and put a hand over his. "I like being good to you. In fact, I wish I could have done more. And you're worth being patient for."

"I know I'm not acting like it right now, but believe me, I know you're special." He kissed her gently on the lips, then hugged her and took a step back. "Have a safe flight back. Text me when you get in, OK?"

She nodded weakly, already missing him. "Will do."

She drove to her parents' house in a fog of conflicting emotions, savoring the feel of his lips on hers, wanting to touch him again, aching for the pain he must be feeling, longing to ease his suffering.

And even though she knew it was a lot to ask, she couldn't help but wish he'd asked her about her speech.

Chapter Fifteen

DETERMINED TO GET back on New York time right away, Cassidy reluctantly woke up to the sound of her alarm clock at eight o'clock the next morning. Part of her was tempted to turn it off and stay nestled in her cozy bed, but she'd learned from experience that the only way to readjust to the time change was to rip off the figurative Band-Aid and get moving—literally. A glance out her bedroom window showed a dark sky and pouring rain, so off to the gym upstairs it was. A ride on the stationary bike was all her injured leg would allow anyway.

She kicked off the sheets and tried not to think about how warm she could be in Palo Alto.

In more ways than one.

That afternoon she called Danielle, expecting to leave her a voice mail. She was pretty sure Danielle was on the road, and she rarely answered her phone even when she was in New York, so Cassidy was surprised when her friend picked up.

"Hey, lady, are you back from California?" Danielle asked.

"I got in late last night. Where are you? And what's this trouble you mentioned in your text?" Cassidy scrolled through the manuscript on her computer screen as she spoke.

"I was in Baltimore for a couple of days, then Boston, but right now I'm in a cab on the way home from the airport, or on the way to the office, I should say. I'm dying to sleep in my own bed tonight. I'll tell you about the trouble the next time I see you."

"Want to do brunch this weekend? I feel like I haven't talked to you in ages."

"I know. I'm sorry, I've been swamped. And I'm back on the road Friday. What about tonight? Want to grab a drink?"

"Sure, as long as it's not too early. I have a manicure at seven."

"Since when do you get manicures?"

"I've recently discovered that rewarding myself with salon treatments is helping me to be more productive on my book."

"Rewarding yourself or bribing yourself?"

"Tomayto, tomahto. Either way, I'm turning over a new leaf in the nail-management department, so it's a win-win for all."

"You're still the only one in the equation, hon. And I'll believe your nail-biting days are over when I see it. Are you going to throw away your sweatpants too?"

Cassidy smiled. "Don't talk crazy now."

"Would Bin 71 work? I could definitely use a nice goblet of wine."

"You say that every time we get together."

"Well, I'm a smart woman. Want to meet at eight?"

"Sounds good."

Cassidy spent the rest of the afternoon at her desk, carefully crafting an emotional turning point for Emma, her increasingly disillusioned heroine. After toiling for weeks to prepare a new business pitch, the night before the presentation Emma confides to Donna, the soft-spoken aesthetician who does her monthly facials, how little she actually cares about bringing in the account, her first since her big promotion.

With a gentle yet supportive nudge, accomplished in remarkably few words, wise Donna prompts Emma to admit—to herself—that her heart just isn't in the career she's chosen.

To admit that she feels unfulfilled.

And lost.

And alone, because her boyfriend thinks she's being foolish for not appreciating the professional opportunity before her.

Then Emma realizes that painful as it may be, her life has to change. And that she's the only one who can change it.

After typing furiously for several hours, Cassidy sat back and smiled at the work she'd done. Darlene's nurturing spirit had now touched both Cassidy *and* her latest heroine, and they were both grateful for it.

She checked the time and was surprised to see it was nearly six o'clock. She stretched her arms over her head, then stood up and walked into the kitchen to pour herself a glass of water. It was still raining outside. She'd been writing most of the day and realized she was still in her workout clothes. She'd meant to shower when she got back from the gym, but she'd sat down for a few moments at her desk and the story had started to speak to her, so she'd listened. When she could go all day without showering, she knew she was in a groove with her writing. But now it was time to clean herself up and rejoin society, starting with her appointment at Annabelle's.

As the hot water rolled over her back and shoulders, Cassidy flushed with pride at having put in a solid day's work. She hadn't heard from Brandon since last night, but given what he was currently dealing with, she wasn't surprised. Plus the break from constant texting had allowed her to get more work done on her book in a single day than she had in ages. She was normally a relatively disciplined writer, but ever since Brandon had entered the picture, her ability to concentrate had unraveled, her cool focus melted by steamy memories of what it felt like to be kissed by him.

And kiss him back.

And hug him.

And hold his hand.

Oh, how she wanted to do all of that again.

When she opened her closet, she saw her new dress hanging there, the one she'd bought for her doomed date with Brandon, the dinner he'd postponed but never rescheduled. It was the first dress she'd bought specifically for a date in ages. She removed it from the closet and held it up in against her in front of the mirror. The hunter-green hue brought out the color in her eyes and highlighted her fair skin—or so the saleslady had told her. She tossed it onto the bed and went to retrieve the ironing board from the hall closet. Maybe wearing a pretty new outfit to meet a good friend at her favorite wine bar would remind her why she'd chosen to live so far away from home.

Cassidy ran into Harper in the lobby on her way out. She was just putting on her coat as he entered the building.

"Well, doesn't someone look nice tonight," he said with a grin. "You got a hot date?"

She smiled at him. "Just meeting Danielle for a drink. But thanks for the compliment."

"When did you get back from California?"

"Last night. I'm already freezing here." She buttoned her coat and wrapped her arms around herself. "It was like seventy degrees in Palo Alto yesterday."

"I'm sure you'll survive. You see, buildings have this thing called *heat*. Did you have fun?"

She nodded. "More or less. We can talk about it later. Did anything exciting happen while I was gone?"

"Actually, yes. I broke up with Vanessa."

Cassidy felt her eyes open wide. "You did? Why?"

"Don't act like you're surprised it didn't last."

"But I thought you liked her."

"I did at first, but then I started to see what all my friends apparently saw from the get-go."

Cassidy made a squeamish face. "Was I right? Gold digger?"

He made guns with his thumbs and index fingers. "Bingo. You called it."

Cassidy shrugged. "I'm sorry. She was nice enough, but she just seemed a bit too . . . *plastic* for you."

He sighed. "I used to be better at spotting the ones who were after my bank account. In my, um, situation, you sort of learn that skill at an early age. Maybe I'm losing my edge."

She smiled. Harper was so modest. "I'm not a handsome banker with a trust fund to boot, so I can only imagine. But I guess it's good that you figured it out before you got in too deep, right?"

"True, but it still bothers me. I really thought Vanessa was different. Or maybe I just hoped she was different."

She put a hand on his arm. "Listen, I'd love to stay and chat, but I'm going to be even later than I normally am. We'll catch up soon, OK?" She turned to leave, then stopped and gave his arm a squeeze. "Just so you know, I'm proud of you for ending things with her. It's not easy to walk away from romance, even when you know it's not right."

He gave her a half smile. "Thanks."

⟨∽

"You're looking quite pretty tonight." Darlene took Cassidy's coat and led her to the manicure table. "Do you have plans with a special someone later?"

"Just a drink with my friend Danielle. She's special, but she's not my special someone."

"Do you *have* a special someone in your life?"

"I think so, maybe." Cassidy smiled. "I hope so."

"Hope is good, always good," Darlene said in a soft voice. She began to smooth lotion over Cassidy's fingers. "Now close your eyes and relax; let your mind just drift away."

Cassidy did as she was instructed, and soon her mind was floating back to the pages of her book, to all the work she'd completed that day. Should she tell Darlene she'd introduced a character based on her? Or would that be awkward because Donna, the fictional aesthetician, was actually inspired by the Darlene who Cassidy had thought owned Annabelle's? Back when Cassidy thought Darlene *was* Annabelle. It was all a bit complicated, but fact or fiction, there was something about the real Darlene's aura that always made Cassidy feel so nurtured, and she was relieved to have realized her young protagonist could benefit from a similar haven, one that could provide just the right vehicle for a critical turning point in the story.

Cassidy tried to relax as her mind began to drift away from her book, from Annabelle's, from New York itself.

All the way back to California.

"Damn, look at *you*." Danielle took off her coat and sat at the bar next to Cassidy. "Do you have a hot date after this?"

Cassidy rolled her eyes. "Just so you know, that's the *third* time I've been asked that question since leaving my apartment. I just thought it would be fun to take my new dress out for a spin, especially on the heels of your sweatpants comment this afternoon. Do you like it?"

"I do, very much. And for the record, you *rock* your sweatpants."

Cassidy laughed. "Thanks. You look nice too, by the way. Did you get a haircut?"

Danielle framed her face with her hands. "I did, and thanks for noticing. So, speaking of hot dates, how did it go with Brandon?"

Cassidy pointed to her. "Let's talk about *you* first. I want to know about this trouble you alluded to. What's up?"

Danielle shook her head. "We'll talk about my problem later. I want to hear all about high-school guy."

Cassidy lightly touched the scrape on her nose. "It wasn't exactly . . . what I expected."

Danielle made a nervous face. "Oh, no. Not good?"

"It was good . . . just complicated."

"Complicated? What do you mean?"

Cassidy took a deep breath, then relayed the story of her tumultuous week in California.

Danielle set down her wineglass. "Damn, Cassidy. That's intense."

Cassidy frowned. "I know. As I said, not exactly what I expected."

"Is his mom going to be OK?"

"They think so, but it's going to be a long, slow road to recovery. Lots of physical therapy."

"So all that happened between you two was one kiss?"

"Basically, yes. He kissed me a couple of other times, but only one *real* kiss, if that makes sense."

"Was it at least a good kiss?"

Cassidy felt her insides stir at the memory. "It was unbelievable."

"So it made your blood rush to all the right places?"

"Danielle!"

Danielle picked up her glass and shrugged. "Don't act all virginal, I'm just trying to get a sense of your definition for *unbelievable*. How did you two leave it?"

"What do you mean?"

"I mean, when are you going to see him again?"

"When I go home for the holidays, I suppose."

"You didn't make any specific plans?"

"No."

"Hmm."

"Hmm *what*? You think that's bad?" Cassidy bit her lip.

"I just like it when a guy makes a point of putting a *next time* on the calendar. It shows that he's into it."

Cassidy gazed glumly at her wineglass. "He's got a lot to deal with right now. And no matter what he may feel for me, I don't think making plans that far out is a big priority."

"I know; I'm not judging, believe me. His plate is clearly more than full. I just want to make sure you're being treated the way you deserve. Your feelings count too, you know?"

Cassidy smiled weakly. "Thanks for always watching out for me. Now enough about me. What trouble are *you* in?"

Just then Danielle's phone rang. She glanced at the display and groaned. "I'm sorry. It's one of my territory managers, so I can't ignore it. Can you give me a minute?"

"Sure, no problem."

Danielle grabbed her coat and went outside to take the call. While she was gone, Cassidy nursed her drink and glanced around the room, enjoying the chance to people watch without feeling self-conscious for being there by herself. She decided to play the character game, this time zeroing in on a distinguished older man sitting alone at the far side of the bar.

What's his name? Harry . . . Harry Winfield.

Where's he from? Westchester. No, Rochester.

What does he do? He's a judge. Retired judge.

What makes him angry? When preppy young lawyers disrespected him in court. Arrogant punks.

Who or what makes him laugh? In his eyes no one will ever be as funny as Johnny Carson. And he loves a good riddle.

Pet phrase? The eyes don't lie.

Biggest regret in life? That he never forgave his father.

Dream job. Already had it.

Secret talent? He can use his tongue to tie a cherry stem into a knot.

A few minutes later, Danielle came rushing back in.

"I've got to get on a flight back to Boston."

Cassidy stared at her. "What? Tonight?"

"Yep. Duty calls, this time in the form of a breakfast meeting. I'm really sorry, but I've literally got to run or I'm going to miss the last flight out. We'll catch up more soon, OK?"

"Sure."

Danielle reached for her wallet, but Cassidy waved her away. "Go, go, I've got it."

"Thanks, hon. Keep me posted on high-school guy."

Cassidy had just taken off her dress and was putting away the ironing board when she heard the chime of her phone. She hurried over to her desk and smiled to see Brandon's name on the display.

> Hi, sorry not to have texted earlier, am buried with work and am still at the office. I think I found a place for my mom, am going to try to get her moved in there this weekend. How was your first day back in NYC? I hear the weather's pretty nasty out there. Missing you.

Still feeling blissful from her productive day, and emboldened by the wine she'd drunk at Bin 71, she typed a flirtatious reply.

> Hi back! So far, so good, got a ton of writing done today. Just got home from meeting a friend for a drink, you've literally caught me in my bra and underwear putting away the ironing board. I must have a serious addiction to texting . . . or to something . . . to be responding right now.

Her phone chimed seconds after she sent that:

> I'd like to see that. You know how to iron?

She hesitated for a moment, wondering if he meant what she hoped he did, then decided to see for herself:

Are you saying you'd like to see me in my bra and underwear? Or see me iron?

Another chime came as she hung up her dress:

Both.

She felt slightly shy but also thrilled. She stared at the screen. Should she do it? She'd never taken a racy photo of herself, much less texted one to a man.

She set down the phone, then stepped into the hall and looked at the full-length mirror hanging on the open bathroom door.

They'd shared only one passionate kiss. Maybe a photo would make him want another one as much as she did.

She bit her lip, then picked up the phone and walked toward the mirror before she lost her nerve. She ran the fingers of her free hand through her hair and took a deep breath.

Am I really doing this?

She turned slightly to one side, titled her hips like the celebrities in magazines always seemed to do, then held up the phone and pressed the photo button.

Click.

Oh my God, I really did it!

She inspected the picture. The automatic flash had blocked out most of her face, which gave the shot an air of mystery, which she liked. Her bra and underwear were both black cotton, which almost made it look like she was wearing a swimsuit. Contrary to what she'd feared, the photo didn't look tasteless at all. She saw it as sporty and a bit fun, adjectives she liked to believe fit her fairly well. She also appeared to be in pretty good shape. Then again, she'd had some wine. Though she didn't drink much anymore, she still knew that *everyone* looked better after a couple of glasses of wine.

She nibbled on her fingernail for just a moment, then decided to act before she changed her mind. She sent the picture, set the phone on the bathroom sink, then shut the door and ran down the hall into her bedroom to change into her pajamas, closing that door too.

She pressed her palms against her forehead and laughed.

I can't believe I just did that!

Less than a minute later, she heard her phone chime through both closed doors.

She exited her bedroom and walked slowly toward the bathroom. She opened the door and reached for the phone.

Her hand flew up to cover her smile as she read the message.

I'm an idiot for not taking advantage of that while you were here.

Emboldened by his reaction, she typed a quick reply:

Is that so?

It is so. I may have to plan another trip to New York . . .

You're welcome to visit anytime.

Let me get through this crazy period at work and get things sorted out with Mom. But I love New York.

Do you want to visit New York, or visit me?

You're the incentive. New York is the bonus.

You're not just saying that?

I don't just say things, Cassidy. I want to see you.

The feeling is mutual.

I'm glad to hear that.

I'll be home in a few weeks for the holidays.

I'm glad about that too. Now I really need to stop texting you and finish this brief. Thanks for the picture. I love it.

Chapter Sixteen

BY THURSDAY IT was beginning to feel like Groundhog Day to Cassidy. For the third day in a row, she awoke to the jarring ring of her alarm clock and reluctantly forced herself out of bed. When she glanced out of the window it was raining again, the sky dark and ominous.

Half-asleep, she shuffled into the bathroom, wishing she felt more motivated to get on the stationary bike. As she brushed her teeth, she looked at herself in the mirror, then suddenly realized something.

That scrape on my nose should have healed by now.

Not so tired anymore, she set down her toothbrush and leaned closer to the mirror. She examined the tiny mark and wondered how long it had been there. Two months? Three months? She couldn't remember the first time she'd noticed it.

Was it a scrape?

Or a scab?

She peered at it.

What is that?

She felt a tightening in her chest as she immediately assumed the worst.

❧

"Hey, neighbor, fancy meeting you here."

She looked up from her magazine and saw Harper standing in front of the stationary bike she was riding. "Hi, Harper. What are you doing here? Shouldn't you be at work by now?" It was just after nine.

He cleared his throat. "I took a personal day. Listen, I'm glad I ran into you because I was going to text you anyway. Are you free for dinner tonight? My treat. I want to talk to you about something."

"Is everything OK?"

"I'll explain at dinner. Are you free?" His voice sounded a little strange, and she wondered what was going on with him. She was worried enough with her concern about her nose right now.

"I think so." She mentally scanned her calendar and was pretty sure it was clear, although she could never be certain without that little book in front of her. "You sure you don't want to talk here?"

He shook his head. "I'd prefer to wait. Plus I'd like to buy you dinner to thank you for getting me started on the essays."

She wiped her forehead with a towel. "OK, but don't think I won't be on your case to *finish* them. You can butter me up all you want, but those essays aren't going to write themselves, and I'm not going to write them for you."

He didn't laugh, which surprised her. Harper always laughed when she teased him. Instead all he said was. "Meet me in the lobby at seven thirty?"

She gave him a curious look. "All right, sure."

❧

Nigel, Cassidy's editor, called her that afternoon while she was sitting at her desk.

She picked up the phone. "I'm working on it right now, I promise. I can text you a photo of my laptop screen if you want."

He laughed. "You make me feel like your mother. How's it coming along?"

"It's getting there. It's not unfolding quite as I'd expected, but then again, they never do. I still have no idea what I'm going to do about the ending, but I'm confident it'll come to me eventually."

"I'm not worried. How did the keynote go?"

Cassidy felt her face get hot. "OK."

"Just OK?"

"I got a bit nervous."

"The powers that be thought you did fine."

"They did?"

"Yes. The program coordinator just called and asked if you'd be up for speaking at another event."

Cassidy sat up straight. "Really?" *A second chance.*

"Their organization's having a similar conference for women in San Francisco, so you'd be speaking on the same topic."

"When?"

"The middle of February. I think she said the sixteenth. Are you interested?"

Cassidy nodded into the phone. "Sure, count me in." Not only was this a chance to redeem herself, but she was thrilled at the thought of another trip to the Bay Area, especially after Brandon's reaction to that photo she'd sent him. Assuming the time they spent together over the holidays went well, it would be nice to know she'd be back in California soon thereafter.

"Excellent. I'll send you an e-mail when I have the details. I also want to get a meeting on the books to talk about your novel. Would the second Wednesday in December work for you? That will give me a little more than a week to read it after you send in the manuscript."

"Are you just doing this to make sure I meet my deadline?"

"Perhaps. Will it work?"

She laughed. "Probably. The fear of letting you down is a powerful motivator."

"I'm not worried. I know you can do it."

"I'm glad to hear that. Now if you'll excuse me, I'm going to get back to writing so I don't let you down."

"Cool beans. Now go get 'em, cowgirl."

She hung up the phone and jotted down their December meeting in her calendar, then slowly flipped through the pages. She nibbled on her thumbnail and stared at another appointment she'd just scheduled.

This one with a dermatologist.

She lightly touched the scape on her nose with her index finger.

It's probably nothing, right?

It doesn't even hurt.

She stood up and walked into the kitchen to pour herself a glass of water. She leaned her hip against the counter for a few minutes, trying to stop thinking about it but not having much luck.

Stop worrying. I'm sure I'm fine.

But what if I'm not?

She finished the water and set the glass in the sink, then walked straight to her desk and picked up her phone. She suddenly wanted to tell someone about her nose, and she wanted that someone to be Brandon. He'd opened up to her, and now she wanted to do the same.

His phone went straight to voice mail, so she left a message: "Hey, it's Cassidy. I, um, I have some news. There's something strange on my nose that isn't going away. I just made an appointment with a dermatologist. I'm sure it's nothing, but I have to admit I'm a bit anxious. Anyhow, I wanted to tell you. I hope you're having a good day."

She hung up the phone and immediately felt better. It had been a long time since she'd allowed herself to be vulnerable in front of a man, even if it was only in a voice mail.

"Where are you taking me?"

Harper held open the cab door. "Landmarc in the Time Warner Center. Have you been there?"

Cassidy shrugged as she climbed inside. "I haven't, but as we both know, that means nothing." She had long ago given up on trying to stay current on the happening places to eat. She gratefully let Danielle and Harper do that for her, since they cared way more about that sort of thing than she did.

The taxi dropped them off at Columbus Circle, and together they took the escalator to the third floor. The place was buzzing, and as the hostess led them through the modern décor to their table, Cassidy was reminded yet again of why she loved living in Manhattan. Where else could you find a trendy, packed restaurant on the third floor of *anything*?

After they'd ordered salads and entrees and each had a glass of wine in front of them, Harper cleared his throat just as Cassidy was about to eat a piece of focaccia.

"I have something important to tell you."

She froze, then slowly set down the bread. She stared at the table for a moment before reluctantly looking up at him, silently praying he wouldn't utter the words a part of her had long feared he might.

"What's up?" She forced a smile and tried to look casual. *Please don't mess up our friendship.*

He paused for a moment, then took a deep breath.

"I'm . . . not applying to business school."

That's the big confession? Relieved, she picked up the piece of bread again. "Why not?"

This time he was the one who stared at the table.

"Harper, you there?" She waved a hand in front of his face.

Finally, he regained eye contact. "I'm not applying to business school because . . . Vanessa's pregnant."

Cassidy dropped the bread.

"She's *pregnant?*"

"Yes."

"But just yesterday you told me you'd broken up with her."

He sighed. "She called me late last night and told me she'd just taken a pregnancy test."

"Oh my God. What are you going to do?"

"I'm going to be a father, apparently."

"She's keeping it?"

He nodded, and despite the dim light she noticed a few bags under his eyes she hadn't seen this morning at the gym. She wondered if he'd slept at all last night. No wonder he'd taken a personal day.

"Oh, Harper. I . . . I don't know what to say." She couldn't believe how wrong she'd been about what he'd wanted to tell her tonight.

He picked up his wineglass. "It's OK, you don't have to say anything. I just wanted you to know."

"So what happens now?"

"I'm not sure. Vanessa and I need to figure that out. We need to figure out a lot of things, so unfortunately, applying to business school's just not very high on my list right now."

Cassidy stared at him, stunned. She felt nothing but compassion and wracked her brain for the right words of support, but despite the thousands she'd poured onto paper over the years, the only ones she could find right now were: "I'm so sorry."

They came out as a whisper.

Back at their apartment building, Cassidy hugged Harper goodbye and exited the elevator on her floor, then walked slowly down the hall to her apartment.

Poor Harper.

Just yesterday he had his whole life ahead of him. Now he was having a child with a woman he'd dated for only a few weeks.

Life really can change on a dime.

That made her think of the spot on her nose, and she reached into her purse, eager to see Brandon's response to her voice mail about it. She hadn't checked her phone all evening, not wanting to be rude after Harper had shared his life-changing news with her. She hoped there was nothing for her to be concerned about, but she couldn't shake the feeling that there might be, and she was grateful to be able to share her anxiety with someone other than her parents, whom she hadn't told. She hadn't even been to see a doctor yet, and the last thing she wanted was to alarm them without knowing if there was anything wrong. She could have told Patti or Danielle, but telling Brandon had felt like a step forward in their relationship.

She looked at the screen.

There were no messages.

Chapter Seventeen

CASSIDY WOKE UP the next morning feeling something uncomfortably familiar.

Dread.

Why hadn't Brandon replied to her voice mail?

She hated that this was her first thought of the day.

She looked at the phone on her nightstand. Maybe he'd texted while she was sleeping?

She hated that this was her second thought of the day.

When did I become so dependent on him?

She sat up in bed and stretched her arms over her head, then reached over and picked up the phone.

There was a new text message.

It was from Brandon, sent last night at just after ten o'clock his time.

Sorry it took so long to reply. Have been swamped.
Sorry about your nose. Sounds like sun damage.

She read it three times.

That was his response?

Had it really taken him that long to get around to listening to her voice mail? Or had he listened to the message but not replied until hours later?

In her mind those were two very different scenarios.

She set down the phone and shuffled into the bathroom.

At least he got back to me, right?

She tried to believe that was what mattered, but she wasn't all that convinced.

From there on out, Cassidy immersed herself in her novel, ordering meals for delivery and leaving her apartment only to ride the stationary bike. The exercise helped clear her head and also kept her from worrying so much about her nose, or Brandon, or about when her injured Achilles tendon would heal.

As for the book, she was approaching the finish line now, and she was pleased with how the story was turning out. The only thing still up in the air was the ending. She kept going back and forth between two distinct scenarios for the final scene with Emma and Jeremy—one happy, one not so happy—and soon she was going to have to stop waffling and make a decision. She was tempted to pick up the phone and ask Nigel for advice on which way to go, but she knew it was important to her growth as a writer to figure it out on her own. The right ending would reveal itself to her if she just relaxed, let go of her preconceptions, and let it happen.

At four o'clock the third day, she hit a wall and decided it was time to take a break from her self-imposed exile. She glanced out the window to see if it was still raining. The sky was cloudy and dark but the street looked dry, so she stood up and pulled a parka and knitted hat off the coatrack. She'd been holed up inside for too long; suddenly she needed some fresh air.

She'd just opened the door when her phone rang. She walked back to her desk and smiled when she saw the name on the display.

"Brandon, hi."

"Hi back. I thought it would be nice to hear your voice for once instead of reading it." He'd texted her a bit during her marathon writing session, but barely.

"It's nice to hear your voice too. How are you?"

"I'm hanging in there. Sorry to have been out of touch lately. Things have been really rough with my mom."

"Is she getting any better?"

"Unfortunately, no. She's still completely paralyzed on her left side."

"Oh, gosh, I'm so sorry."

"And suddenly Jack is having more trouble at school."

"Because of the lisp?"

"Yes. It's getting worse, so the teasing is getting worse too. Or maybe the lisp is getting worse because of the teasing. We're not sure what's really going on."

"Poor little guy. What are you going to do?"

He sighed. "Juliette and I aren't quite seeing eye to eye on that. She wants to put him in a special school, but I'd like to give speech therapy more of a chance first before taking such drastic action. I want the boys to be together, if possible."

"Sounds complicated. I'm . . . sure you two will figure something out." Was that the right response? Or was she supposed to take his side? She was at a loss as to how to react.

He cleared his throat. "Anyhow, enough about all my problems. How's the book coming along? I know your deadline is looming."

"Pretty well, thanks for asking. I'm going to have to push hard to finish on time, but I think I can do it. I was just about to go for a walk, actually. I've been hunkered down in my apartment and need to get outside."

"Well, I'll let you get going then. I just wanted to say hi."

"I'm glad you did."

They said good-bye and she headed out of the door with a smile on her face, wondering why she'd been so insecure about him.

It wasn't until she was in the elevator that she realized he hadn't asked her anything about her nose.

The next afternoon Cassidy was absorbed in her novel when she was startled by the chime of a text. It was a message from Harper:

> Frozen yogurt tonight? I know it's cold outside, but I've got me a hankering.

She typed a quick reply.

> Sure. Meet me in the lobby at seven thirty. Trying to write until then. See ya.

Less than a minute later her phone chimed again, and she silently cursed Harper. Had she not been clear enough that she was working? She picked up the phone and was surprised to see Brandon's name on the display.

She caught her breath as she read the message.

> I've been looking at that photo you sent me.

She put her free hand on her cheek, which suddenly felt a bit flushed.

She read the message again, then looked at the manuscript on the screen in front of her. She knew she should keep writing and wait until later to respond, but it didn't matter either way. Her focus was shattered, which meant the same for her momentum, reply or no reply.

The next few hours were dotted with a playful exchange of messages that kept her heart aflutter even as she tried her best to be productive. Brandon was in her head again now, and she was helpless to resist:

You've been looking at my photo again?

I have

You're making me blush.

Good

You're a man of few words today. Very little punctuation too.

I'm working

You're working? It certainly doesn't seem like it.

I'm multitasking

I thought men weren't good at that.

I'm not like most men

I think I've figured that out.

I'm looking at the photo right now, you're beautiful.

Cassidy smiled and felt a small tear form in the corner of her eye as she read the text. *He really likes me too. I'm not the only one feeling this.*

She chewed on her pencil as she pondered something she'd been thinking about for a while now.

Should she ask him?

Was it too early?

She pushed the thoughts away and worked on her book a bit more, then stood up and stretched her arms over her head before heading into her bedroom to change out of her sweatpants. As she pulled a pair of jeans from the drawer, she began to craft a new text message in her head. From there she moved to the bathroom, where she fixed her hair and applied a bit of makeup and mentally tweaked the message. When she was all dressed and ready to meet Harper for yogurt, she picked up her phone. She read Brandon's last text again, then began to type:

I know people's schedules fill up way ahead of time during the holidays. Would it be wildly inappropriate for me to invite you to something now?

The response time from both of them had varied all afternoon, but this time he wrote her back right away:

What day?

She typed again, practically holding her breath as she did so:

My family has an annual dinner at a restaurant downtown. It's my parents and Tyler and Jessica and the
girls, plus Jessica's parents and a few assorted friends
and relatives, usually around 20 people including kids.
My dad pays for everything, and it's the only night all
year he wears a tie. This year it's on the Friday before
Christmas at the Westin. Do you have the boys that
weekend?

Within a minute he replied:

I just checked my calendar. No kids that weekend!
Dinner sounds fun.

The corners of her lips turned upward. *He said yes!*
She glanced at the clock and typed another message:

Great. I'll tell my parents you're in. They'll be happy to
see you again. So will I.

Her phone chimed again:

The feeling is mutual.

With a huge smile on her face, she tossed the phone into her
purse and rushed out the door to meet Harper.

Her relationship with Brandon had just taken a big step
forward.

"So how's it going with Vanessa?" Cassidy said, then scooped up a
spoonful of peanut butter yogurt.

Harper shrugged. "The same. She's still pregnant. How's it going with that guy in California?"

"For the record his name is Brandon, and I think it's going pretty well."

He raised an eyebrow. "You *think* it's going pretty well? Talk about hedging your bets."

She pointed her spoon at him. "Hey, now. Given the inconvenient geography of the situation, that's the only answer I can give you, and I *think* it's a pretty good one."

"If you say so."

"That reminds me: I need your help with something."

He put a hand on his heart. "You need *my* help with something? That's new. I'm not sure I'm comfortable about this."

She rolled her eyes. "Give me a break. You helped me get those prints in my living room to hang straight, remember?"

"You're right, I did do that. So what do you need me for now?"

"I want to give Brandon a Christmas present, but I have no idea what to get him."

He dipped his spoon into his cup. "Maybe a new phone? His is probably fried, given the amount of texting going on between you two."

"Come on, I'm *serious*. He actually reminds me of you a little bit, so I thought maybe you would have some good ideas of what he might like."

Harper sat up straight. "He reminds you of me how, exactly? Is it that he's smart, charming, and sexy as all hell?"

Cassidy smiled. "Well, of course. But I meant more in his aesthetics."

He gave her a look. "In his what?"

"His aesthetics."

"Could you say that in English, please? Not everyone at this table is a professional writer."

"He's . . . I don't know . . . *fancy.*" She put the word in air quotes.

Harper leaned back in his chair and crossed his arms in front of him. "Fancy."

"Yes, but I mean that as a compliment. He dresses well, likes nice things, that sort of thing. I guess you could say he's your classic well-heeled metrosexual. He definitely spends way more on his shoes than I do, for example." She pointed her spoon at him. "And he wore a lavender button-down when he took me out to dinner."

Harper scooped up some more yogurt. "I see, I see. I do like me some lavender."

"So you understand what I mean?"

"I do."

"And you're not offended?"

He finished his yogurt and shook his head. "I am not."

"Good. Do you have any ideas for a gift?"

"You said he has kids, right?"

"Yes, two boys. Henry and Jack."

He thought for a moment, then snapped his fingers. "You know what I bet he'd love?"

She set down her cup and held up her palms. "*Obviously* I don't."

"Get him a set of cuff links."

"Cuff links?"

He tapped a finger to one wrist and then the other. "Sterling silver. Engraved. From Tiffany."

"Engraved? You think?"

"Yes. One initial on each cuff link, for each son's name."

Cassidy raised her eyebrows. "Ooh, I like that." *An H and a J.*

Harper nodded. "Tiffany cuff links are very classy, and an engraving like that makes them special—and a super thoughtful gift. He'll love them."

"I love the idea, but do you think it would be too much? I mean, as you can clearly tell, it's not like he's my boyfriend or anything."

"How many text messages did you say you two have exchanged?"

Cassidy felt her cheeks turn a bit pink. "I'm not exactly sure what it's at now, but around . . . three thousand?" The frequency had dropped off considerably since his mother's stroke, but it was hard to discount the sheer volume of messages they'd exchanged.

"*Three . . . thousand . . . text . . . messages.*" Using his spoon, Harper tapped the side of his yogurt cup as he said each word. "I think that answers your question."

She gave him a hopeful smile. "He's also coming to my family holiday dinner."

"Is that so?"

"Yes. I just asked him today."

Harper nodded. "Then he'll dig the cuff links. Don't worry."

Chapter Eighteen

DANIELLE WAS STILL out of town that weekend, so Sunday morning Cassidy went for a power walk in Central Park, then planned to get a pedicure. She hoped the mental break of taking the entire day off and spending much of it outside, infused with some much-needed fresh air, sunlight, and pampering, might provide a final burst of inspiration to finish the book. Though she was tempted to try to run, she knew it would set her back in the long haul.

She played the character game as she plugged along on her walk, first eyeing a diminutive redhead who sped by her in a spandex blur:

What's her name? Rebecca Black, but her family calls her Becky, which she hates.

Where's she from? South Boston, but she says Boston.

What does she do? Investment banker.

What makes her angry? When her cleaning lady doesn't dust the top of the refrigerator.

What makes her laugh? Laughing is overrated.

Favorite food? She says it's brown rice and vegetables with tofu, but it's really Nacho Cheese Doritos. You'll never see her eat them in public, though.

Biggest life disappointment so far? She'll say none, but it's really that she didn't get into Harvard Business School and had to settle for Wharton.

Biggest secret? She's not a real redhead.

Dream job? She wishes to God she knew. But she'll tell you it's investment banker.

Next up was a thin, pale man who looked about Cassidy's age, sitting alone on a bench with his hands folded on his lap.

What's his name? Buddy Hawthorne.

Where does he live? Queens.

What does he do? He was a firefighter.

Favorite hobby? He played basketball three times a week before he got sick.

Favorite food? Anything he can keep down.

Biggest life disappointment so far? Knowing he probably won't live to marry and have children.

Cassidy turned back for another look at the man on the bench, wondering why her imagination had taken her down such a dark path. She felt a pang of guilt for the life she'd just imagined for him and hoped he was in fact healthy and happy. Same went for the redhead, who in all likelihood was nothing like the unsympathetic character she'd just depicted in her mind.

Cassidy blinked a few times and decided to stop playing this game. If she was going to take a break from actual writing today, she should also take a break from thinking like a writer. She let her mind wander to Brandon.

Of how he'd been looking at her photo.

Of how much she was looking forward to seeing him again.

And kissing him again.

And again.

After more than an hour in the park, she stretched on a bench for a few minutes, then slowly headed east toward the exit. Once she reached Fifth Avenue she put her hands on her hips and looked in the direction of Central Park South.

Hmm.

She stood on the sidewalk, thinking.

Should I buy them today?

She began to nibble on her fingernail but quickly stopped, then began walking.

South.

Next stop: Tiffany & Co.

An hour later, as Cassidy strolled back through the park on her way home, she called Patti.

"What's shakin', bacon? Is it freezing out there yet?"

Cassidy looked up at the clear skies all around and wondered when the first snowfall would be. "It's not too bad. It's getting there, though. I can't believe how fast this year has gone by. Pretty soon there will be holiday decorations in all the shop windows."

"Oh God, don't remind me that Christmas is just around the corner again. Being Santa for three kids is a logistical pain in the hee-haw. Thank God for online shopping. You should see how many boxes get delivered to Roy's office every year."

Cassidy glanced at the shopping bag she was carrying and cleared her throat. "Actually, speaking of Christmas presents, I just bought one for Brandon."

"Already? Nice work."

"I know it's a little early, but I couldn't help myself. Is that bad?"

"It's not bad, it's adorable. What did you end up getting him?"

"Engraved cuff links. From Tiffany. That's what Harper suggested."

"Tiffany cuff links? How elegant. What did the engraving say? It had to have something to do with texting. Was it LOL? TTYL? Or maybe a smiley face?"

Cassidy laughed. "OK, I deserve that. But I ordered one cuff link engraved with a *J* and one with an *H*, for his sons' names, Jack and Henry."

"I love it! Did Harper suggest that too?"

"Yep. He's barely out of his twenties, but sometimes I feel like he's more mature than I am."

"Well, he came up with a *great* idea, that's for sure. I'd love to get Roy something classy like that, but he'd probably think they were earrings. He's not too up on fashion."

Cassidy kicked a pebble. "Have you settled on a date for the Jingle Jog yet? My leg should be healed by then."

Patti had been on the cross-country team with Cassidy in high school, and while her exercise now mainly consisted of chasing after her kids, every year she organized a casual holiday run through San Carlos. It ended with a stroll through a decoration-crazed neighborhood that attracted visitors from up and down the Peninsula.

"No, but I'll let you know as soon as I do. When's your big family dinner this year?"

"The Friday before Christmas, so don't pick that."

"Got it."

Cassidy cleared her throat again. "I . . . invited Brandon."

"To the Jingle Jog?"

"No, to the dinner."

"Wow. Already?"

Cassidy kicked another pebble. "I realize it's early, but you know how fast people's schedules fill up over the holidays, right? Plus with his kids and everything, I just wanted to—"

"Stop it. I love that you invited him early. It's cute. Shows how much you like him."

Cassidy smiled into the phone. "You're such a good friend."

"I know I am. Now apparently it's time to start my holiday shopping, so I'd better run. Talk soon?"

"Talk soon. Bye."

"Your nails are doing better, love."

Cassidy peered over her magazine. "They are?"

Darlene nodded up at her. "I know we're doing a pedicure today, but I can tell you haven't been nibbling on those fingers quite as much."

"I've been trying, but I can't say I'm succeeding with any regularity. It's so hard to break the habit."

"You're on your way. I can see a change in you, and not just with your nails, mind you." She gave Cassidy's feet a gentle squeeze.

Cassidy felt her eyes get a little bigger. "You can?"

"I can."

"But what do you—"

Just then the front door opened and Annabelle Polanski strolled in, her enormous dark sunglasses covering half her petite face, her outsized personality overtaking the limited air space without her having to utter a word. Darlene stiffened and immediately looked down at Cassidy's feet, filing the nails intently. Cassidy glanced around the room and noticed the other attendants reacting in a similar manner. Her fellow patrons seemed equally startled, and the already subdued volume of the salon dropped to a hush, amplifying the sound of Annabelle's stiletto heels clicking on the hardwood floors as she strode across the room. When she reached the pedicure chair, she gave Cassidy a polite smile, then quickly disappeared into one of the back rooms.

When the door shut behind Annabelle, Cassidy felt her shoulders drop and realized she had tensed up as well. She leaned toward Darlene and lowered her voice to a whisper. "She scares me."

Darlene didn't reply or look up, but Cassidy could see the hint of a smile had formed on her lips.

That afternoon Cassidy took a nap, spent a couple of hours answering a backlog of e-mails before making dinner, then finally curled up on the couch to watch a movie. At just after eight o'clock, her phone chimed with a text message from Brandon, the first she'd received all day.

Want to adopt two boys? I'm exhausted.

She paused the movie and replied:

What's the going rate for that sort of work? I could use some spending money.

LOL. They're finally asleep. Thank God.

I assume you're not talking about your feet.

I love when you make me laugh. Did you have a good day?

I did. I bought your Christmas present, actually.

You got me a gift? You are too nice.

Now you can't ditch me until after Christmas, promise?

I can't believe you already got me a gift. I'm flattered.

Do you promise?

Yes. ☺

I'm excited for the holidays. I'll have finished my book by then! Maybe we can celebrate in style.

I would like that. I could use some fun.

Maybe we could go bowling. I have my own shoes.

Please tell me you're joking.

I'm joking. Maybe we could go ice skating? There's a rink in Belmont that I've taken my nieces to a few times. It's sort of cheesy, but they play fun holiday music.

That does sound fun. Could we hold hands while we
skate? Would be a good excuse to touch you while also
keeping me from falling on my out-of-shape ass.

I'd be honored to keep you from falling on your out-of-
shape ass. How is your mom doing?

About the same. I don't really want to talk about it.

Oh, sorry.

Don't be sorry. I'm just tired of talking about it. Hey,
I've got to run now, the boys woke up and are going at
it. Have a good night.

OK, good night.

She stared at the phone for a few moments before gently setting it on the coffee table. Had she said something wrong?

Chapter Nineteen

"I'M SURE IT'S nothing." Harper peered at her nose as he opened the cab door. "It doesn't even look like anything."

Cassidy climbed inside and took a seat. It was a couple of days later, and they were on their way to the dermatologist's office. "I hope you're right. Thanks for taking the morning off to come with me, by the way. I feel like a baby for not wanting to go by myself, but for some reason I just don't want to."

He climbed in behind her. "That's what friends are for, right? You've certainly been a good one to me lately."

She put a hand on his arm and squeezed. "I'm not sure where this neediness is coming from. Usually I'm more independent than this."

"It's OK to need people, Cassidy."

"I know," she said with a sigh. Before calling Harper last night, she'd spent the day expecting to hear from Brandon at some point, even if only to say he was thinking of her. But her phone had remained silent, and as her anxiety about her appointment grew, she'd felt an urge to talk to someone. She'd called Patti, and then Danielle, but neither had picked up, so she'd confided in

Harper, who then offered to come with her. She knew Brandon was extremely busy with his own problems, but she wished that just once he had time to pay attention to her when she needed a little support.

"I'm sorry to keep you waiting so long. It's been a hectic morning. Thanks for being patient." The doctor shut the door of the examination room and held out a hand. "I'm Dr. Zimmerman."

Cassidy shook his hand, then nodded toward Harper. "Cassidy Lane. This is my friend, Harper Gold."

"I'm the neighbor," Harper said. "Just here for moral support."

"Nothing wrong with a little moral support." Dr. Zimmerman smiled curtly as he glanced down at her chart. "I understand you've got a little something on your nose."

Cassidy cleared her throat and felt her hand move involuntarily to touch the area in question. "Yes. I think it's been there for about three months. For a while I thought it was just a scrape that had turned into a scab, but then recently I realized it should have healed by now." As she said the words out loud, the reality of why she was there hit her, and she felt her blood turn cold at what might happen. Her anxiety must have shown in her face, because Harper reached for her hand and squeezed it. She squeezed back, grateful to have him there.

"Let's have a look, shall we?" Dr. Zimmerman set the folder down on a counter and picked up a magnifying glass, then walked over to Cassidy. Leaning in close, he switched on a bright light attached to the instrument. He peered at her nose briefly, then turned off the light and set down the magnifying glass.

He smiled. "There's nothing to worry about."

Cassidy felt her whole body loosen. "There isn't?"

He shook his head. "I believe what you have there is a wart."

Harper laughed, and Cassidy hit him playfully on the arm. Then she looked back at Dr. Zimmerman. "A *wart?*"

He nodded. "Most likely it's a wart, but if it's something else, it hasn't yet turned into anything to worry about, so we'll freeze it off and that should do it."

"You mean right now?"

"Yep." He opened a cabinet and picked up a large aerosol can, then held it up to her face. "Close your eyes. This might sting a little bit."

She shut her eyes tight. He sprayed for literally one second and then it was over.

"All done," he said.

Cassidy opened her eyes. "That's it?"

He smiled. "That's it. It will crust up and may look a little unsightly for a few days, but then it will fall off. The wart, not your nose."

Cassidy exhaled. "I'm so relieved. Thank you, Dr. Zimmerman."

"You're very welcome. I like it when the news is good."

"I can't believe I took the morning off of work for a wart."

Cassidy narrowed her eyes at him. "Hey now, don't make fun of me. I thought maybe I was dying."

"It's well within my rights to make fun of you for a *wart*. Dying. Please."

She laughed and stirred sugar into her latte. "OK, you can have this one. You have no idea how relieved I am."

"As you should be. Melanoma is no joke. You dodged a bullet in there."

"No kidding. I feel really lucky." She sipped her latte, then pointed outside the Starbucks window. "Want to wander for a bit before you head to the office? We could walk toward Broadway."

He nodded, and together they slowly made their way west. They strolled for half a block in silence before Cassidy spoke. He'd been there when she needed him, and she wanted to repay the favor, or at least try. "So what's the latest with Vanessa? Do you want to talk about it?"

He shrugged. "The same. She's still pregnant. The question now is, where is she going to live?"

Cassidy looked over at him "Are you thinking of having her move in with you?"

"I'm thinking about it. I haven't made any decisions, but I'm thinking about it."

"Where does she live now?"

"Hell's Kitchen. But she has two roommates in a walk-up. Not doable for raising a baby."

"Where do her parents live?"

"Texas."

"Yikes. And she doesn't want to go back there?"

"No, she's set on staying here."

Cassidy closed her eyes. "Oh, Harper. I'm so sorry about all of this."

He tossed his empty coffee cup into a trash bin. "It could be worse. She's a nice person, and we get along pretty well."

"You think she's a nice person?"

He nodded. "I do. She's a bit shallow, but she has a good heart. I mean, the whole situation is far from ideal, but I could do a lot worse for the mother of my child."

They were hardly the words of a proud father-to-be, but he was clearly trying to do the right thing, whatever that was, and Cassidy's heart ached for him. She knew how much he'd wanted to fall in love, get married, and have a family—in that order. Her thoughts turned to Danielle: independent, confident Danielle, who didn't share Harper's dream of a white picket fence but had been tied in knots for having given in to temptation, however briefly. Then there was her own relationship with Brandon, which was admittedly unconventional but recently seemed to have careened far from the idyllic. She lightly touched the bandage on her nose and wondered when she'd hear from him.

However different, she and her friends had all embarked on journeys that had been sparked by the irresistible pull of physical attraction. She wanted to believe the roads they were traveling would lead to a future of love, or fulfillment, or whatever *happiness* represented to each of them. But she knew better. She knew there was no guarantee any of them would end up with the life— or the person—they really wanted.

She took a sip of her latte and frowned at the uncertainties of life.

This must be why people like my books.

By bedtime that evening, Cassidy had had enough of waiting. After nearly two days of not hearing from Brandon, she gave up and texted him:

Hi, I don't have skin cancer, in case you were curious.

He wrote back a couple minutes later.

That is great news.

She was glad he'd replied so quickly, but she couldn't help but wonder if he would have asked about her nose had she not brought it up first. And now she would never know.

She shut off her phone. For the time being, she figured it was best to say nothing more. Rationally, she knew how stressed he was, but she couldn't help but feel disappointed that he hadn't been there for her when she needed him.

She also felt guilty for being disappointed.

Despite her conflicting emotions, as she turned off the light and climbed into bed, all she could think about was what it would feel like to be falling asleep in his arms.

Chapter Twenty

FROM THEN ON things were different.

Brandon kept reaching out, but less and less with each passing day. Where he had once sent Cassidy a message first thing in the morning, he began waiting later and later to get in touch, as well as longer to reply. The tone of their conversations was also shifting. He grew more reserved, so she followed his lead and shared less. They continued to text regularly and exchange information, but the intimacy was slowly disappearing, the witty banter gradually replaced by a bland neutrality more suited for a coworker than a romantic interest. She tried several times to inject a jolt of playfulness into their conversations, but he rarely reciprocated, and if he did, it didn't last longer than a message or two. In striking contrast to the sexual innuendo that once leaped off the screen, she now found herself searching for any hint of suggestion or flirtation in everything he wrote her.

She rarely found it.

Long day today. I'm exhausted. Need to get a good night's sleep tonight.

Me too, have been working hard on the book, not getting as many naps in as I should.

I think I'm coming down with the flu.

Sorry to hear that. Wish I could be there to take care of you.

I hate being sick.

Drink hot tea with lemon.

Henry has the flu. That means we're all going to get it.

Feel better. Listen, we're clearly both tired, so I think I'm going to hit the sack now.

OK, good night.

He was also grumbling more and more about his hectic life—in addition to managing the care of his mother and sons, he was working crazy hours and looking for a new school for Jack—and inquiring less about hers.

Hi there, how's your day going?

Not great. Too much work, too little time. Never seems to stop.

Are you feeling any better?

Unfortunately, no, but I have too much going on at the
office right now to take a sick day.

Sorry to hear that. When I'm not feeling well, I can't
get any writing done. My brain basically shuts down
and tells me to climb into bed. You know how I am
about sleeping.

I wish I could climb into bed right now.

I wish I could cheer you up. I'll be home in a few weeks,
so at least that's some good news.

That is good news. I hope I won't have as much on my
plate then, but it's doubtful.

Soon he was down to sending a single message after she'd
already gone to sleep, and a couple of days went by when she didn't
hear from him at all. By the first Monday in December, after not
hearing from him all weekend, she was on the verge of tears.

What had happened?

Long gone were the spirited flirtations, playful teasing about
her daily naps, or any mention of a visit to New York.

She'd once felt they were growing closer with each conversation, but now it was as if they were moving in opposite directions.

Fast.

Early one evening she was at her desk, working on her novel, when
she heard the unmistakable chime of a new text message.

I feel bad that I haven't been in touch much lately. I'm
not being a good friend.

She caught her breath.
He was finally doing it.
She began nibbling on her fingernail. She knew what was
coming but tried to stop it by pretending everything was OK.

It's OK, I know you've had a rough few weeks. How is
your mom doing?

The back-and-forth ensued:

Not great. I'm not sleeping very much. Very stressed.

I'm sorry. I wish I could help.

You've been very supportive.

It's because I care about you.

I wish I could give you what you need from me.

You're doing your best. I'm just glad you want me in
your life at all right now.

She felt sick with desperation as she continued to pretend she
didn't mind, hating herself for not having the strength to agree
he'd let her down.
To tell him she deserved better.

To let him go.

She held the phone in her hand and waited. She already knew what his next text would say, but she wondered which words he would use to say it.

The phone chimed about a minute later. She closed her eyes for a moment, then opened them and looked at the screen.

> I just feel like I'm being pulled in too many directions.
> Maybe it's best if we just stay friends until things settle down for me.

She stared at the message.

There it was.

The other shoe.

Clattering against the hardwood floor.

Cassidy squeezed the phone, trying to process what had just happened. She'd been expecting it for days, even weeks, but she still couldn't believe it was real. *Thousands* of text messages had come down to . . . this?

She tried to remember when he'd dropped the first shoe. Was it their first date, when he didn't kiss her until she asked him to do so? She'd been more or less teetering between bliss and eggshells ever since. Or maybe it was the morning they'd met for coffee to talk about his mother. There was no denying how different he'd been then. Then there was the time he hadn't asked how her keynote address had gone . . . long before he hadn't asked about her doctor's appointment. Both instances had hurt her feelings, which in turn had made her feel guilty. Given what had happened to his mother, it wasn't fair to expect much in the way of emotional support from him, if any at all.

Had it been over even before it began?

She paced around her apartment, not sure how to respond, humiliated that this was happening via text message. No matter how busy he was, didn't he realize how insensitive it was to end a romance this way? How *callous* it was? Didn't he care about her feelings at all? What had happened to the gracious and polite man she'd fallen for? He'd once joked about how they were texting like teenagers, but they weren't teenagers. They were adults.

She threw her phone on the couch.

He should have called her.

She was furious but didn't know if she had a right to be, which made her more furious.

Is this what the world has come to?

Ending a relationship via text message is acceptable behavior?

She put her hands on her head, wanting to pull her hair out.

The man is thirty-eight years old!

He has children!

He owns a law practice!

After pacing around her living room for several minutes, she picked up her phone and typed a brief reply:

Got it.

Her phone chimed immediately, and the back-and-forth resumed:

Are you mad?

No.

I just can't handle being more than friends right now. I hope you understand.

I understand, but I have plenty of friends.

What are you saying?

I'm saying I have enough friends.

That's not fair.

Why isn't that fair?

Because this isn't about us.

What do you mean, it's not about us? Of course it's about us. Two weeks ago you said you wanted to come visit me, and now you're dumping me over text message.

No, that's not it.

Then what is it?

I'm sorry.

That's not an answer.

I don't know what else I can say.

I also invited you to my family holiday dinner AND sent you a photo of myself in my underwear. Now I feel like a complete idiot.

Please don't feel like an idiot.

Easy for you to say.

You told me you'd been hurt before, so I'm just trying to protect you, because right now I can't give you what you want. I don't want to end up hurting you too.

I think it's too late for that.

I'm sorry. I wanted to be ready to be in a relationship with you, but I'm not.

Nice of you to tell me.

I didn't expect this to happen. I think the world of you.

Then what do you want from me?

I want us to be friends.

Stop saying that.

I'm just messed up right now.

That sounds like an excuse.

It's not an excuse.

I'd rather you be honest with me than try to spare my feelings.

I am being honest. You're perfect, and I'm a wreck.

Don't say that. If I were so perfect, you wouldn't be
doing this.

It's true.

She stared at her phone, incredulous that they were still
talking over text message. Why hadn't he picked up the phone to
call her? Wasn't she worth at least *that*?

Why did you even bother to contact me if you weren't
ready for a relationship? You started all of this.

Things were different then. Maybe it was wrong to
engage with you, but I had no way of knowing this
would happen to my mom. I'm really sorry, Cassidy.

She closed her eyes. Could this really be because his mother
had had a stroke? Didn't people overcome much bigger obstacles
all the time, especially where love was concerned? Weren't people
supposed to do anything for love?

She threw the phone on her couch again.

No.

She'd been an idiot to believe he could fall for her.

She'd been a fool to let herself fall for him.

She never should have opened up and told him how much
she'd been hurt in the past, but now it was too late. She'd shown
her hand and he'd rejected her.

He wants to be friends? *Give me a break.*

Everyone knew *let's be friends* was a euphemism for *I'm not
interested.*

She wanted to chew her nails but stopped herself.

NO.

She balled her hands into fists and started pacing around the living room again, her budding fingernails digging into her palms.

He's the one who pursued me.

He's the one who initiated everything.

I was doing just fine before.

Why did he bother?

Why did I let him in?

Suddenly she wanted to run, her Achilles be damned. Running would calm her down. Running would make her feel better. It always made her feel better. She rushed into her bedroom and changed, then grabbed her keys and left the apartment, slamming the door behind her.

She ran for less than a block before her lower leg started hurting too much to continue.

Damn it!

She slowed to a brisk walk and began pumping her arms, trying to outrace the feeling of despair she knew would inevitably catch up to her and crush the shell of indignation still protecting her. Right now she felt only anger toward Brandon, for what he'd done to her, for how he'd made her care so much about him.

For how he'd made her believe he cared too.

How dare he?

Had this all been a game to him? He'd had her on her heels early on, making a point to say he wasn't a Boy Scout, then behaving like one when they were together, seeming smitten from afar yet not acting on it when he had the chance.

Inviting her to Tahoe before they'd even had an official date.

Suggesting he'd like to come visit her in New York.

Accepting her invitation to her family's holiday party.

He'd clearly dipped his toe in the water, but something had stopped him. She tried to pinpoint when he'd begun to pull back.

Had he been playing with her all along?

If that was the case, he'd won. Handily.

How dare he?

She walked as fast as she could, pumping her arms, breathing hard, doing her best to escape from what she knew was coming. But it was unavoidable. The anger was fleeting, and soon it turned inward, releasing a toxic insecurity into her psyche.

Then the real pain hit, and she wanted to cry.

What did I do wrong?

She thought of their dinner date in Palo Alto, remembering how she'd peeked out the window as he approached the front door of her parents' house, her body literally buzzing with anticipation at the prospect of finally being with him. Then, after all that buildup, all that flirting, all that chemistry, he hadn't even tried to kiss her.

Why not?

Am I that unattractive?

Am I that unappealing?

Was that why he'd kept his distance?

She pumped her arms harder, increasing her pace.

Is there something wrong with me?

She knew he was consumed with his mother's health, and rightfully so, but he was a *man*, for God's sake. Men craved physical intimacy, no matter how they were feeling upstairs.

Yes, they'd shared a passionate kiss that had left her dizzy, and there was no denying the heat it had sparked between them. But they weren't sixteen anymore. From an adult perspective, Brandon had barely touched her.

She felt the tears welling up and shook her head in a feeble attempt to keep them at bay. She didn't want to cry. She didn't want to let a man hurt her like this again. After Dean she'd told herself her heart had had enough.

But her heart had had other ideas.

And now it was broken once more.

She pressed her palms against her eyes, physically trying to hold back the tears, but it didn't work. The salty drops began sliding down her cheeks, the wind quickly turning them cold and icy.

She coughed and choked back a sob, then looked down to hide her face as two joggers ran by in the opposite direction.

Why doesn't he want me?

Why doesn't anyone ever want me?

She slowed her pace and cried silently as she walked, aching at the loss of what could have been, wishing she'd never gone to that reunion, yet already missing Brandon so much her chest hurt.

Wishing he weren't hurting too, in his own way.

Wanting to help him but wishing she didn't.

Wondering if a man like him could ever fall in love with her.

Wondering if it would ever be her turn.

The tears streamed down her face, but she kept walking.

And thinking.

And longing.

Eventually she stopped crying. She looked up at the sky, which was nearly pitch black now, save for a few flickering stars. In her haste to leave her apartment, she hadn't brought a watch and wondered what time it was. She had no idea how long she'd been in the park.

She felt empty inside.

And cold.

It was time to go back.

She wiped the remaining tears from her face, then put her hands on her waist and stood still for a few moments, staring in the direction in which the sun had set.

Then she took a step forward and slowly made her way home.

"Ms. Lane, a package arrived for you while you were out."

"Thanks, Carson." Cassidy approached the doorman, who was standing behind the lobby desk holding up a clipboard. She signed the delivery slip, and he handed over a small cardboard box. She squinted at the unfamiliar return address. Who could it be from? It had been a long time since she'd received a package that didn't say Rio Media on it.

Once inside the elevator, she pulled open the cardboard lid and removed a layer of bubble wrap. Underneath, gracefully swathed in more bubble wrap, was a small box.

An iconic blue box.

The Tiffany cuff links had arrived.

Chapter Twenty-One

"OH, JEEZ, I'M so sorry to hear that. I was really rooting for you two."

Cassidy leaned back against the couch and closed her eyes. "Thanks, Patti. I knew it was coming, but I didn't expect it to hurt this much." She felt her fingers squeezing the phone.

"Don't let it. It's not like he's rejecting you."

Cassidy opened her eyes. "What are you talking about? Of course he is."

"I don't see it that way."

She sat up straight. "He said he wanted to be *friends*, Patti. *Friends*. Even my mom knows what that means."

"I think he's being sincere, Cassidy. You should cut the poor guy some slack. I mean, look what he's dealing with."

"You really think that's why he broke things off?"

"It doesn't sound like he broke things off. To me it sounds like he just put things on ice."

"You really believe that?"

"I really do."

"Well, I don't. I knew I shouldn't have invited him to our holiday dinner. I should have waited."

"Stop it. There's no use beating yourself up about that now."

"It was too soon. I scared him and he bolted."

"You're being ridiculous. And besides, people *do* plan things early over the holidays. That reminds me, I've got the date for the Jingle Jog: December twenty-third. Think you'll be able to run by then?"

"I hope so. If not, I'll just meet you at the end."

"I hope so too, because otherwise Amy and I will probably be running by ourselves." The Jingle Jog's numbers had hovered around ten in the early days but had dwindled since.

"I'm putting it on my calendar right now." Cassidy reached for the pad of sticky notes on her coffee table and jotted down the date.

"Why don't you ask Brandon to run with us?"

Cassidy stifled a cough. "Are you joking?"

"Why not? You said he wants to be friends, and friends help friends get in shape, right?"

Despite being so sad, Cassidy couldn't help but laugh. "I just spent an hour crying my eyes out over the guy and now you want me to invite him to go *running*?"

"Yep. God knows we could use the boost in attendance. It's hard finding people willing to run around dressed like reindeer. And if he's saying he needs you to be his friend, then be his friend."

Cassidy pulled her knees up to her chest. "The thing is, I *have* been a friend to him. I've been a really good friend to him." She thought of all the conversations they'd had about his mom, his hectic work schedule, his kids. In a way, a friend was all she'd been. Or all she'd had the chance to be.

"I'm sure you have. And I'm sure he knows that."

Cassidy sighed and rested her chin on top of her knees. "But I want to be *more* than just his friend, Patti. I'd be kidding myself to think otherwise."

"I think it will happen if you're patient. You said he wanted to be ready for a relationship with you but isn't, right?"

"Yes."

"Why would he bother to say something like that if it weren't true?"

Cassidy bit her lip. "I don't know."

"Exactly. I think you should just take a deep breath and try not to be so upset about all of this. I don't think it's over yet."

"You really don't?"

"I really don't. But for the time being, I think you should let him focus on himself, and you should focus on yourself. He'll reach out to you when he's ready."

"How do I go about focusing on myself?"

"Come on, you know the answer to that question."

Cassidy glanced over at her desk.

She *did* know.

She needed to finish her novel.

Cassidy worked until after eleven and surprisingly got a lot done. She was still sad, but Patti's pep talk had almost erased the sting of rejection she'd felt earlier, and she was no longer wallowing in self-doubt. When she was finally done for the night, she brushed her teeth and put on her pajamas, then picked up her phone and returned Brandon's last text, which he'd sent hours earlier.

Hi, Brandon, I've had some time to think about what you said and realize I may have overreacted because I tend to associate the word *friend* with *not interested.* But I know this is about more than that. You mean too much to me now for me to bail when you might need me the most, so I'm not going anywhere. If you need a friend, I'm here.

Within a minute he replied.

Thank you so much for understanding. How about I reach out when things are a little better for me, and we'll see where things go from there?

She typed a quick text back before climbing into bed:

Sounds great. ☺

As she turned off the light, she was proud of herself for putting his need for support and understanding above her own for self-preservation, because that's what true friends did.

Or so she hoped.

Chapter Twenty-Two

"AND YOU HAVEN'T heard from him since?" It was more than two weeks later, and Danielle was finally back in town. They were seated on bar stools at the Amsterdam Ale House on a Wednesday evening. Danielle was sitting normally, but Cassidy was slouching visibly.

Cassidy picked up her beer and frowned. "Not a word. So much for being *friends.*"

Danielle shrugged. "I wouldn't read too much into it. I'm sure he'll get in touch soon. Like he told you, he just needs some time until things settle down for him. It has nothing to do with you."

"You sound like Patti."

"Well, Patti is clearly a very smart woman, if I may say so."

Cassidy set her glass on the bar and looked at her lap. "I just feel so . . . foolish."

"Do *not* feel foolish."

"Believe me, I have good reason to."

"Why?"

Cassidy made a pained face, then leaned forward and lowered her voice. "I . . . sort of . . . texted him a racy picture of myself."

Danielle's raised her eyebrows. "Nude?"

Cassidy shook her head. "God no. Just in my underwear."

Danielle waved a hand dismissively. "Then don't worry about it. Not even for one second."

Cassidy kept her voice hushed, "Have you ever done something like that?"

"Of course. Many times. Who hasn't?"

"*I* haven't, or hadn't. Not even close."

"That's not surprising, coming from you. Can I see it?"

"You really want to?"

"Hell yes, I do."

Cassidy pulled her phone out of her purse and scrolled to the photo, then hesitated before showing it to her. "You promise you won't laugh?"

"Please. Your butt is *way* smaller than mine." Danielle wiggled her fingers at the phone. "Now hand it over."

Cassidy bit her lip, then did as she was told.

Danielle raised her eyebrows at the screen. "Looking *good*, Ms. Lane."

Cassidy made a sheepish face. "I still can't believe I did that. It was so unlike me."

"Now that's what you writer types would call an understatement. But you look really good in this picture, especially for a woman our age. If I looked that good in my skivvies, I'd be posting photos of myself all over the Internet."

"No you wouldn't."

"OK, you're right, I wouldn't. But you shouldn't regret having sent him that photo. If anything, it will be a reminder of what he could have had."

Cassidy smiled. "Thank you for always being so nice to me."

"It goes both ways. Remember that. I'm not nice to everyone."

"I just can't believe we went from texting *all the time* to nothing so quickly. I even changed the chime of my message alert the other day. It was making me too sad because I kept hoping they were from him."

"Oh, hon, I'm so sorry. After the frenzy you two were in, the silence must be really difficult. But you're right to give him his space until he's ready to get in touch again. Have you been staying busy to keep your mind off him?"

Cassidy sat up straight on her stool and managed a genuine smile. "Actually, *yes*. I finished my book two full days before the deadline, a new record for me. My editor was elated. I'm meeting with him tomorrow to talk about it."

"You really finished it?"

Cassidy smiled again. "I *did*. I sat down at my desk and focused, and the ending that needed to happen finally revealed itself, and then everything leading up to it came pouring out of me. Funny how getting your heart broken can stir up the creative juices."

Danielle gave her a sad look. "I'm glad you finished it, but I hate that you have a broken heart. It hurts me to hear you describe yourself that way."

Cassidy's smile faded. "It hurts me too, but it's the truth. Looking back, we were clearly doomed practically from the start, but for some reason I thought things were going to work out. I really did. Maybe it was because I write romances for a living, but after the promising beginning of our story, I certainly didn't think it would end before it even got off the ground."

"Why would you have thought it would end? No one ever thinks it's going to end at the beginning, right? Even I don't think that way."

"Yes, but even when the red flags were staring me in the face, I kept holding on to the hope of a fairy-tale ending." She felt her shoulders droop slightly. "In a way I still am, which I know is crazy, but I can't help myself. I still have all these . . . *feelings* for him, which makes me feel so foolish."

Danielle squeezed her arm. "Don't feel foolish. That's the last thing you should be feeling. If anything, *he's* the one who should feel foolish for letting you go. Given all that he's going through with his mom, not to mention his kids and the baggage he's probably carrying around from his divorce, one day he'll realize how lucky he was to have you. It can't be easy to find a woman willing to walk into that situation, much less a woman as sensational as you."

Cassidy wiped a small tear from the corner of her eye. "Thanks for saying that."

"I think he'll figure it out and come around. And if he doesn't, you're better off anyway."

Cassidy picked up her beer, which she had hardly touched, and took a sip. "I appreciate your letting me bend your ear like this, but I think I'm officially sick of talking about Brandon Forrester. What about you? I haven't seen you in weeks. Where have you been besides London?"

"Just Paris. Spent a full week there relaxing after the conference."

"That doesn't sound like you. I figured you'd be raising hell all over Europe."

"We did venture outside the city for a couple day trips, but it was nice to stay put in the same hotel for once."

"We? You weren't alone?"

Danielle hesitated, which Cassidy took as confirmation. "Did you meet someone?"

Danielle remained silent.

"Well? Please tell me you met someone. I could use a romantic story to cheer me up."

When Danielle still didn't respond, it clicked. And Cassidy knew.

She set down her glass. "Danielle, were you with . . . your CFO?"

Danielle covered her eyes with her hand and nodded. "His name is Jonathan."

"Have you been . . . *seeing* him? Is that the trouble you were talking about weeks ago?"

"Sort of."

"Danielle!"

"Shhh." Danielle looked around the bar. "Keep your voice down."

"What's going on?" Cassidy whispered.

"I couldn't help myself, Cassidy. I *can't* help myself."

Cassidy kept her voice hushed. "You're having an affair?"

"Technically, yes. But it's not like that."

"That doesn't make any sense. It's not like *what*?"

Danielle sighed. "I mean . . . I think I'm in love with him."

Cassidy caught her breath. "Oh, wow."

Little tears formed in the corners of Danielle's eyes. "It's bad, really bad."

"I've never heard you say you were in love."

Danielle tried to laugh as she wiped away a tear. "I guess there's a first time for everything."

"What are you going to do?"

"I'm not sure. I want to walk away from it, but I just can't."

"Is he going to leave his wife?"

"I think so. I hope so."

"You *hope* so?"

"Well, it's not like he can just up and take off. It's not that simple when you have kids."

"He has kids?"

Danielle nodded. "Three."

Oh, Danielle. Poor Danielle.

Danielle took a sip of her beer. "He says it's been over between them for a long time, and not just for him. His wife has checked out emotionally too."

Cassidy narrowed her eyes. "Isn't that what they all say?"

"Maybe, but this is different. Even if I hadn't entered the picture, he wouldn't want to stay with her. That's what he says, at least."

"So he's getting divorced?"

"I told him I'd give him two months to make a decision."

"And you think he'll choose you?"

Danielle nodded, but just slightly. Cassidy had never seen her ever-confident friend look so uncertain.

"And if he doesn't?"

"I hope I won't have to face that. He's really serious about this, Cassidy."

Cassidy raised an eyebrow. "So he's never cheated before?"

"Never."

"Are you sure about that?"

"That's what he says."

"And you believe him." It wasn't a question.

"I do. I know it sounds bad, Cassidy, but I have a feeling it's going to work out in the end."

"But how do you *know*? That's what I hoped about Brandon, and look what happened. I ran right into a tree."

Danielle set down her glass. "That's why I think you should give Brandon space to let him decide what he really wants."

Cassidy laughed weakly. "For all these years, you and I have talked about how different we are when it comes to romance, but look at us now, our heartstrings both entangled with unavailable men. What a pair."

Danielle laughed weakly. "I guess I'm a late bloomer. I know it was wrong to get myself into this situation, and I wish things were different, but what's done is done and I'm invested now."

"But what about all the women we know who've been down this same road? The guy never leaves his wife. I don't want you to be one of those women, Danielle. I feel sorry for them."

"I don't think I will. I know that sounds naïve, but I really don't."

Cassidy held up her palms. "All right, I guess we'll see what happens. What do I know about relationships anyway? Clearly nothing."

Danielle smiled. "Thank you for not judging me. It means a lot."

"That's what true friends do, right? Or *don't* do, I mean."

"Yes. You're a true friend to the core. And just so you know, you're the only person I've told about this."

They sat quietly together, both of them absorbing the shift that had just occurred in their friendship. Love was a powerful drug, something Cassidy knew all too well, and while she didn't enjoy seeing anyone in this position, she was grateful that Danielle trusted her enough to open up about something so personal.

The revelation stirred something else inside Cassidy. She feared Danielle was in for a painful awakening, but her willingness to straddle a moral line in the name of love certainly shed new light on Cassidy's own relationship with Brandon, which didn't seem so complicated anymore.

Or so special.

Had she made it all up in her head?

Danielle said she *knew*.

Cassidy had never *known*.

She'd desperately wanted to, but it had never happened.

Her thoughts must have been written all over her face, because after a few moments of silence Danielle reached over and squeezed her hand. "I hope Brandon figures things out, because he would be really lucky to have you."

"Welcome to Rio Media, Ms. Lane. It's nice to see you again." The receptionist greeted Cassidy with a warm smile.

"Hi, Tina, and please call me Cassidy. Otherwise I'll feel like you're talking to my mother."

Tina picked up her phone. "Sorry, force of habit. Nigel's in his office, if you want to go on back. I'll tell him you're here. Can I bring you anything? Coffee? Water?"

"I'm fine, but thank you." Cassidy made her way through the busy corridors until she reached Nigel's back corner office. The door was ajar, so she lightly rapped her knuckles against the wood and poked her head inside. "Anybody home? I know I'm early."

Nigel looked up from his computer and motioned for her to enter. "Hi there, Cassidy. I was just about to watch your video. Have a seat." He gestured to a chair across from his desk.

She removed her coat and sat down. "Oh my gosh, the video shoot! I forgot all about that. How did it turn out?"

"See for yourself." He turned his monitor toward her, and together they watched as the screen flickered to life.

**INSIDE RIO MEDIA: BEHIND THE SCENES WITH
BESTSELLING AUTHOR CASSIDY LANE**

Cassidy let out a small gasp when she saw herself appear on the screen.

Professionally groomed for the cameras and swathed in flattering light, she looked vibrant, graceful, poised, self-assured.

And happy.

Everything she hadn't felt in weeks.

For the next five minutes she watched herself discuss the journey she was on with Rio Media and how much she was enjoying life as a full-time author. She joked around with the interviewer, admitted her delight at receiving fan e-mails, shared a few blunders she'd made when she was just getting started, and wondered aloud what her next novel would be.

As she enviously watched the person she'd been just two months ago, Cassidy wondered what had happened to her.

I want to be her again.

"Thanks for coming in. I know it's a pain making the trek when it's this cold outside," Nigel said after the video was over.

"I don't mind. I feel like I became a bit of a shut-in working on the manuscript toward the end, so it's nice to get out of my apartment." She kept her hands interlaced on her lap, determined not to chew on her fingernails in front of him. Not only was it unprofessional, but she had a manicure in a couple of hours and couldn't bear to face Darlene if she let her nerves slip her up after having been so good all week. She tried to shift the focus of her anxiety to Nigel's countenance, doing her best to read him before he got to the point of the meeting: her new book. What did he think of the way she'd ended it? Not knowing had been eating at her since the moment she'd e-mailed him the manuscript.

He spread his hands on his desk and studied them for a moment, as though deciding what to say next. Or how to say it. His hesitation only exacerbated her angst, and now she wasn't sure she wanted to hear the words he was preparing to utter. Had she blown it by trying something different? Had her effort to demonstrate growth in fact revealed her limitations? Tiny stabs of insecurity began to claw away at her self-confidence. She was tempted to pull out her phone to read some fan e-mails when Nigel made eye contact and spoke.

"Cassidy, I've got to say, the hard work you've been putting in really shows. You did a fantastic job on the manuscript."

She put a hand on her heart. "I did?

"Yes. You surprised me, actually, and that doesn't happen very often."

"I surprised you? You mean . . . you didn't think I'd do a good job?"

He chuckled and shook his head. "I'm sorry, that came out the wrong way. Of course I knew you'd write a great book. What I didn't expect was the ending, but I love the direction you chose, and I understand why you felt the need to do it. I don't think a traditional happy ending would have worked for Emma and Jeremy. It would have seemed . . . forced."

Cassidy felt herself leaning forward in her chair. "That's exactly what I was feeling as I was writing it. I think that's a big reason why I was struggling for so long with how to finish it."

"Because your books usually have happy endings?"

She nodded. "When I started this one, I completely expected Emma to wind up with Jeremy at the end, but as the book unfolded, it just didn't seem right, and I knew I had to listen to what the story was telling me, what *Emma* was telling me. I'm not sure how my readers will react to a different type of ending from me, though. Do you think it will be a problem?" She began to nibble on her fingernail, then yanked her hand away when she realized what she was doing. *Stop it.*

Nigel shook his head. "If a book tells a good story with interesting, believable characters, readers respond accordingly. And that's what you've done with this book, even though it's different from what you've done in the past. Plus I think the shift in tone will help position you as a more versatile writer. While happily ever after is what a lot of readers want, not everyone buys into the idea."

Cassidy sighed. "The thing is . . ." Her voice trailed off.

"The thing is what?"

"The thing is . . . *I* still buy into it, which is another reason why I had so much trouble writing the end. Even though I knew it wasn't right for them to be together, I still wanted them to walk off into the sunset." She glanced at her hands and shifted uncomfortably in her seat. This conversation was hitting dangerously close to home.

He tapped his pen on the desk. "I'm really proud of you, Cassidy. You listened to what your gut was telling you, even though it wasn't necessarily what you wanted to hear. That takes talent and maturity, and as a result you wrote a terrific book that is going to sell very well. I can't wait to see what you come up with next."

She smiled. "I'm so relieved."

"Enjoy the feeling. You worked hard for it."

"It's funny to be discussing how the characters—and the story itself—talk to me, because I had a similar conversation a few weeks ago with . . ." Her voice faded as the tiny seed of an idea began to take shape in a far corner of her brain. She quickly opened her purse and pulled out her pad of sticky notes. "Sorry, Nigel, I just thought of something and I want to write it down before I forget it."

He made a sweeping gesture with his palm. "By all means. I don't want to interfere with the creative process."

"It's nice to see you again. Are you going anywhere for the holidays?" Darlene asked.

Cassidy smiled as she took a seat. "Leaving tomorrow, actually. Off to California for a couple of weeks."

"That sounds lovely."

"What about you?"

Darlene shook her head. "We'll be here. My husband doesn't like to travel."

"Do you live nearby?"

"Not too far." She reached for Cassidy's hands, which ended the small talk. "Now let's have a look at those nails."

As Darlene studied her hands, Cassidy glanced at the hefty diamond set in a gold band on Darlene's left ring finger and tried to imagine what her husband was like. She bet he wasn't too tall but was brawny and barrel-chested, most likely sporting a mustache; tough but like a teddy bear inside. Maybe his name was Mack. Hank? Or Carl? Carl seemed like a good name for the manager of a tire factory.

Before she could ask, Darlene spoke. "They're looking better, but I suspect you've been cheating."

"I'm trying to be good, I swear I am. It's just such a habit, especially when I get anxious."

Darlene gave her fingers a squeeze. "Think you can make it through the holidays for me without a nibble?"

"I can try, but it might be hard. Holidays are always a little stressful."

"Stressful? What does a pretty young woman like you have to be stressed about?"

"The mistletoe, for one. I *hate* the mistletoe."

Darlene raised an eyebrow. "Too many suitors, have you? Not sure which one to pick?"

Cassidy couldn't help but laugh. "If you only knew."

"I see what I see, and let's leave it at that. Now you hush and relax, OK, love?"

"OK." Cassidy closed her eyes. She wondered what Darlene could see that she couldn't. Maybe the mistletoe would be her friend this year? Would Brandon have a change of heart? She tried to remember the last time she'd had a real kiss during the holidays. Dean had never come to California with her when they were dating, preferring instead to visit his own family in Chicago. Looking back, part of her had always known their relationship wasn't going anywhere, and she wished she hadn't held on for as long as she had.

She wondered where Dean was now. She hadn't heard from him in months. Was he even in New York anymore? The last time she'd spoken to him, he'd been thinking about moving to London, but then again, he'd always been thinking about moving to London to advance his career.

Maybe he was gone now.

Cassidy half smiled to herself as she realized she didn't know—and didn't care. That was one sure benefit of a new romance. Even if it didn't work out, at least it got you over the last one.

The circles of life, the circles of love.

"Darlene, I need to speak to you. Please come to my office when you're through here, will you?"

The hushed yet harsh sound of a woman's voice yanked Cassidy out of her musings. She opened her eyes and saw Annabelle Polanski standing next to the manicure table, in a huff as usual. Darlene, visibly flustered by the interruption, nodded politely. "Yes, Annabelle. I'll be there as soon as I finish with Ms. Lane."

"Thank you. Please pardon the interruption, Ms. Lane. I hope you enjoy your treatment." Annabelle smiled politely and nodded at Cassidy, then turned on her stiletto heel and disappeared down the hallway.

"She still scares me," Cassidy whispered.

Darlene stole a quick peek to make sure Annabelle was out of earshot, then turned her attention back to Cassidy's nails. She curled up her lips ever so slightly and whispered back: "It's OK, love, she scares me too."

Chapter Twenty-Three

CASSIDY SETTLED INTO her seat and looked out the window at the darkening sky above. It was still clear, but a big storm was supposed to hit the entire East Coast tonight, and the last place she wanted to be during a snowstorm was on the tarmac. But that was out of her control, so she pulled down the window cover and tried not to think about the weather.

Instead she focused on the trip ahead of her. Assuming they got off the ground, in a few hours she'd be back in Palo Alto.

At her parents' place, less than a mile from Brandon's house.

Before Nigel had pushed up her deadline, she'd expected to spend a good chunk of her time at home in a mad rush to finish her book. Now, instead of being chained to her laptop those two weeks, she'd be able to relax, celebrate the early completion of her sixth novel, and treat the trip like an actual vacation, with plenty of time to soak in the spirit of the holidays.

She had friends to visit.

Parties to hop.

Dinners to attend.

There would be laughter and good cheer all the way around.

She closed her eyes and leaned against the headrest.

This was supposed to be the happiest time of the year, and all she wanted to do was cry.

The sound of a woman's voice startled her. "Excuse me, ma'am, you need to shut down your phone now. The captain's preparing for takeoff."

Cassidy opened her eyes and nodded at the flight attendant. "Will do. Sorry." She picked up her phone and checked the screen one last time before turning it off.

No new messages.

"Well, hello there. You're looking very pretty tonight." Cassidy's sister-in-law approached her as she entered the private dining area at the Westin.

Cassidy opened her mouth to respond, but before she could utter a word, Jessica pointed to her dress and continued. "It's probably just because I'm used to seeing you in jeans, if not sweats, but I do love that outfit. It's good to see you wearing nice clothes now and again."

Cassidy wasn't surprised or offended. For Jessica this was practically fawning. "Thanks, I like it too." She'd decided to wear the hunter-green dress she'd bought specifically for that fateful date with Brandon that had never happened. She'd hoped doing so would make her feel strong, but unfortunately it was having the reverse effect, and all she could think about was how she'd invited Brandon to be her date tonight.

Jessica gave her a polite yet slightly cool smile, just as she always did. "How are you?"

Cassidy tried to force Brandon to the back of her mind, to focus on the positive things going on in her life. "I'm doing well, actually. I just finished a new book."

"I heard. Your brother and I were talking about that on the drive here. Congratulations."

"Thanks. I have a lot of editing ahead of me, of course, but the heavy lifting's behind me."

Jessica sipped her champagne. "What's this one about?"

"It's the story of a bright yet naïve young advertising executive whose life isn't quite turning out the way she expected. I think I'm going to call it *Miss Perception*."

"Ooh, I like that double entendre. Sounds mysterious. So no street-name title this time?"

"The book is pretty different from the kind of stuff I normally write, so I thought it might be a good idea to take the title in a new direction as well. I hope it all works."

"Different how?"

"It doesn't exactly end with a walk into the sunset."

"Is that a bad thing?"

Cassidy played with her earring. "I'm not sure yet, but it's a bit of a gamble to change course; my regular readers won't be expecting it." She wondered if it would pay off, despite what Nigel had said. She didn't want to disappoint her fan base. "It's also a little depressing to write a book without a happy ending, to be honest. I didn't realize that until it was sort of too late."

Jessica shrugged and glanced over her shoulder. "Well, even if it's a huge flop, you should be proud of yourself for trying something new."

"If what's a huge flop?" The sound of her brother's voice made Cassidy turn her head. Before she could reply, he lifted her a couple of inches off the ground in a bear hug, then set her down.

"Hey, Tyler, happy holidays. We were just talking about my new book."

"I hope there's a dashing character named Tyler in this one. It's about time you gave me my just deserts."

She gave him an I'm-sorry shrug. "Unfortunately, I just couldn't fit it in. But if you want dessert, I hear the pumpkin pie is quite tasty here."

He held up his palms. "Where is the love?"

"Maybe the next book?"

"That's what you say every book. Call me a super sleuth, but I'm beginning to detect a pattern here. When did you come in?"

"Yesterday."

"Nice. You still coming over to open presents with us on Christmas morning? You're totally invited, so long as you bring me a fat box of doughnuts."

"Wouldn't miss it. And yes, I'll bring your doughnuts."

Jessica looked annoyed. "You'd better watch it or you'll end up *looking* like a doughnut."

Tyler put his arm around her. "My lovely wife, eating enormous quantities of crappy food on holidays is practically a requirement. The rest of the year you know I'm a lean, mean exercise machine."

Cassidy poked him in his flat stomach. "I think you look great." Gaunt Jessica, on the other hand, looked like she needed to eat a sandwich. Or ten. Plus a few bags of marshmallows. God forbid she balloon to a size two.

"Auntie Cassie! Auntie Cassie!" Caroline and Courtney came running over and wrapped their tiny arms around Cassidy's legs.

"Girls, watch your manners now," Jessica said.

Cassidy leaned down and hugged them. "Hi, munchkins. You both look so pretty tonight. Can I see your holiday dresses?"

The girls took a step back and held out their arms, then each did a little twirl.

Cassidy laughed. "Let me guess: you've been practicing that."

Both girls nodded and curtsied. "Mommy taught us."

Cassidy clapped. "She did a great job, well done." She looked at her brother and Jessica. "I was thinking we could all go ice skating next week. What do you think? Wouldn't that be fun?"

Jessica didn't look too excited at the suggestion, but Tyler did. "I think it sounds great," he said.

"Ice skating! Ice skating!" After giving their aunt another hug, the girls darted off in the direction of Cassidy's dad, who scooped them both into his arms for the original Lane bear hug. Tyler followed along after them, and as Cassidy watched her nieces squeal with delight in their grandfather's arms, she again wondered what it would be like to have her own children. When she was in New York she was focused on her career, but at times like this she couldn't help but imagine what her life would be like had she taken a different path.

Somewhere along the way, would she have become a mother? Or a stepmother?

Jessica's hand on her arm snapped her back to the present.

"So what happened?" Jessica asked.

Cassidy blinked. "I'm sorry, what did you say?"

Jessica lowered her voice. "We heard you were bringing a date, and then suddenly you weren't anymore. What happened?"

Cassidy winced. "Ugh."

"Ugh? That's the story?"

"You really want to know?"

"Of course I do. I was so curious to meet the man you'd finally deemed worthy of an invitation. You're so picky, I figured he must be Superman or something."

Cassidy stifled a laugh. "You think I'm *picky*?" Was that really how Jessica saw her? Talk about a misperception.

"Are you saying you're not? It's a good thing, though. Women like you should be picky; it's not like you're looking for a meal ticket or anything. So tell me about the guy."

Cassidy cleared her throat, then gave a quick, elevator version of the Brandon saga, doing her best to recount the most salient moments along the way—while also minimizing the most painful ones.

When she was done, Jessica took a sip of her drink and looked over her shoulder again. "Sounds like the timing was just off. I wouldn't take it personally."

"That's what I'm trying to tell myself. It still just . . . hurts."

Jessica shrugged. "You'll forget about him faster than you think."

"I will?"

"Sure. It's not like it was a real relationship or anything. You'll bounce back."

Cassidy caught her breath. The words stung—hard—but she tried not to show it. "I guess so," she mumbled, suddenly feeling foolish.

And sad.

Jessica looked across the room and held up a finger. "Hang on a second, will you? Caroline's got something stuck to the back of her dress. I'll be right back." She walked over to her daughters and her husband, who were chatting with Cassidy's parents and Jessica's mother and father, who were even more formal than Jessica. As Cassidy watched them all together, she tried to see things from Jessica's perspective. She'd been with Cassidy's brother for twelve years, married to him for ten, had two children with him, a home with him, a life with him.

That was a real relationship.

Jessica had made a measure of effort, however minor, to express concern for Cassidy's situation with Brandon. But from her point of reference, a two-month text affair wasn't even a blip on the radar of reality. And rightly so, given her own life experience. Cassidy knew her sister-in-law, despite her inherent iciness, hadn't meant her comments to sound harsh.

But they did.

Cassidy forced an outward smile, but inside she was hurting, no matter how much she didn't want to be. The fact was that her life experience had taken her, for better or for worse, in a different direction from Jessica's. Her contribution to the world was in the form of novels, not children, and she should be proud of that.

She *was* proud of that.

She'd decided what she wanted out of life and made it happen, all on her own.

All on her own.

She took another look at the festive gathering across the room, then balled her hands into fists and stared at the floor, willing herself to keep it together.

Don't cry.

Don't cry.

There was no doubt that she loved her career, but she still longed for a different type of love.

She looked up and took a deep breath, then did her best to smile as she began walking toward her family on the other side of the room.

Maybe it was nothing to the rest of the world, but it was real to me.

"You still haven't heard from him? Text? E-mail? Nothing?" Patti finished tying a small silver bell onto her shoelace.

Cassidy shook her head "Not a peep."

"Wow. I'm really surprised."

Cassidy leaned her hands against the wall and pressed down her heel to stretch her calf and Achilles. "Join the club."

"How long has it been now?"

"About a month. Radio silence."

"And this was after he made a big deal of wanting to be your friend?"

"Yes. I told him I had enough friends, and he got upset with me, so I swallowed my pride and agreed to be his friend, whatever that means." She held up her palms. "Apparently *friends* is the new term for *not speaking*."

Patti stood up and put her hands on her hips. "I hate to say it, but Brandon Forrester sort of sucks. He's hot, but he sucks."

Cassidy laughed. "I adore you. Can I just tell you that?"

"Of course you can. I'm quite adorable, despite what my kids think."

"I guess I was right when I wondered if he seemed too good to be true. He certainly seemed perfect for a while there."

Patti handed her a pair of reindeer antlers. "You should have gone for pothead Trent at the reunion. Did you let him know when you were coming home?"

"You mean Brandon or Trent?"

Patti pretended to stick a finger down her throat. "Yeah, right. Barf."

Cassidy put on the headband and adjusted the antlers in front of the hall mirror. "He knows."

"Maybe you should just tell him you made it here safely?"

"That sounds a bit desperate to me."

Patti shrugged. "Maybe he forgot the date. Guys are terrible with dates. Roy can barely remember our anniversary."

"Hey now, it's sometime in July," Roy said, emerging from the kitchen. "Give a guy some credit."

Cassidy pulled on a thin pair of gloves. "Tomorrow is Christmas Eve, Patti. Even if he forgot the exact date of my arrival, if he's thinking about me at all, he's got to assume I'm home by now. Don't you agree, Roy?"

Roy offered a reluctant nod. "I know men can be clueless when it comes to women, but it's pretty rare that we're *that* oblivious."

Cassidy looked at Patti. "See? From the horse's mouth."

Patti walked over and gave Roy a quick kiss. "I like your horse mouth. Where are the devil children?"

Roy pointed down the hall. "They're supposed to be quietly watching a video in the den, but I give it five minutes before I hear a crash and/or a scream."

"Good luck with that, babe." Patti pointed toward the front door. "We're off to do some jingle jogging."

Roy saluted. "Heigh-ho."

After their run Patti, Cassidy, and Patti's friend Amy followed tradition and drove to a local bar called the Office for their annual post–Jingle Jog drink. Huddled around one of the outdoor fire pits in the chilly patio area, they clinked their glasses together in a toast.

"To my leg finally being healed!" Cassidy smiled. "I'm so happy to be healthy again."

"And to the most successful Jingle Jog yet!" Patti added. "I can't believe we had ten other people come out tonight. I didn't think I had that many friends."

Amy glanced around the bar, which was decorated with red and silver tinsel and looking quite festive. "Personally I think joining us for the post-jog festivities—which is my favorite part of the evening—should be a requirement for participation. What's up with bailing at seven thirty? Everyone just took off."

"We're old now," Patti said with a shrug. "People need to get home to their families."

"We're in our thirties," Amy said. "We're not dead."

Cassidy laughed. "I like your attitude."

"How's the job search going?" Patti asked Amy.

Cassidy looked at Amy. "Are you out of work?"

"No, I just hate my job."

"You're a lawyer, right?"

"Yep. And I hate it. I literally want to hang myself every single day. Except for the weekend, of course."

Cassidy sighed. "Brandon's a lawyer."

"Who's Brandon?" Amy asked.

Patti took a sip of her beer. "He's that guy from high school I told you about, the one who asked Cassidy out after our reunion."

Amy's eyes lit up. "Oh, yes! I loved that story. So romantic. How are things going with him?"

Cassidy frowned. "Not so great."

"What happened?"

Patti stood up. "Life got in the way, *that's* what happened." She looked at Cassidy. "Tell her. I'm going to get us another round."

As Patti disappeared inside, Cassidy filled Amy in on the highlights. By the time Patti returned a few minutes later with their beers, Amy was caught up on the situation, and Cassidy's good mood had gone a little sour.

"I'm sorry, Cassidy. He sounds like a good guy."

Patti sat down. "He *is* a good guy. But in my opinion he's kind of acting like an ass right now."

Amy nodded. "Being a good guy and acting like an ass on occasion aren't mutually exclusive. If I've learned anything after seven years of marriage, it's that."

Cassidy picked up her glass. "I don't know what to do with his Christmas present."

Patti made a pained face. "Oh no, the cuff links."

Cassidy nodded. "The dreaded cuff links. I was just telling Amy about how stupid I feel for having jumped the gun like that."

Amy shook her head. "Why would you feel stupid? They're a superthoughtful gift."

"Yes, for someone you're *dating*. He and I weren't even dating," Cassidy said. "I think I may have projected all of it."

"Stop it," Patti said. "You did not project it."

"Stop what? It's true. Embarrassing to admit, but true. Besides two dinners and a couple of coffee dates, our entire relationship was via text, with a few phone calls thrown in to spice things up. I can't pretend it was more than that."

"Come on, you know it was more than that."

Cassidy shook her head. "It was more than that to *me*, but it clearly wasn't to Brandon." She looked at Amy. "Isn't that how it sounds to you, from an outsider's perspective? Like the whole thing was silly and fake? And sort of pathetic?"

"I wouldn't call it silly or fake, especially given how it began, and I certainly wouldn't call it *pathetic*, but it does sound like a lot of the relationship was . . . you know . . . virtual," Amy said.

Cassidy pressed her palms against her eyes. "I'm so humiliated. I feel like the victim of a cruel hoax."

"I'm sorry," Amy said, a rueful look on her face. "That came out wrong."

Cassidy took a sip of her beer. "Don't be sorry. My sister-in-law had the same reaction the other night, and you've both brought some much-needed clarity to the situation." She lowered her voice to a whisper. "We barely even kissed."

"Really?" Amy said.

"Really. So how can I feel so heartbroken? What the hell is wrong with me?"

"I think the fact that you *didn't* hook up with him shows that your feelings are real," Patti said.

"You do?"

"I do too," Amy said. "Don't be so hard on yourself."

Patti sipped her beer. "You know how they say most women can't differentiate between romantic feelings and sexual attraction, right?"

"My friend Danielle can," Cassidy said. *Or can she?* She wondered how Danielle was faring with the whole Jonathan ordeal.

Patti set down her glass. "Well, most women can't. But sex wasn't a factor in this equation and you still opened up to him, Cassidy. This wasn't just some physical thing. Sure, a lot of it was via text message and phone, but that doesn't mean you two weren't connecting, and to most men an emotional connection is more intimate than sex. Don't you agree, Amy?"

Amy nodded. "Affirmative, your honor."

Patti looked back at Cassidy. "So who knows what really happened? Maybe he just got scared."

Cassidy stuck out her tongue. "Blech. I feel like we're back in seventh-grade science class right now, only we're dissecting a relationship instead of a frog. And I still feel sick."

Amy laughed. "Do you ever think that maybe the fact that you live in New York is what made you so attractive to him?

Cassidy looked at her. "What do you mean?"

Amy lifted her glass. "I'm just wondering if the fact that you don't live here was part of the appeal, given that he's clearly in no position to be in a relationship right now, much less a serious one. And then when it started to become more than he was ready for, he decided to throw some ice on it."

"You mean like when I asked him to my family's holiday dinner?"

Amy nodded. "Maybe."

Cassidy frowned and chewed on her thumbnail. "I hadn't thought of it that way. Now I feel even more stupid."

"I don't entirely agree," Patti said. "No one over the age of sixteen engages in that level of texting if it doesn't mean something, and no one over the age of thirty breaks off a promising relationship without a legitimate reason." She put her hand on Cassidy's arm. "I think he had real feelings for you, and I think he probably still does. He's just in a bad place right now, and that has absolutely nothing to do with you. And for what it's worth, I think you should give him the cuff links."

Cassidy gave her an are-you-crazy look. "Why should I give them to him? To make myself look even more like an idiot?"

"Stop talking like that. Because that's the kind of person you are, that's why."

"You mean an idiot?"

"Stop it right now or I'm going to throw this beer in your face."

Cassidy looked at Amy. "What do *you* think?"

Amy shook her head. "I wouldn't do it. If he doesn't react the way you want him to, you may regret it."

Cassidy turned back to Patti. "I think Amy's right. And she's smarter than you; she's a lawyer."

Patti reached for a napkin. "I will choose to ignore that assumption, even though you're probably correct. But regardless, who cares how he reacts? I'm concerned about you, not him. You can be the bigger person here, Cassidy. He said he wanted to be friends, right? So even if he's not acting like one right now, that doesn't mean *you* can't. You can never go wrong in life by being the bigger person."

Cassidy frowned. "Easier said than done. I'm the one who's hurting, remember?"

"I think you're underestimating what he feels for you. Even though we all agree he's kind of being a jerk right now, I'm sure he's hurting too," Patti said. "And you can't discount what he's dealing with. Watching your mother crumble like that? It has to be tough."

"I know, but I still think that if he felt anything for me, I would have heard from him by now. Even Roy said as much."

Patti shook her head. "I disagree, and Roy doesn't know the extent of how much you and Brandon were in contact. Men are different from us. While we tend to look at how our actions impact others, I think Brandon can't see beyond his own awful situation right now, and unfortunately you're just collateral damage."

Amy smiled. "Collateral damage. That's pretty good."

Patti sat up straight, a proud smile on her face. "Isn't it? I just made it up right now, and I didn't even go to law school."

Cassidy smiled weakly. "I wish he could hear you guys saying all this. I wish . . . he knew how hurt I am. I hate feeling this . . . defeated," she practically whispered the last part of the sentence.

Patti pulled her car keys out of her pocket. "Want me to tell him? If so, just give me his address, because I have no problem driving right over to his house and telling him. No problem at all."

Cassidy rolled her eyes. "Yeah, that wouldn't make either of us look crazy at all."

Patti put her keys away. "OK, I admit I was joking, sort of. But what about the cuff links? You want me to drop them off for you? *That* would be far from crazy."

"Thanks, but if I'm going to give them to him, I need to do it myself."

"Do it," Patti said.

Cassidy turned to Amy. "Should I?"

Amy shook her head. "I probably wouldn't, but Patti's known you much longer than I have, and she knows Brandon too, so maybe her opinion should trump mine."

Cassidy looked back at Patti, then sighed.

"Do it," Patti said again.

Cassidy sat there for a moment, then slowly began to nod. "OK. But I just . . . I just wonder . . ." Her voice trailed off.

"You wonder what?" Amy asked.

Cassidy stared at the table. "I just wonder . . . if it's ever going to happen for me."

"If what's ever going to happen for you?" Patti asked.

Cassidy gave her a sheepish look. "You know, the fairy-tale romance, the prince, the wedding, the happy ending, all of that. All the stuff I write about in my books."

Amy and Patti both started laughing.

"What's so funny?" Cassidy said.

Patti squeezed her shoulder. "I know you make a living pretending that marriage is a bottomless love fest, but believe me, it isn't. No one talks about what it's like sleeping next to a man who ate an enormous burrito for dinner."

Amy raised her hand. "Don't forget the perpetual argument about what constitutes something as *clean*. Hot tap water alone does not a clean dish make, am I right?"

"Are you saying you'd rather *not* be married?" Cassidy asked them. "There's no way either of you is saying that."

Patti shook her head. "No, I'm not saying that. What I'm saying is that marriage is not all breakfast in bed and picnics in the park, especially when you throw kids into the mix. And being married is hardly the only relationship that matters in a person's life. I'd kill to have parents like yours, for example. I barely speak to mine anymore, and they've made zero effort to get to know their own grandchildren. Do you have any idea how hurtful that is?"

Amy nodded. "I completely agree. My husband hasn't spoken to his dad in years, and as you just heard, I absolutely loathe my job. Being married is hardly the only key to happiness."

Cassidy smiled. "I guess I have a pretty cool family."

Patti nodded. "Hell yes you do. And you have a sick job too."

Cassidy nodded. "I do love my job, if you can even call it a job."

"It pays the bills. It's a *job*," Patti said.

Amy sighed. "I spend all day watching the clock."

Patti pointed at Cassidy. "See? No one has *everything*. I know it hurts right now, and I'm not discounting your feelings. But when you look at the whole picture, romance is just one part of life. It may not be clicking the way you want it to right now, but don't forget to appreciate the things that *are* clicking, because they're just as important."

Cassidy touched the part of her nose where the scrape had once been. "You're right."

"I told you so."

Cassidy reached for Patti's hand and squeezed it. "I think I'm doing pretty well in the friendship department, if I may say so myself."

Patti squeezed back. "Damn straight you are. Now let's order another round before it's my bedtime."

Chapter Twenty-Four

THE FIRST DAY of January, Cassidy decided to call Brandon. She told herself she was just following Patti's advice, that she was being the bigger person by reaching out to see how he was doing, just as a true friend would. But deep down she knew the truth—that she wouldn't be able to move on until she had some kind of contact with him. She'd had enough of texting and decided the grown-up thing to do was to pick up the phone the old-fashioned way.

She didn't really expect him to answer, but he did.

On the second ring.

"Cassidy, hi." He sounded surprised. "How are you?"

She was briefly frozen at hearing his voice, but she forced herself to speak. "Hi. I'm good, thanks. Um . . . I know it's a little awkward, but I still have your Christmas present, and since it's something I can't return, I thought maybe I could bring it over to you." The last thing she wanted to do was stop by unannounced, or worse, run into him while trying to drop off the gift surreptitiously. She already felt like a stalker just for thinking about him so much, and now she just wanted this to be over.

He didn't reply right away, and for a crushing moment she wondered if he was going to turn her down completely.

She felt her palms begin to sweat.

He wouldn't do that, would he?

After all we've been through?

Oh my God.

He's going to say no.

After an excruciating silence, he finally spoke. "I've got the boys today, but maybe tomorrow afternoon. Around one?"

She swallowed. "OK, sure."

Another uncomfortable pause followed, so she decided to end the conversation before it got even worse. She couldn't take anymore.

"Good, I'll come by then. Bye, Brandon."

"Bye, Cassidy."

She hung up the phone and stared at it.

Her hand was shaking.

How had things changed so much, so fast?

At 12:56 the next afternoon, Cassidy made a right turn onto Brandon's street. She drove slowly down the block, wondering which house was his. Was this where he'd lived with his ex-wife? The fact that she didn't know the answer reminded her of how little she actually knew about him.

She spotted the address and pulled her mom's SUV over to the curb. As soon as she turned off the ignition, her heartbeat became more pronounced, and she felt a wave of nausea hit her. Nearly two months had passed since she'd last seen him, but given how raw her emotions were right now, it felt like yesterday. When he'd kissed her good-bye outside of Mayfield Bakery that day, she never would have guessed it would be for the last time.

She sat in the car for a few moments, trying to calm her jittery nerves. She could feel tiny beads of sweat on the back of her neck, much like she'd felt before her keynote address back in November. She closed her eyes and searched for the strength she knew was still inside her, however hidden.

Believe in yourself, Cassidy.

Finally, she opened the car door, then reached for her purse and slowly approached Brandon's house, admiring his holiday decorations as she made her way to the front door. A reindeer grazed next to a sleigh on the front lawn, and all the windows facing the street were lined with white lights. Two tiny pairs of muddy rain boots were lined up on the front step.

She took a deep breath, then slowly raised her hand toward the doorbell and pressed the button. Her heart was still beating faster than she would have liked, and she willed it to slow down.

Deep breaths, deep breaths.

She heard footsteps on the other side of the door, then a clicking sound.

And there he was.

"Hi, Cassidy."

"Hi, Brandon." She was slightly taken aback at his appearance. As usual he was dressed impeccably, in dark jeans and a dark-blue V-neck sweater over a white collared shirt, but he looked . . . awful. His skin was ashen, his forehead deeply lined, his shoulders drooping.

And his eyes . . .

His piercing gray eyes, which had once mesmerized her, now looked . . . hollow.

He looked hollow.

She was tempted to hug him but didn't dare.

He stepped outside onto the porch. "How are you? I'm sorry for not being in touch. I didn't want to bug you."

She tried not to laugh. He didn't want to *bug* her? If he only knew how many times she'd stared at her phone, desperately wishing he would *bug* her.

"I'm good, thanks. How is your mom?"

He crossed his arms in front of him. "Not well. She's back in the hospital. She's exhibiting signs of brain damage."

Cassidy's hand flew up to cover her mouth. "Oh my God."

He scratched his chin, which now was nearly covered with a full beard. "So needless to say, that complicates her situation a great deal."

"What happens now?"

"I need to find a live-in facility that can help with both the mental and physical issues she's dealing with, and then I've got to put her house on the market."

"I'm so sorry, Brandon."

"Thank you. It's been a rough couple of months, to say the least. I'm hoping this year will be better. It certainly can't get much worse."

She nodded slowly. No wonder she hadn't heard from him.

They stood there in silence for a few moments, and then he finally spoke. "So how have you been? Did you have a good Christmas?" He recrossed his arms, and she could feel a chill in the air.

"I did, thanks, just spent it with my family, nothing too exciting. What about you?"

He shrugged. "I had the boys for Christmas Eve, then spent most of Christmas Day at the hospital." His eyes were vacant, glassy.

Distant.

"Oh," she said softly.

He glanced at her leg. "Did your Achilles finally heal?"

She smiled. "Yes, finally. It took long enough. I really missed running for a while there."

"Glad to hear it. So what else is going on?"

She swallowed. "I, uh, I finished my novel."

"Good for you. That's great news."

"Thanks. It was a challenge for a bit, but I finally got through it."

"You must be thrilled."

"Right now I'm more drained than thrilled. This one really took it out of me, especially at the end. I think I'm better off writing happier books, to be honest."

"It's not a happy book?"

"I wouldn't say that. It's just . . . *different* from my other books. At least the ending is. I guess you could call it bittersweet."

He nodded but didn't say anything, and she knew he understood. She wondered if she might have had a different reaction to *Miss Perception*'s ending had their own romance not imploded so unceremoniously.

She stared at the ground for a few moments, then slowly raised her gaze and looked at him.

At his eyes.

Those eyes had once captivated her, not only for their beauty but for how he'd allowed her to see beyond them, to see *within* him, and also for how they'd seen something special inside her. Now, as she studied them intently, she saw nothing . . . and realized they were seeing nothing in return. The intense connection between them was broken.

It was almost as if he were staring right through her.

It was almost as if she were standing there by herself.

A car drove by, breaking the silence, and she suddenly remembered why she was there. "Oh, your gift." She reached inside her purse and pulled out a small box, which she'd wrapped in shiny red paper and white ribbon. "Sorry for the delayed delivery. I guess better late than never, right?" She wondered what this scene would look like from the perspective of the passing driver, the two of them standing on the porch of a charming house decorated for the holidays, pleasantly exchanging gifts. No one would have guessed that the storybook presentation was anything but.

He took the box but barely smiled. He didn't look ungrateful, just weary. "Thanks. Do you want me to open it now?"

She shrugged. "Sure, why not?" This was hardly going as she'd hoped it would, but by now she'd pretty much given up hope, at least where he was concerned. She was eager to get back on the plane to New York as soon as possible and put all this behind her. She had her answer, and there was no point in drawing it out.

He carefully removed the wrapping paper and opened the signature light-blue box. He removed the cuff links and held them up for a moment, then put them back. "Thank you, Cassidy, these are very nice." He said the words without any visible emotion. Had he seen the engraving? If so, he hadn't reacted.

She tried to prod him with her eyes, but it wasn't working, so she abandoned tact for directness. "Did you see the engraving?"

He glanced at the box again. "Yes."

She gave him a confused look. "Do you know what they stand for?"

"No."

She cleared her throat. *What is wrong with him?* "The *H* is for Henry, and the *J* is for Jack."

He nodded slowly. "Ah, got it. I'm sorry. I thought the *J* was an *I*, so I didn't put it together. My mind is a little fuzzy right now. I haven't been sleeping very much."

"I can tell." It was like talking to a robot.

He tried to smile, but it looked painfully forced. "Thank you for these. That was very thoughtful of you." It was clear he had nothing for her—but then, she hadn't really expected him to.

"You're welcome. Obviously, um, I bought them a long time ago, you know . . . when things were different." *When I thought there was something magical happening between us.*

He nodded, then changed the subject.

"When do you head back to New York?"

"In a couple of days. But I'll be back in about six weeks for another speaking engagement. Another keynote, actually. In San Francisco."

"Good for you."

She felt he wanted her to leave now, that he had nothing more to say to her. Then again, did she have anything more to say to him? She didn't want to admit that the answer was no. She still didn't want to admit that it was really ending this way.

She forced a smile of her own. "Well, I guess I'd better get going. I'm so sorry about your mom. Will you keep me posted on how things are going with her?"

He nodded. "I will. Thanks again for the gift."

She stood on her tiptoes and gave him a quick hug before turning to leave. He hugged her back, but there was no intimacy in his embrace.

It felt stiff.

Cold.

Empty.

It felt . . . over.

As she drove away, she forced herself not to look back at the house, even though she'd seen him disappear inside before she'd even reached her car. Then she realized he hadn't asked her to come in.

Their entire conversation had taken place on the front steps. She wiped a small tear from the corner of her eye.

How fitting.

Later that afternoon Cassidy drove up to Portola Valley and went for a long run. Besides the Jingle Jog, this was the first time she'd broken a sweat outdoors in months, and she felt . . . *free.* The air was crisp and clear, the only sounds those of her breathing and the crackling of an occasional leaf beneath her shoes on the dirt trail. The quiet solitude was a stark difference from Central Park, where even on the bleakest day she encountered dozens of other joggers.

As she ran she replayed the stilted conversation with Brandon in her head, or what she could remember of it. In addition to his chilly demeanor, the only thing she could recall with absolute clarity was the haunting, vacant look in his eyes. She hadn't gotten much of a reaction to the cuff links, but what did she expect? He clearly had nothing to give, at least to her, at least for the time being and maybe never. Seeing him in such a state finally made her understand—and believe—that his behavior had very little to do with her. There was no denying she'd been shaken by it, but their conversation had also altered the sorrow she was feeling, and for the first time in weeks, she didn't feel like crying. Maybe Brandon did still care for her, or maybe he didn't. But it didn't matter; right now he needed to focus on his family and his livelihood. That was just how it had to be.

Her mind reached further back, to the day he'd told her he couldn't handle more than a friendship, when she'd wanted so desperately to run but her injured leg wouldn't allow it. She vividly remembered how upset she'd been as she walked through

Central Park, how her chest had hurt physically, how she'd fought back the tears . . . and lost.

How she'd felt so rejected.

So misled.

So unlovable.

So . . . sad.

At the time, and for weeks after, she'd asked herself what was wrong with her, why he didn't want her.

After seeing him today, she wasn't asking those questions anymore. She was still disappointed their romance hadn't worked out, but now she understood he was hurting just as deeply as she was, if not more so, and despite her own heartache, she felt compassion for him. Though her parents were getting older of course, they were still very healthy, and her relationship with them was a source of joy, one that brought her love and support, not anguish and stress.

As she continued to run along the trail, the crisp air whistling past her, she remembered what Patti had said about life, how romantic love was just one piece of the picture. She began to mentally tick off other areas of her life that were on track:

She'd finished her sixth novel.

Her career was moving forward.

She had Patti.

And Danielle.

And Harper.

Her leg had healed.

Next month she'd be giving her second keynote address—and was determined to do better this time.

She had her own apartment in one of the greatest cities in the world.

She was living the life of a writer, which countless others only dreamed of.

She didn't even have to wake up early if she didn't want to.

She felt the tiniest of smiles appear on her face as she finished her run.

It's time to stop feeling sorry for myself.

She'd been unable to stop the tears that day in the park, but she'd fought through them, and she would continue to do so. While the fog of heartache was far from lifted, she hadn't let the emotional pain stop her from experiencing happiness in other parts of her life, although she hadn't quite realized that until today. She could now see—albeit with bittersweet clarity—what Patti had been trying to tell her.

No one's life was perfect, but in the grand scheme of things, hers was going pretty well.

When Cassidy returned to the parking lot, she leaned against a tree to stretch out her leg, thrilled that it had held up for the duration of the run—and not oblivious to the symbolism. Once inside the car she removed her phone from the glove compartment, then clicked to open the marathon chain of text messages between her and Brandon, containing every note they'd shared. She was briefly tempted to scroll back to the beginning of the exchange, as she'd done several times before, reliving the fleeting promise of romance one last time while also trying to pinpoint when everything had begun to go south. But now she knew it was pointless to revisit any of it, the good or the bad.

It was time to stop asking what had gone wrong. It was time to move forward.

She hesitated for just a moment, then clicked *delete this thread.*

Chapter Twenty-Five

CASSIDY FLEW HOME two days later, grateful to be beginning a new year in Manhattan despite the freezing sheets of sleet that greeted her at the airport. She'd long ago given up making New Year's resolutions she never kept, but she always enjoyed the chance to start fresh, and this year was no exception. Assuming the revision went smoothly, *Miss Perception* would be coming out in the fall, and the time had come to start thinking about what to write next. It was always a daunting process, but she now knew from experience that she'd think of something eventually. She just had to let it come to her.

That evening she met Danielle for a glass of wine at Bin 71. They hadn't spoken much over the holidays, and Cassidy was eager to get caught up on the CFO Jonathan saga.

The moment Danielle walked through the door, Cassidy could see something was wrong from her seat at the bar. She set down her glass and stood up as Danielle approached.

"I got fired," Danielle said.

"What? When?"

Danielle took off her coat and gestured toward the bartender to bring her a drink. "Yesterday. Jonathan's wife went to the board when she found out I work at the same company he does. Actually, her lawyer went to the board."

"She knows?"

Danielle nodded. "He told her right after Christmas."

Cassidy covered her mouth with her hand. "Wow, he really did it."

"Yep, and she's pissed. Although I can't blame her, really. I'd be pissed too. I *am* pissed. The whole situation sucks."

"And they fired *you*? Why not him? Is what you did illegal?"

Danielle laughed weakly and sat down on a bar stool. "I love you to death for supporting me, but you clearly don't understand corporate America."

"I thought you said his wife wasn't into the marriage anymore."

"She's not. She's into an enormous divorce settlement, which she'll get if she can prove he was unfaithful, even though he's pretty sure she's had several affairs herself."

"I'm so sorry, Danielle. What happens now?"

Danielle picked up her glass. "I'm having a drink, that's what happens now."

"Are they giving you a severance package?"

"Hell yes, and a large one. Technically I'm *resigning,* but we all know that's a corporate euphemism for *I got thrown out on my ass without cause.* So don't worry about me, I'll be fine. I feel gross about the whole situation, but I'll be fine."

"What are you going to do?"

Danielle pointed at her glass. "Did you not hear what I just said? I'm having a drink."

"Very funny."

Danielle shrugged. "I'm not sure yet. I'll probably take a few months off, do some traveling. I've already gotten a few calls from headhunters, so I'm not too worried about finding another job. I'm more worried about forgiving myself for getting into such a mess."

"See what you were missing all those years you didn't let your heart get involved? Isn't it fun?"

"Oh, yes, it's awesome. I wish I'd done this much sooner. I wouldn't have spent all that time feeling independent and good about myself."

"And Jonathan? What's going to happen with him?"

"I guess we'll see. I think we both need some space. I love him, but he's knee-deep in it right now, so I think the smart thing to do is just stay away from him until things settle down."

Cassidy squeezed Danielle's knee. "I love how levelheaded you are, even in the middle of a nightmare like this. I wish I were more like you."

Danielle smiled. "Thanks for saying that. But enough about me; I want to talk about *you*. Did your editor like your book?"

"Yes! I'm so relieved, you have no idea."

"I knew he would. And what about Brandon? Did you see him when you were home?"

Cassidy nodded.

"Well? What happened?

Cassidy spread her fingers wide to show off her nails. "What do you think? I've gone more than two weeks without a nibble. Darlene's going to be so proud of me."

Danielle peered at her over the rim of her wineglass. "That is a truly sad attempt at deflecting a question. So I'm guessing it didn't go so well?"

Cassidy dropped her hands and shook her head. "It went the opposite of well."

"Did you give him the cuff links?

"That also didn't go so well."

Danielle frowned. "I'm sorry, hon."

"Me too. But it's a new year, and I don't want to talk about it. I'm all about new beginnings right now."

Danielle lifted her glass. "Then here's to a new year and new beginnings."

Cassidy clinked her glass against Danielle's. "Amen to that."

"Hello there, welcome to Annabelle's. Do you have an appointment?" A young woman approached with a polite smile and spoke in a hushed voice as Cassidy shut the door behind her.

Cassidy smiled back and glanced around the salon, which for the first time she noticed wasn't scented. "Yes, my name's Cassidy Lane. I have a five o'clock with Darlene."

"Oh, yes, Ms. Lane. I'm Denise. I'll be taking care of you this evening. May I hang that up for you?" She gestured to Cassidy's coat.

"Is Darlene ill?" Cassidy asked as she removed it and handed it to the woman, then took off her gloves and glanced at her nails. She'd been looking forward to showing off the fruits of her nibble-free holiday, plus the two weeks she'd been back in New York. Earlier that afternoon she'd turned in the revision of *Miss Perception* right on schedule, and after so many hours at her desk she'd been looking forward to pampering herself. In addition to a manicure, she'd also scheduled a facial, her first.

After hanging up Cassidy's coat, Denise explained, "Darlene doesn't work here anymore. Would you like a cup of tea?"

Cassidy stopped walking and looked at her. "What? What happened?"

Denise kept smiling as she nudged Cassidy toward the manicure station. "I couldn't say, Ms. Lane."

"Is she OK?"

"I really couldn't say, ma'am. I'm new here. Do you prefer peppermint or chamomile?"

Cassidy stared at her, feeling a bit stunned. "Oh, um, peppermint, please." She took a seat.

Darlene was gone?

Why did she leave?

Where did she go?

Why didn't she say anything when she did my nails before Christmas?

Cassidy looked around the salon. Though the room was filled with customers, it suddenly felt a bit empty.

And a bit cold.

Denise soon appeared with a steaming cup of tea and sat down across from Cassidy. "Have you had a manicure here before?" she asked gently.

Cassidy nodded. "Several times, always with Darlene. She was lovely."

Denise smiled. "Well it's nice to have you back. I'll do my best to fill her shoes. Go ahead and relax now."

As Denise went to work on her nails—without putting a warm wrap on Cassidy's neck—Cassidy closed her eyes and let her mind drift to thoughts of what had happened to Darlene. After a few minutes of daydreaming, she came up with the following scenario:

Carl, Darlene's beloved husband of thirty-five years, retired from his job at the tire factory with a comfortable pension. After much thought they decided to make a big change and sell their modest two-bedroom house in exchange for a condo at a community for active seniors in Vero Beach, Florida. Their new place will have plenty of room for the children and their families to visit regularly, and the happy couple will welcome loved ones with open arms to their new home. Carl will focus on losing weight and lowering his blood pressure through regular walks and games of golf, and Darlene will dip into their nest egg to finally fund her own dream, a small nail salon in the center of town called Darlene's. The space will be bright and inviting and will always smell wonderful, and soon Darlene will have a base of regular customers who appreciate her friendly, nurturing, and gentle demeanor.

It will be a perfect next chapter in her life.

And well deserved.

Cassidy looked up from her hamburger. "She's moving in with you next month?"

Harper tossed a fry into his mouth. "That is correct. She just gave her thirty-day notice."

"And you two are getting along OK?"

He shrugged and picked up another fry. "As well as can be expected, I guess. It's all a bit stressful."

"And business school? Still on the back burner?"

He nodded. "Way in the back."

"Ah, got it." Cassidy tried to look cheerful but failed.

"I'll be fine," Harper said.

"I know you will."

It was the following Saturday, and the two of them were

having lunch at the New Wave Café on Broadway and Seventy-Eighth. Harper was facing his own new beginnings, albeit not necessarily the ones he would have chosen for himself.

He reached for the ketchup. "What about you? What's new and exciting in the world of Cassidy?"

She picked up her water glass with a shrug. "Compared to what's going on with you, pretty much nothing, although I did finish my book."

"Oh, yes, finishing a book is definitely nothing. Please. What about that guy from home? Anything happening there?"

"Over."

He raised his eyebrows. "Over?"

"Over."

"From the one-word answer, I'm guessing you don't want to talk about it."

She shrugged. "It's last year. Why dwell on the past?"

Harper laughed. "You mean last year as in not even three weeks ago?"

"Touché, but I still don't want to talk about it."

"Come on, you've got to give me something. Did he turn out to be a douche? What happened?"

She shook her head. "Bad timing. He couldn't handle a relationship right now."

Harper realized she wasn't kidding around. "Oh, man, I'm sorry Cassidy. I just assumed that if it ended, you were the one who ended it."

She smiled. "Ah, Harper, my biggest cheerleader. So loyal but so delusional."

He winked at her. "Always will be."

"And I love you for it, but let's talk about something else, OK? I've pitied myself enough and I have to move on."

"Excuse me, Ms. Lane?"

The sound of a woman's voice made them both turn their heads.

Cassidy looked at the young woman standing there. Her face was familiar, but Cassidy couldn't place it.

Just then Harper's phone rang. He pulled it out of his pocket, then sighed and stood up. "It's Vanessa, so I should take it. Be back in a minute, I hope."

"Sure, go ahead," Cassidy said.

As he walked away, Cassidy looked at the young woman. "We've met, right?"

The woman smiled. "My name's Molly Benson. I sat next to you on a plane from New York to San Francisco a couple of months ago. I was on my way to a wedding in Napa."

Cassidy's eyes lit up with recognition. "That's right, of course! How did the wedding go? Do you want to sit?" She gestured to Harper's empty side of the booth.

Molly glanced toward the exit. "Are you sure? I don't want to intrude."

"It's no trouble. My friend won't be back for a few minutes. Please, have a seat."

Molly sat down tentatively. "Thanks. My friends already took off, but when I recognized you I had to come over and tell you that I've read some of your books since meeting you. I think they're great."

Cassidy smiled. "That's always nice to hear. I'm glad you enjoyed them."

Molly frowned slightly, which Cassidy wasn't expecting. She focused on the table between them. "And well, the truth is, they've really helped me get through a tough time."

"A tough time? How so?"

Molly looked up at her, and Cassidy immediately recognized the pain in her eyes. She'd seen that look in the mirror too many times lately. Molly tapped her fingers on the table. "Well, at that wedding I met this guy, Patrick, who also lives here in New York, and we really hit it off."

Cassidy nodded, and Molly continued.

"For a few weeks I was on cloud nine, like happier than I'd ever been. I know it sounds silly, but I truly thought he was the one for me, like I'd finally found him." She smiled weakly.

Cassidy nodded again, knowing Molly had more to say and knowing it wasn't good.

Molly's voice cracked a little. "But then out of the blue it all fell apart, or I guess he lost interest or something, because he basically . . . disappeared."

Cassidy gave her a sympathetic nod. "I'm sorry."

Molly kept tapping the table. "Since then I've been so sad. So, so sad. My friends keep telling me to snap out of it and forget about him, and I know I should, but I just . . . *can't.* I feel so stupid for thinking he could be *the one* after such a short time, but I really did. I really . . . did." Her eyes were watery now, the sadness radiating out of them.

She was basically a stranger, but Cassidy felt for her.

In a way she *was* her.

Cassidy spoke softly. "If it's any consolation, I've been there."

I am there.

Molly smiled and wiped a few tears away with the back of her hand and sniffled. "Thanks. I know I'm sharing way too much, and you probably think I'm a nut job for telling you all this, but I wanted to let you know that your books have given me hope that maybe the right guy for me is still out there somewhere."

"I bet he is," Cassidy said.

I hope the same thing for myself.

"I sure hope so." Molly forced another smile. "Anyhow, I wanted to thank you for writing the stories you do. Please keep at it, because we all need to believe."

"We all need to believe what?" a male voice asked.

They both turned to see Harper standing next to the booth.

Cassidy gracefully changed the subject. "Harper Gold, this is Molly Benson. She and I met on a plane ride to San Francisco."

Harper bowed his head. "It's a pleasure, Molly." Then he looked at Cassidy and gestured over his shoulder with his thumb. "Listen, I hate to eat and run before dessert, but duty calls. I've already paid the bill if you two want to stick around."

Molly quickly stood up and exited the booth, wiping a tear from her eye. "That's OK, I was just leaving anyway."

Cassidy stood up too and gave her a hug. "Hang in there," she whispered into her ear.

Molly hugged her back. "Thank you for listening. Really, thank you." She turned and hurried out of the restaurant, clearly a bit embarrassed.

"What was that all about?" Harper asked when Molly was out of earshot.

Cassidy smiled. "Girl talk."

It had begun snowing during lunch, so Cassidy rushed home to avoid getting too wet. She was halfway there when she heard a beeping inside her purse. As she walked she reached inside her purse to check her phone.

BUY MARSHMALLOWS!

She clicked *dismiss*, then turned around and headed in the opposite direction, toward CVS. She could handle being out of a lot of things during snowy weather, but not marshmallows.

She moved quickly yet gingerly along the sidewalk, which was now covered in a fresh layer of powder. She'd nearly reached the CVS entrance when she heard the tiny yap of what had to be an equally tiny dog. She looked to her left and spotted a small white poodle in the arms of a diminutive woman huddled under the awning of a restaurant. She was wearing what looked like a very expensive fur coat, one that wouldn't take well to snow.

Cassidy's eyes moved from the woman's coat to her face.

It was Annabelle Polanski.

Should she say hello?

Maybe not.

She was about to turn and duck into CVS when Annabelle made eye contact and smiled.

"Hello," she said curtly.

Cassidy smiled back. "Hi."

"You're Ms. Lane, right? You've been to my salon a few times, Annabelle's? I'm Annabelle Polanksi."

"Yes, my name's Cassidy. I love your place."

She knows my name? Why is she being so nice?

"Thank you. I must say I love it too." Annabelle peered out at the street, then smoothed a hand over the miniature dog. "I *hate* getting caught in the snow, and poor Muffin here gets so scared. We're just waiting for my driver to come pick us up."

Cassidy nodded toward the entrance next door. "I'm on my way home too. I was just running into CVS to pick up a few . . . staples." She realized most people wouldn't view marshmallows as a staple, but to each her own.

Annabelle smiled again and shooed her away. "Go on then, I don't want to hold you up. It's only going to come down harder. I hope to see you in the salon again soon."

"Thanks." Cassidy turned to go, then stopped and brushed a few snowflakes out of her hair. "Do you mind if I ask what happened to Darlene?"

Annabelle's eyes went a bit dark. "Darlene?"

"Yes, she always did my manicures. Do you know where she went?"

Annabelle kept petting Muffin but didn't answer.

"Mrs. Polanksi?" Cassidy said.

"Please, call me Annabelle. And Darlene . . . resigned."

"What? But why? She seemed so happy there."

She sighed. "If you must know, it was that awful husband of hers."

Cassidy felt her eyes get big. *Awful husband?* "What happened?"

Annabelle nodded and looked down the street for her driver. "He came into the shop . . . *again* . . . and caused a bit of a scene . . . *again*, griping as always about her spending too much time away from home, and then they left. She called the next morning and said she wasn't coming back."

Cassidy put a hand on her heart. "Is she OK?"

Annabelle shrugged. "I hope so. She's a nice woman, but she didn't choose a nice husband. Well, there's my car, so I'm off now." She darted toward the street. "I hope to see you at the salon soon. Stay warm now."

"Bye." Cassidy stood there for a moment, in a bit of a daze, as she watched Annabelle climb inside a large black town car, which quickly disappeared into the traffic. The snow was coming down harder now, swirling under the awning where Cassidy was standing, but she didn't move.

Instead she tried to process what she'd just learned.

Darlene's life wasn't anything like she'd pictured it to be.

Her high-school-sweetheart husband, the kind and loving father of her children.

Her move to Florida to open her own salon.

Her happily ever after.

None of it was true.

It was all just Cassidy's imagination.

Darlene had always made her feel nurtured, but she had never opened up about her personal life. Had she told Cassidy anything at all? Looking back, Cassidy wasn't sure she ever had. Cassidy had painted a picture of Darlene's home life that was clearly far from reality, and now a version of that picture was sprinkled among the pages of her new manuscript in the form of Donna, one of her favorite characters.

A small character, but an important one.

A character whose storybook marriage would live forever in Cassidy's imagination, as well as those of her readers.

Did that make it real on some level?

She'd filled in the blanks with Darlene and had been dead wrong.

Had she done the same thing with Brandon? Expected him to be something he wasn't?

She blinked.

Fiction isn't real.

Wishful thinking doesn't make it true.

After a few moments, she dusted off the thin layer of snow now covering her like powdered sugar, turned, and entered the store.

When Cassidy had made it back to her warm and dry apartment, she brewed a pot of coffee, changed into her favorite sweatpants, pulled her hair up into a bun, and sat down at her desk with a full bag of marshmallows.

Then she clicked to open a new Word document.

She was still trying to wrap her head around what she'd just learned about Darlene, but her mind also kept returning to the conversation she'd had earlier with Molly Benson.

One thing in particular that Molly had said to her jumped out. *Please keep doing what you're doing. We all need to believe.*

Cassidy stared at the screen for a few moments, then glanced at the sticky note she'd pasted on a corner of her desk, the idea she'd jotted down after watching the video at Nigel's office.

Hmm.

I need to believe too.

A new story was talking to her. And it was time to listen.

She opened the bag, popped a marshmallow into her mouth, and began to type.

Chapter Twenty-Six

one month later

CASSIDY BOARDED THE ten o'clock train, which had arrived right on schedule and was barely half-full. She smiled at the ease of it all. After nearly a decade of living in New York City, her tolerance for freeway traffic had effectively disappeared, so she'd opted for Caltrain over her mom's car for the thirty-five-mile trip from Palo Alto to San Francisco.

She settled into a comfortable window seat, and within moments the train pulled out of the station. While reviewing her notes, she occasionally glanced out the window as they wound their way up the tree-lined Peninsula. The experience could not have been more different from the New York subway, which bustled even in off-peak hours. As she did every time she visited home, she wondered what her life would be like if she lived here again. Would the calm be a welcome change? Or would she eventually become bored and crave the energy of the big city? Though she'd had the same conversation with herself countless times, she still didn't know the answer.

She smiled as she realized that she had the best of both worlds. For now, at least, she still liked it that way.

Her thoughts turned to the keynote speech ahead. This time she was determined to open up more to the audience, which meant she'd soon be sharing her personal story of repeated failure with nearly a thousand women.

She hoped to inspire them to follow their dreams, as she had. To stand up in the face of rejection and keep trying, as she had.

To keep trying.

And trying.

She glanced out the train window.

Please don't choke.

"Thank you so much for being so honest. It makes all the difference to know you had to work at it too. You've really inspired me to follow my dream of opening my own flower store."

"You're very welcome." Cassidy smiled and peeked over the woman's shoulder as she handed her a signed copy of *Hanover Square*. The line of enthusiastic conference attendees waiting patiently to speak to Cassidy had snaked down the hall at one point, and she was exhausted.

But also exhilarated.

She'd done it this time.

While she'd wanted to open up more than she had at her first keynote, she hadn't expected to share quite so many of her own shortcomings. This was the first time she'd divulged such intimate, wrenching details about her professional insecurities in a public forum, and the warm reaction she'd received had touched her deeply, in a way she hadn't expected.

Being forthcoming about her failures wasn't such a scary thing after all.

When the line had finally cleared, she smiled to herself. *I need to speak at events like this more often.*

Cassidy was collecting her things to leave when her phone beeped on the table in front of her. It was a text from Harper.

CALL ME IMMEDIATELY. AS IN NOW.

She did as instructed, wondering what the big news could possibly be. She hadn't talked to him in nearly a week.

He answered on the first ring. "I'm not the father."

"What?"

"I'm not the father. The baby's not mine."

Cassidy gasped. "Oh my God."

"Can you believe it? After all that?"

"I'm stunned."

"Join the club."

"What happened?"

"Vanessa took a paternity test."

There was no one within thirty feet of her, but Cassidy lowered her voice to a whisper anyway. "Why?"

"We were out to dinner the other night, and as we were leaving, we bumped into a couple of women she knows. One of them, who had clearly been drinking, made a joke about wondering who the father was. When Vanessa didn't laugh, I knew something wasn't right. When we got home I pressed her about it, and it turns out I wasn't the only guy she was sleeping with when she got pregnant."

"Wow."

"Yep. So I insisted on a paternity test just to be sure, and we just got the results today. Negative."

Cassidy slowly shook her head. *"So you're . . . off the hook? I know that sounds horrible."*

"It's not horrible. It's true. She was playing me, and she knew it."

Cassidy remembered how Harper had used the phrase dodged a bullet *after her skin-cancer scare. Now he'd dodged one of his own. "I knew there was a reason I didn't quite trust her," she said.*

"You and everyone else. So when are you coming back to New York? We have to celebrate my newfound bachelorhood. Not to mention my business school essays. I want to get that ball rolling again so I can have my applications in by March."

"I'll be back early Friday evening. Maybe dinner?"

"Perfect."

"Cool, it's a date. I'll text you when I land." She hung up the phone and stared at it for a moment, thinking once again how quickly life can change.

"You have a date on Friday?"

The sound of a male voice startled her.

His voice.

No way.

It can't be.

She looked up and saw Brandon standing there.

He was holding a bouquet of pink tulips.

"What are you doing here?"

He handed her the flowers. "I came to hear you speak. You were really, really good. I was impressed."

She looked at the arrangement, then up at him. "But . . . how did you know I was here?" They hadn't had any contact in weeks. Had he called her parents? Or Patti?

"I checked your website."

"Oh." Suddenly she was back at Diablo Royale in the West Village, when he'd told her he'd read her bio. What was going on? Had he really come all the way up to the city . . . for her?

"Thanks for the tulips, Brandon. They're beautiful."

"You're welcome." He cleared his throat. "Listen, do you think we could talk somewhere private?"

She pointed down the hall. "There's a bar next to the lobby. Want to get some coffee?"

"Sounds perfect."

"Let me just get my things, OK?"

He waited in the hallway as she ducked into the speakers' lounge to pick up her coat. She willed her nervous system to keep calm, but it was futile. She was now more anxious than she'd been during her keynote.

Why is he here?

What does he want?

She wiped her palms on a napkin, hoping they weren't too sweaty.

She took a deep breath, then stepped out into the hallway and forced a smile. "OK, I'm ready."

As they walked toward the bar in silence, Cassidy wondered if it would be too early to order a real drink. She could certainly use one. They chose a high table in a far corner near the windows.

"What can I get you?" Brandon gestured toward the bar as she climbed onto a stool and set the bouquet of flowers on the table.

"I'll have a glass of wine. What the hell, right?" She gave him an awkward smile.

"Sauvignon blanc?"

"You remember?" She'd ordered sauvignon blanc on their one official dinner date.

He smiled. "I remember. I think I'll have the same."

Her mind began to race as he walked over to the bar.

Is this really happening?

Is this what I think it is?

After all this time?

Has he really come around?

Brandon returned with two glasses of wine, then took a seat next to her.

"Congratulations again on an excellent keynote." He lifted his glass for a toast. "You were quite an inspiration up there."

She tapped her glass against his. "Thank you. I think you might have been the only male member of the audience."

"Nah, I saw a few male waiters milling around."

She smiled. "Ah, yes, of course."

"So you have a date on Friday?" he asked.

She blushed and looked at the table, startled at the quick change of topic. "Oh, no. That's just my friend Harper."

"I doubt that."

She regained eye contact with him. "It's a long story, but trust me, he's just a friend. So how's your mom doing?"

He shrugged. "She's OK; stable but not great. The good news is that we finally got her settled into an excellent facility, and they're taking really good care of her. That's made my life a lot easier."

"I'm glad to hear that."

He set down his glass. "Listen, Cassidy, I didn't come here to talk about my mom. I came to apologize to you."

"Apologize? Why?"

"For ending things the way I did. I should have called you instead of texting."

She felt a pang of humiliation at the memory of how he'd broken things off. "Oh, that's OK."

"No, it wasn't OK. I also want to apologize for basically disappearing on you, especially after I made you feel bad for not wanting

to be friends with me. I know that wasn't fair to you either. From the moment we started talking, you were nothing but kind to me, and you deserved better than that."

She took a sip of her wine, not sure how to respond.

He continued. "It's just that I got hit by a firestorm. I tried to manage it all, but I wasn't doing a very good job, so I had to retreat and focus on my family. I know I hurt you because of that, and I'm truly sorry."

She smiled, albeit awkwardly, and interlaced her hands on the table. "It's OK. I understood where you were coming from." That wasn't exactly true, but she didn't want him to know how crushed she'd been, or how much she'd agonized over what she might have done wrong, over what she should have done differently.

Over what was wrong with her.

Before she could speculate further over where this was going, he put his hands over hers. "I want to try again."

She caught her breath. "What?"

He squeezed her hands. "I want to try again. With you. With us."

She looked at him. His beautiful gray eyes were alive again, staring at her with an intensity that suggested he meant what he said. But she couldn't forget the emptiness that had been there the last time she'd seen him. That memory still haunted her.

"Why?" she whispered.

"A couple of weeks after you came by to give me those cuff links, things finally began to settle down a bit. At first my thoughts were still consumed with the well-being of my mom and my kids, but when my head finally began to clear, I started thinking about what makes me *happy."*

Cassidy stared at him, still in shock that he was really here, that this was really happening.

He took a deep breath and continued. "What I'm trying to say is, my mom's situation made me realize how important it is to hold on to happiness when you're lucky enough to find it, because life can change so fast. Then I started thinking about you again, and soon I couldn't stop."

She still didn't respond.

He squeezed her hands. "I kept thinking about how much you make me laugh. About how smart and thoughtful you are, and how patient you were with me. About how you've been so good at creating a life that makes you happy, and how you never give up when something is important to you. I kept thinking about how much I loved getting to know you, and how I didn't want that to end."

She felt tears welling up in her eyes. She didn't want it to end either, but she was too afraid to say so out loud.

She was too afraid to utter a word. So she remained silent.

He squeezed her hands again. "Can you please say something?"

Finally, she found her voice. "You don't think it's too complicated? With your mom, and your boys, and the distance?"

"It's always going to be complicated, but I want to make room in my life for you, Cassidy. I need to make room in my life for you. I thought I couldn't do it before, but I realize now how important you are to me, and I'm willing to fight to make it work. I'm willing to fight for you, to fight for us."

She stared at him, still thunderstruck by what was happening. How many times had she dreamed about this moment?

Finally, he released her hands, then gestured to his wrist. "What do you think?"

She realized he was wearing the cuff links. "Are you referring to the cuff links or your offer to try this again?"

"Both."

"Well, the cuff links look fantastic. Someone clearly has exquisite taste, if I do say so myself."

"That is most definitely true. Now what about my offer?"

She smiled. "I think . . . I think you're making a compelling argument for my acceptance, Counselor."

He smiled back. "I'm glad to learn my debating skills serve a purpose beyond the courtroom. You know, I wore the cuff links today because I was hoping this would be a special occasion. If you're up for it, I have the whole evening planned for us."

"You do?"

"I want to treat you the way you've treated me, and I plan to start right now, if you'll let me. Want to hear the agenda?"

"I could be convinced to hear the agenda."

"I was thinking we could spend the rest of the afternoon wandering around North Beach, then enjoy a romantic dinner at Cafe Jacqueline. Afterward, if we're not too tired, I thought it would be fun to stop by the Starlight Room, perhaps the one place in the entire Bay Area we can go dancing without feeling old."

She laughed. "That's probably true. But dancing? For real?" Outside of Harper's birthday party, she couldn't remember the last time she'd danced anywhere other than at a wedding.

"Consider tonight the prom, just a couple of decades removed. I want to make up for all the knuckleheads in high school, including yours truly, who didn't ask you back then."

She glanced down at her simple black dress. It was pretty but plain. "You, as always, look quite dapper, but I'm hardly dolled up for the prom."

"You always look stunning. Have I ever told you that?"

"If you did I probably forgot. If I remember anything, it's that I remember nothing."

He chuckled. "Well, it's true. Cassidy Leigh Lane, you are a truly beautiful woman. So what do you say? Will you be my prom date?"

She wiped a tear from her eye and nodded.

He reached for her hands again. "Is that a yes?"

"That's a yes."

They stared at each other for a few moments, and then his face slowly broke into a smile. "Just so you know, I'm not going to wait for you to ask me to kiss you this time. Are you OK with that?"

She smiled back. "I'm OK with that."

"Good." He squeezed her hands one more time, then leaned over and kissed her.

Cassidy stared at the words on the screen in front of her, a weary half smile on her face.

She sighed and slowly shook her head.

Oh, Brandon Forrester . . . what could have been.

Just then the sound of an ambulance screeching by outside snapped her mind back into the present. She also noticed the humming of her air conditioner.

I'm in Manhattan.

I'm in my apartment.

It's summer.

She glanced out of the window for a moment, then back at her laptop to read over the final scene once more before typing *THE END* into the last page of the manuscript. She hit save, then took a deep breath, stood up, and stretched her arms over her head.

She'd done it.

She'd written a book not so loosely based on what had happened between her and Brandon.

Only with a very different ending.

A happy ending.

She glanced at the clock on the lower right-hand corner of her monitor. It was nearly eight o'clock. She'd been at her desk all day and was looking forward to getting outside for a run, especially now that it had probably cooled off a bit. It wouldn't be dark until nearly nine, so she still had time.

She walked into the kitchen and poured herself a glass of water, then leaned against the counter.

This time she smiled for real.

I've really done it.

Now she just had to go back and change the names of the main characters, plus some identifying details. While all her novels had autobiographical elements to them, this was the first manuscript in which she'd actually used the real names of those people who had inspired the central figures—Brandon, Patti, Harper, Danielle, even herself. She'd written the initial draft with real names to bring authenticity to the writing and planned for them to be temporary placeholders, but seeing those names in front of her had unleashed a creative energy she hadn't expected, so she'd run with it. Then she'd become immersed in the writing, and after that she hadn't looked back. Perhaps it had been the timing of when she'd begun writing the book, shortly after that dark yet illuminating encounter with Brandon on New Year's Day, after she'd run into a brokenhearted Molly Benson and learned that Darlene was in a less than ideal marriage. At that moment in her life, nothing had been the way she wanted it to be, or imagined it would be, so she'd poured her disillusion and disappointment into the novel, where she could right wrongs and let the good people win.

It was bittersweet—if not outright painful—to put the heartache of her doomed relationship with Brandon down on paper, but doing so had helped her heal, and accept, and begin to move on, however reluctantly.

And now she'd created a novel out of it.

One in which Cassidy would become Melanie.

And Brandon would become Andrew.

Their story, told a different way.

A tale of what could have been.

In truth she'd never heard from Brandon after that conversation on his front step. She'd reached out a couple of times to say hi, but he hadn't responded. After that she'd spent weeks, which slowly melted into months, quietly hoping he'd get in touch—and trying, albeit unsuccessfully, to stop herself from doing so. She'd cried more than she wanted to admit, something even Patti didn't know, but eventually the medicinal benefits of time began to replace the pain with insight, and now she felt genuine compassion for him. He was a decent person faced with an extraordinary combination of difficult circumstances, and he needed to put his family first. As a man should.

Or . . . maybe he'd just lost interest.

Or . . . maybe there was someone else.

She'd probably never truly know why their romance had imploded, but for whatever reason, their story was over, and she wished him the best. In a strange way she was grateful to him; he'd shown her she could open her heart again after Dean, whose rejection she once feared would haunt her forever. Plus the heartache she'd suffered from their ill-fated entanglement, while extremely painful, had led to the idea for this new book.

And now, nearly seven months later, she had written it.

With the ending she'd once wanted so desperately for herself, but which she no longer needed.

I'm whole again.

That recognition alone was enough to make her smile.

I'm me again.

She set the glass in the sink, then lightly skipped into her bedroom to change into her running clothes.

Life was good again.

On the way out of her building, Cassidy ran into Harper and Vanessa, baby in tow. Little Morgan was nearly a month old now.

"Hi, Harper; hi, Vanessa." She peered into the stroller and waved. "Hi there, little girl."

"Off for a run?" Harper asked.

Cassidy smiled as she stood up. "A celebratory run. I just finished my book."

"Already?" Vanessa said. "That's wonderful, Cassidy."

Cassidy put her hands on her hips. "Thanks. It didn't take quite nine months, but I guess in a way it's like I just gave birth too."

Vanessa put her hand on her stomach. "I'm jealous. I wish *I* could go running right now. It's all I can do to waddle my fat body into the elevator."

Cassidy rolled her eyes. "Please, you look great." She had been pleasantly surprised at how down-to-earth Vanessa had turned out to be, especially since she'd had Morgan. Despite the unconventional way they'd fallen into their roles as parents, she and Harper seemed to be getting along well, and Cassidy was rooting for them as a couple. She was glad Harper had never read her books, and she knew for a fact Vanessa only read magazines. The pregnancy storyline she'd written into her new novel ended with a less than flattering portrayal of Vanessa, but she didn't want to hurt anyone's feelings. She might need to change how that storyline was resolved, in case either of them ever did read it. Harper certainly appeared happy enough, so perhaps fatherhood wasn't the worst thing for him.

As for Brandon, if he ever read the book, she could only hope he'd realize how much she had cared for him, and how sad she'd been when things hadn't worked out, for whatever reason.

Cassidy pointed toward the lobby exit. "I'm going to head out before it gets dark. See you soon?"

Harper touched Morgan's nose. "Say good-bye to Auntie Cassie, little girl."

Cassidy waved good-bye, then set out for Central Park. It was a gentle, balmy summer evening, and she wanted to enjoy it before the sun set.

Chapter Twenty-Seven

one year later

"I ABSOLUTELY LOVED *Rocky Road*, Cassidy. Loved it!" Crystal Hightower Bryant clapped her hands together cheerleader style, just as she'd done at Paly football games.

Cassidy looked up from the signing table. "It came out the day before yesterday. You've already read it?"

Crystal patted the side of her enormous purse. "I preordered it on my Kindle, but of course I had to come here to buy an autographed print copy from you for my bookshelf."

"That was so nice of you, Crystal. I'm really glad you enjoyed it."

Crystal turned to the bearded man next to her. "You remember my husband, Stanley, from our last reunion?"

Cassidy nodded and smiled. "Of course. Stanley, it's nice to see you again."

Crystal poked his arm. "*Tell her*, Stanley. Tell her how I couldn't put her new book down."

Stanley shrugged with a nod. "It's true. I got up in the middle of the night to use the bathroom and she was still awake reading it."

Crystal lowered her voice, then put her hands on the table and leaned forward. "This one was just so *realistic*, Cassidy. You've got to tell me: Did that happen to you? Did you run into an old college classmate at a wedding and strike up a long-distance romance?"

Cassidy felt her cheeks flush. "Actually, no, that didn't happen to me." *Not exactly.*

Crystal looked surprised. "Really? Well, you could have fooled me. Well done."

"Thanks." *If you only knew.*

"I was biting my nails the whole time, wondering what was going to happen. I laughed, then I cried, then I laughed again, and then I cried again, and then, when Andrew showed up after Melanie's speaking engagement with flowers and wearing the cuff links, I cried *again*. And the prom date thing? I was a mess, a blubbering mess. Poor Stanley here didn't know what to do with me by then."

Stanley shrugged again. "I was just trying to get some sleep."

Cassidy smiled and felt a bit sorry for Stanley. "I'm glad you liked the way it turned out. I toyed around for a bit with the idea of having him never call her again, but I just thought that after all they'd been through, they both deserved a happy ending."

We all do.

Crystal nodded and lowered her voice. "I'm so glad. I enjoyed *Miss Perception* and know it got good reviews and all that, but reading it sort of made me sad, because in spite of it all, I wanted Emma and Jeremy to wind up together, you know what I mean?"

Cassidy pointed a pen at her. "I *do* know what you mean, because to be perfectly honest, writing that book sort of made me sad too. That's another reason why I wanted *Rocky Road* to turn out differently. What's wrong with a little happiness, right? We all need to believe in fairy tales now and then, especially when things get a little rough." She inadvertently glanced toward the entrance—not for the first time tonight.

Her website listed all the details for the book signing, which was free and open to the public.

For anyone to come by and say hello.

Stanley put a hand on Crystal's arm and discreetly gestured to the line of people waiting patiently behind her. "Pumpkin, we should probably let her get on with it," he whispered, clearly not wanting to embarrass his wife but well aware that she was hogging Cassidy's time.

"Thanks, sweetie. I totally lost track of time." Crystal quickly slipped the book Cassidy had autographed into her bag, then slung it over her shoulder with a smile. "I'll be waiting for your next book, that's for sure! And you'd better come to our twenty-fifth reunion. Scary as that may sound, it's not that far away, you know."

Cassidy pointed toward the back of the room. "Thanks, Crystal. I'll do my best to be there. And speaking of high school, Patti Bramble's over there talking to my brother, if you'd like to go say hi before you leave."

"Perfect!" Ever the cheerleader, Crystal clapped her hands together again. Then she hooked her arm through Stanley's, and they drifted away in search of Patti.

Cassidy spent the next hour or so chatting with fans, and eventually the line thinned to a trickle. When she'd autographed the last book and shaken the last hand, she stood up and smoothed the front of her dress. She had feared that the crisp white sheath with navy trim looked a bit too nautical, but the saleslady had insisted it flattered her figure. She was drained but did her best not to appear so, just in case anyone was watching her. Being *on* like this for so long was exhausting, at least for her, and she hadn't been able to sneak in a nap today. Plus her feet were hurting from her new heels.

Tyler and her parents approached the table. "You had quite a turnout tonight," her mother said.

Cassidy looked at the small stack of novels left on the signing table. "I know, way more than I expected. I almost ran out of books."

Her dad winked at her. "Your fame is growing, kiddo."

Tyler put a hand on his dad's shoulder. "Hey, now, don't let her head get too big. We don't want her to forget she once wore neck gear."

Cassidy's hand instinctively flew up to her throat, visions of junior high school flashing before her. "If you *ever* want to make it into one of my books, you'd best keep that information to yourself."

Her mom began putting the remaining books into a cardboard box. "We'll take care of these for you, angel. Go relax and have a drink with Patti. We'll see you back at the house."

Tyler gave her a bear hug. "I've got to get going as well or Jessica will have my head. Way to represent the Lane clan, little sis. I'm proud of you."

"Thanks, big bro. Give the girls a kiss for me." She hugged him back, then wandered across the nearly empty room to Patti, who was listening to Crystal tell a story. Stanley just stood there patiently as his wife chattered on about something to do with their daughter's teacher. Cassidy wondered if he ever got a word in edgewise.

"You all done over there, hotcakes?" Patti said to Cassidy as she approached.

Cassidy laughed. "Truth be told, not feeling like hotcakes right this minute."

Patti held up a hand. "Stop it. This is your hometown book launch party! You, my friend, are the belle of the ball. And look at that dress. You are *definitely* hotcakes tonight."

Crystal grabbed Patti's arm. "Oh my gosh, the way you just said *stop it,* it sounded exactly like the Peggy character in *Rocky Road.*"

Patti looked at Cassidy and slowly raised an eyebrow. "The *Peggy* character?"

"You haven't read it yet?" Crystal asked.

Patti laughed. "Given that it came out two days ago, Crystal, that would be a no." She returned her gaze to Cassidy. "So you based a character on me, did you now?"

"I think she was my favorite. So sassy," Crystal said.

Patti kept looking at Cassidy "Is that so?"

Cassidy shrugged. "I have to draw my inspiration from somewhere. Sometimes I get a little desperate and have to fish off the company pier, so to speak."

"Does this sassy Peggy character, who I imagine is strikingly beautiful and off-the-charts intelligent, live in San Carlos and have three children with a penchant for misbehaving?"

Cassidy held up a palm. "She does live in San Carlos, but she doesn't have kids. She does, however, have a scruffy yet lovable husband named Roy who may or may not like to wear flannel."

"No kids? I envy the woman. Am I getting royalties for this inspiration?"

"Do you pay me when I babysit your children?"

Patti held up her wineglass. "Touché."

"Wow, this is like reading a conversation between Peggy and Melanie in the book," Crystal said. "I feel like Harrison is going to walk in any moment."

Patti looked at Cassidy. "Harrison?"

Cassidy shrugged. "He might be a little bit like Harper."

"I think Harper and I need to revisit this royalties situation," Patti said.

"I think I need a drink." Cassidy pointed across the room.

They said good-bye to Crystal and Stanley, then walked over to the bar area. Cassidy never drank alcohol during book signings so she could stay sharp while chatting with her readers, but now that the official part of the evening was over, she was looking forward to a glass of wine.

As they each took a seat at the bar, Cassidy stole a quick glance at the entrance.

"Are you watching the door to see if creepy Trent is going to show up? I could use a smoke right now, dude." Patti briefly turned her eyes into slits, then squeezed Cassidy's knee and gave her a knowing look. "Here you go, superstar." She handed her a glass of wine, then held up her own for a toast. "To another bestseller."

"To a lifelong friendship," Cassidy said.

"To my future royalties."

Cassidy laughed. "In all seriousness, thanks for coming tonight. I know it's hard for you to get out during the week."

Patti waved a dismissive hand. "Please. I would never miss one of your book launch parties. It's fun to be in the inner circle of a C-list celebrity now and again. Crystal's so jealous of me, it's sort of funny and sad at the same time."

"Did you just say C-list? Have I been promoted from the D-list?"

Patti nodded. "I think you're ready for a bump up."

Cassidy put a hand on her chest and bowed her head. "I'm honored."

"As you should be. When do you fly back to New York?"

"Tomorrow morning. I don't want to miss the rehearsal dinner."

"Is your bridesmaid's dress crazy ugly?"

Cassidy shrugged and took a sip of her wine. "Not as ugly as the one you made me wear."

"I'll take that. I should have known better than to listen to fashion suggestions from Roy's grandmother."

They chatted until they finished their drinks, then Patti reached for her purse and pointed a thumb over her shoulder. "OK, missy, my hall pass is up. I've gotta hit the road."

Cassidy yawned. "Me too. I'm just going to run to the ladies' room before I leave. I guess I'll see you when I'm home for Halloween."

Patti stood up and put her hands on her hips. "It's on October thirty-first. That's a little over two months from now. Do you want me to put an alarm in your phone to remind you?"

"Very funny." Cassidy stood up too and hugged her. "Tell Roy and the kids I said hi."

After Patti left Cassidy walked alone toward the restrooms. As she washed her hands, she admired her manicured fingernails, which she hadn't nibbled even once in more than a year now. She hadn't been back to Annabelle's either. She found that not returning made it easier to keep the fond memories of her visits there intact, which for some reason was important to her.

She looked at herself in the mirror and couldn't help but recognize the significance of tonight's event, of how much she'd accomplished since that last trip to Annabelle's.

Not just professionally but personally.

She'd kept going and she'd come out on the other side, with a novel that made her feel proud, one she'd written not just for her readers but for herself.

And for Brandon.

And most of all, for what could have been.

By channeling the intense feelings she'd once had for Brandon into the world of Melanie and Andrew, she'd given those emotions a meaning, a purpose, and that was something for which to be thankful, even if she never saw Brandon again.

She returned to the bar stool and picked up her lightweight wrap, then slung her purse over her shoulder and took one last look at the entrance.

She'd lingered long enough.

It was time to go now.

He wasn't coming.

Real life was calling.

She made her way slowly to the door. Once outside she walked through the parking lot toward her mom's SUV, then turned for one last glance back. Though it had been bubbling with activity just an hour earlier, the place was now quiet and still.

She got in the car and headed south on El Camino. When she reached the left-turn stoplight at Embarcadero, she glanced over at Palo Alto High School on one side of the street, then at Town & Country Village—and Mayfield Bakery—on the other.

To the right buzzed a massive, blurry memory of being a teenager, too many individual moments to count or even categorize.

To the left hovered a single vivid memory from adulthood, of the day she'd met Brandon for coffee. The last time he'd held her hand, the last time he'd kissed her. That story hadn't had the ending she'd hoped for, but she was happy again, and that was all that mattered now. And who knew what would happen this weekend? Maybe life would imitate art, and she *would* run into a college classmate at Danielle's wedding. Maybe the irresistible promise of romance would call her name again.

Or maybe not.

Either way she'd be just fine; she knew that now.

At least Danielle had gotten a fairy-tale ending, and after quite a shaky beginning, to say the least.

The stoplight switched from red to green, and for the briefest of moments Cassidy hesitated before turning onto Embarcadero Road.

High school to the right.

Heartache to the left.

She squeezed the steering wheel and drove straight between the memories on either side, trying her best to keep focused on the road ahead.

She had just parked in her parents' driveway when her phone began to ring.

She dug it out of her purse and caught her breath when she saw the name on the display.

Brandon.

Thanks!

After pouring my life into four Waverly Bryson novels, to describe crafting something brand-new as *daunting* is an enormous understatement. The simple truth is that I couldn't have written *Cassidy Lane* without the help of a few trusted friends, whose early feedback and encouragement helped shape a story I hadn't imagined at the outset. Thanks to the following people for their candid advice and unwavering support throughout the process: Tami May McMillan, Patti Castaneda Bennett, Alberto Ferrer, Katie Mahon, Terri Sharkey, and Lori Rosenwasser. A special hug goes to my lifelong pal Peggy Prendergast, whose valuable ideas for authenticity included throwing in a reference to the quintessential "mixtape," a lost art of which the sheer mention will forever stir up pangs of teenage angst for countless Generation Xers.

I openly admit that at this point in my career I would be lost without my editor, Christina Henry de Tessan. Sometimes when I'm writing the first iteration of a story I feel like I'm pushing an enormous boulder up a mountain and fear I'll never reach the top. Christina helps me get there with her brilliant insight and suggestions, and then together we nudge the manuscript over the crest and joyfully watch it roll down the other side as a fully developed novel. Christina, at this point I trust your opinion as much as I do my own, and it's a sheer honor to work with you. Thanks as well to Terry Goodman and Alex Carr at Amazon Publishing for encouraging me to stretch my literary wings—plus to Jessica Poore for her tireless efforts to keep Waverly's world alive and well! And kudos of course to the most loyal (and free) proofreader in town, my dear, sweet, beautiful mother, Flo Murnane. Mommy Dearest, you will never know how much I love you.

I'd also like to thank a handful of friends whose own life experiences, observations, and expertise influenced this book in various ways: Lauren Battle, Steph Bernabe, Kathy Carter, Diane Fishman, Joe Guggemos, Rob Henderson, Ariel Hoffman, Jenny Jongejan, Kristin Law, Courtney Carroll Levinsohn, Jen Livingstone, Mitch Miller, Manny Palugod, Brett Sharkey, and Anh Vazquez. Thanks for the insight, information, and inspiration!

About the Author

A former PR executive who abandoned a successful career to pursue a more fulfilling life, Maria Murnane is the bestselling author of the romantic comedies *Perfect on Paper*, *It's a Waverly Life*, *Honey on Your Mind*, and *Chocolate for Two*, which garnered a starred review in *Publishers Weekly*. Originally from California, she now lives in Brooklyn.